MINDFIELD

BOOK 8 IN THE *SPIES LIE* SERIES

D. S. KANE
(dskane@dskane.com)

ISBN-13: 978-0-9862321-5-2
(paperback)
ISBN: 978-0-9996554-0-5 (Kindle)
ISBN: 978-0-9996554-1-2 (ePub)

Cover design by Jeroen Ten Berge
[www.jeroentenberge.com]

Print and ebook layout by eBooks By Barb
for booknook.biz

Praise for DS Kane's *Spies Lie* Series

Bloodridge

"A globe-trotting spy thriller dense with intriguing insider's knowledge."—*Kirkus Reviews*

"I thoroughly enjoyed this book ... It is definitely a page-turner."—*Judge, 22nd Annual Writer's Digest Self-Published Book Awards*

"This is a sizzler torn straight from tomorrow's headlines. *Bloodridge* by D.S. Kane is one you won't want to miss." —*John Reinhard Dizon, author of* **Nightcrawler** *and* **Wolf Man**

"What a wild ride! Filled with adventure and suspense and kept me on the edge of my seat. There wasn't a slow moment in it. Reminiscent of Ludlum and Follett." —*Sharon Law Tucker, author of* **How To Be A BadAss, A Survival Guide For Women**

DeathByte

"Readers who adore action-packed thrillers in the vein of Robert Ludlum's Bourne series will enjoy its many double-crossings."—*Kirkus Reviews*

"This was a great thriller...and the speed of the plot was breathtaking."—*Judge, 22nd Annual Writer's Digest Self-Published Book Awards*

Swiftshadow

"A must read for lovers of this genre." —*Sheri A. Wilkinson, book blogger*

"...the high stakes and dizzily paced action will hook genre fans from the first page."—*Kirkus Reviews*

GrayNet

"Conspiracy theorists are sure to devour this novel."
—*Mallory Heart Reviews*

"Nonstop action and suspense starring the definition of a strong female lead."—*Kirkus Reviews*

Baksheesh (Bribes)

"More wild, violent adventures in the world of international espionage.."—*Kirkus Reviews*

"This Story Should be an Audible Selection... Could be a Major Motion Picture."—*Charles W, TOP 500 REVIEWER*

ProxyWar

"The latest adventure in a series that only grows more engaging with each installment."—*Kirkus Reviews*

"Mr Kane saved the best for last of course he left open the next installment. And he brought back accidental spy Jon Sommers to finish things up. Please write fast Mr Kane so we can see what happens next!" —*Richard L. Cooper, Amazon Reviewer*

CypherGhost

"After working as a covert operative for over a decade and travelling the globe, DS Kane now writes fictions about how intelligence agencies craft lies to sway and manipulate their national policy. His latest techno-thriller **Cypher-Ghost** is a fast-paced and gripping story which will keep you up reading the whole night. DS Kane, without a doubt, is a great storyteller. When we picked up the latest installment of Kane's Spies Lies series, we got hooked from the beginning. The author does a wonderful job of fictionalizing the crossroads of politics, technology and national security in an entertaining plot.

The book is written is a very easy language and can be read in one sitting. Although we can categorize this novel as a thriller, the author has toyed to some extent with some science fiction themes which make the story more absorbing. Overall, a highly recommended read for the lovers of popular thrillers."—*Mystery Tribune*

"Packed with enough terrifying detail to feel at least moderately plausible, if not horrifyingly prescient."
—*Kirkus Reviews*

"If you are into spy novels then look no further. The 7th book in the Spies Lie series is every bit as good as the 6 that preceded it. D.S. Kane is the pseudonym of a former CIA covert operative who clearly knows what he is talking about. Characters are well developed and plots are exciting and not far removed from what the operations of a modern intelligence agency might get up to. Do yourself a huge favour and read the book, you won't be disappointed . . .

then once you have finished that you have 6 other books in the series that you need to get your hands on as soon as possible! Other books in the series are as follows 1. Bloodridge, 2. DeathByte, 3. Swiftshadow, 4. GrayNet, 5. Baksheesh, 6. ProxyWar. They are all available from Amazon. Do yourself a huge favour and read them now!"

—*N G McKenzie*

The *Spies Lie* Series by DS Kane:

Bloodridge, Book 1
(http://www.amazon.com/dp/B00K0029J0)

DeathByte, Book 2
(http://www.amazon.com/dp/B00L2LLKSC)

Swiftshadow, Book 3
(http://www.amazon.com/dp/B00MJ5KXKG)

GrayNet, Book 4
(http://www.amazon.com/dp/B00P8HRT9U)

Baksheesh (Bribes), Book 5
(http://www.amazon.com/dp/B010NR3RD6)

ProxyWar, Book 6
(http://www.amazon.com/dp/B018YS91CM)

CypherGhost, Book 7
(http://www.amazon.com/dp/B01MTPXRZ5)

Mindfield, Book 8 ...with more to come.

For certain faculty and administration of the Naval Postgraduate School in Monterey (you know who you are), my guides into the political side of how our military functions.

Contents

PART I

PART II

PART III

PART IV

Disclaimer

This is a work of fiction. All of the characters and events depicted here are the work of the author's mind. Most but not all of the places are real.

PART I

The whole program appeared to go classified, hidden from view and was presumed to be funded by either the KGB, the military or some other 'government interest' ... There was evidence that they were particularly active in long distance telepathic communication. Also in PK that they call telekinesis and possibly in telepathic hypnosis to disrupt individuals in key positions or handling sensitive equipment.

—Major General Edward Thompson,
Assistant Chief of Staff for Intelligence,
US Army, 1977–1981

CHAPTER 1

Ann Silbey Sashakovich embedded her presence within the CypherGhost's to make it more difficult for the other woman to detect her. The Bug-Lok nanodevices embedded in their brains enabled each woman's consciousness to travel vast distances using the internet, while their living bodies rested intact and far away.

The CypherGhost stood behind the large, leather couch in the hunting room of Cyrus DeSpain's Akron, Ohio, mansion. De Spain was pacing the room, right in front of her, but he couldn't "see" her. And the CypherGhost was too busy hacking Cyrus DeSpain's medical device and his cellphone to notice Ann.

In fact, at about five-foot-six and one hundred twenty pounds each, Ann and the CypherGhost were nearly identical in height and weight, and it was easy for Ann's projection to stand within the other woman's without much chance the other would notice.

It took only a few seconds for the CypherGhost to administer a fatal bolus of insulin to the old man. Ann could almost feel the smile on the other's face before the other woman's presence faded away. Where had the CypherGhost gone? It would take Ann some time to reacquire her location.

Ann was not sure if the CypherGhost had noticed Ann. She tried to deny the attraction that had drawn the two together before everything went sideways.

Then Ann's brain kicked in and she pondered the obvious. *Why had the CypherGhost murdered DeSpain?* She scanned the hunting room of DeSpain's compound for clues. Ann dropped her mindspace into DeSpain's cellphone's directories. *I need to know what's so important in these.* She began searching through everything she'd copied from the CypherGhost.

When she heard Avram Shimmel's voice coming closer from the front door, she forced her consciousness to exit the hunting room. She reentered her body where it lay in the bed of her room and brought herself to wakefulness back in the Swiftshadow safe house in Washington DC, a thousand miles from DeSpain's home.

The shades were drawn and the door was closed. She enjoyed the warmth from the radiator under the window.

She knew Avram and his United Nations Task Force would remain at DeSpain's home to investigate the murder site. She knew how frustrated he would be at losing his only clue to what was happening. *But now I know,* she thought, *and I can get him back on the track of the CypherGhost if I can figure out where she's gone.*

Ann knew soon all her own Bug-Lok devices would cease their functioning and she would once again be "normal." Helpless.

She forced herself back into a near-reality fugue, trying to determine if there was any way to transform her own neural clusters to accomplish the functions performed by a Bug-Lok module. Some of the functions were easy to imitate, others impossible. The most difficult and most valuable one was using her brain to access a nearby local area network. A cyber function of wireless internet—something the Bug-Lok was designed to do—seemed impossible to duplicate neurally, but she kept trying. And she kept failing. This was her most important project: *Hack my own brain.*

She had another project to complete, and this one was almost as important, but absolutely impossible until she successfully completed the first one. She already knew that when a Bug-Lok unit was failing she could alter or stop its functioning within her and force it to detach from her brainstem. What she wanted to be able to do now was to use the internet to reach into another person who had ingested Bug-Loks, by employing the power of her own Bug-Loks. Was it even possible to control another person's Bug-Loks by using just her own brain? She was sure it was impossible, but she knew she would have to try.

She wasn't aware of time passing. She knew that after about two hours she would become run down, tired, and hungry. Then, she'd have to become conscious again to find food before she slept. But even after two hours must have passed by, she still felt strong. So, she kept trying.

An unwelcome thought emerged into her mind. She ejected the eighteen nearly dead or damaged units and counted only eleven Bug-Loks still operating within her. She emerged back into the real world. Time was running out faster now.

Since she had witnessed what the CypherGhost had done to Cy DeSpain, she was now sure the CypherGhost and she were on opposite sides of this battle. She knew the hacker's abilities were at least as good as hers, but she couldn't fathom what drove the CypherGhost.

Ann wondered if she had enough power left in her remaining Bug-Loks to defeat the CypherGhost. How to do just that was something she hadn't even thought about.

Would Ann have to kill her? If necessary, she was certainly willing. But, how to do it was a mystery to her.

* * *

The CypherGhost exited the bus at a stop in the northern suburbs of Washington DC, close to Baltimore. She wouldn't be noticed in the section of town she'd chosen. It was a run-down block and the cheap, old motel she'd chosen had no redeeming features. She settled into her room, sat on the ratty couch in the corner of the room across from the ancient television, and closed her eyes to facilitate entry into the alternate realm. She would have to complete a list of tasks to ensure her survival.

* * *

Ann lay back on the bed and focused into her mindset as hard as she could. She already knew the harder she worked the Bug-Lok devices, the faster they failed. Now only nine Bug-Loks remained active inside her. She forced them to look outward, through the local network, into cyberspace. Now, while the Bug-Loks held the outward passway open, she tried using her own brain to push her thoughts through with them, to accompany them. Last time she tried, she had no success, but this time, she was able to sense a single additional signal. She tried to Google "brain chemistry" with the signal, searching by using her own brain. The result was foggy, but it was real. She was able to hold the search pathway open for perhaps two seconds before it crashed.

She felt totally exhausted but she blinked her eyes, roused herself, and managed to walk into the kitchen. *I've finally succeeded. I'll need to practice.* She ate leftover grilled pork and linguini with clam sauce stored in the refrigerator from last night's dinner, and then opened and ate the contents of cans of green beans, peaches, and stewed tomatoes she found in the pantry.

* * *

Hours later, when Cassie had returned to the safe house, she poured herself a cup of black coffee and sat at the kitchen table across from Ann. They smiled warmly at each other. Cassie was two inches taller, but when she was seated her longer legs and shorter torso made the two women appear about the same height. She bore her age well, and as a result, they looked more like mismatched sisters than mother and adopted child. Cassie had chestnut-brown short-cropped hair and brown eyes, while Ann had blonde hair and blue eyes. Cassie was very thin, while Ann was slightly more substantial.

Cassie replaced her smile with a look of relief. "I'm glad that troublesome woman is gone." She looked at Ann expectantly, as if her daughter was required to answer.

Ann smiled with arched brows. A beginning of a question forced itself through her lips. "Mom, I need to ask you for a huge favor."

"Uh, sure, sweetie. Ask away."

"I think I can turn off a Bug-Lok that another person has ingested. But before I try this when I face off with the CypherGhost, I need to see if it's even possible."

"No. Absolutely not. I just had two of those nasties surgically removed. I won't ingest another just so you can see if you can do what I already know is impossible."

Ann sighed. "Can you contact William? Maybe he'll let me try to turn one of his off."

Cassie thought for a second. "He's eleven thousand miles away. Do you think you can really do this? From here?"

"Only one way to find out."

Cassie pulled her cellphone from her pocket. "It's nearly

midnight there." She punched in a long number. William Wing and his wife Betsy were in Hong Kong, undercover and using alternate identities. Betsy was now "Alice" and William was now "Warren." Since the call could be tracked and traced, Cassie knew to use their cover names.

"Alice? This is Cassie. Is Warren there?"

The voice sounded as if it had just been roused from sleep. "Calling us is dangerous. But, okay, he's right here with me."

William's voice was more alert than Betsy's had been. "Hi. Can we come back to America now?"

Cassie handed the phone to Ann. "He's all yours. Good luck."

Ann, took a deep breath, organizing her thoughts. "It's Ann. I need to ask you to volunteer for something."

"Ann? How are you?"

"Uh, I'm okay. But I have a serious problem and I think you can help me out."

"Ah, sure. As long as it's not dangerous."

Ann considered the risk. "I think this is safe, but, of course I could be wrong."

"Tell me."

"Is your Bug-Lok unit still active?"

Seconds passed. "Just tested it. Yeah. Still works, for another week or two at least."

"May I try to turn it off?"

"Huh? Are you going to try to hack me with a computer?"

"No. Not with a computer. I want to try to hack your Bug-Lok with my brain."

William laughed for nearly thirty seconds. "Very funny."

Ann sighed. *Yes, it's difficult to believe this.* "Not funny. For real. Can I try to turn off your Bug-Lok using my brain from over ten thousand miles away?"

William stopped laughing. "You mean for real? This is too funny. Sure, okay. Give it a go."

Ann frowned, doubting her unique abilities. She tried to use her brain, not her Bug-Loks to enter into her alternate mind world. She focused on William, on his approximate locale in Hong Kong, and visualized him, seeing him suddenly emerge within her mind's field of vision. She tried to enter into his mind. She failed. She tried again. Three more times. It didn't work.

"Warren, it's not working. Can I have your permission to try after we get off the phone?"

"Sure, Ann. Keep trying. But I'm sure what you're trying isn't even possible."

"Thanks. If I think I've been successful, can I call you back?"

"Yeah. Good luck." William terminated the call.

Ann was sure she was missing something. But what was it? What was both necessary and sufficient to communicate with the mind of another? She headed back to her notebook computer. *Hadn't the CIA and the Russian KGB been active in mind-control experiments a few decades in the past? I wonder if there are any studies from that time still in their archives?*

* * *

As dusk turned into night, the CypherGhost sat on her stained, smelly couch in the dingy, darkened motel room. She brushed back her dyed bright-red hair and stared at her notebook's screen.

She had used Google to locate the aircraft that Avram and his mercenaries were on, flying back to Washington. She knew Avram would soon know it was she who had murdered DeSpain. She assumed he would place her death high on his priority list of things he had to accomplish.

She figured she could hack their Cessna and make it crash in about an hour, after she was sure the aircraft had reached its peak altitude.

* * *

Ann practiced as she sat in the darkened bedroom, testing her ability to employ her brain to access the internet. As time passed, her ability became even stronger. She was still trying the next phase of her plan, to turn off a Bug-Lok inside another person. So far, over two hundred failures. But, if the Bug-Loks were accessible using near-field communication, she might be able to use the internet and a local network to... to do what? Was this even possible?

She sighed. She reread the technical specifications and functional specs for the Bug-Lok device. Not clear.

She finished reading about experiments that the CIA and KGB had separately done, trying to harness the higher powers of the human brain. Telekinesis. It had never worked, or so they reported. In effect, she realized, *that's what I'm trying to do.*

She kept trying. Nearly an hour had passed, and, every time, she failed.

* * *

It just happened. Thinking about how Ann had turned into her enemy made the CypherGhost furious, and she threw her hands up in the air and screamed with anger. To her surprise, she felt ash fall into her hair. She saw burn marks in the ceiling.

She tried the same thing several more times and just once she saw sparks fly from her fingertips. After that, she spent hours practicing until she had mastered her ability to send fire from her hands.

Soon, the CypherGhost had set fire to the telephone

directory book, the hotel room's New Testament, and a roll of toilet paper by aiming her hands at these objects, closing her eyes, and thinking "fire!" She looked at her hands. Her fingertips emitted a thin wisp of smoke as she focused intently on them. Sparks, small ones. Then she threw her hands at the motel room's unplugged lamp and it burst into flames. She extinguished it with the pitcher of water she'd prepared beforehand. *Cool! Just like the Emperor in Star Wars!*

* * *

The aircraft carrying Avram and sixty of his mercs was nearing Dulles International Airport. The sky was dark outside. Avram was angry, and given his huge height and muscular bearing, the mercs all sat as far away as they could.

He and Jon Sommers had nearly finished their conversation on cellphones but still had no actionable plan. No next step. They both knew they needed to find proof of guilt for the ninety-three associates of Cy DeSpain before they could terminate them, but neither could formulate a plan that had even a remote chance of working.

The pilot's voice advised them through the sound system to secure their seat belts. Still cruising at twenty thousand feet, the Cessna awaited tower clearance for landing.

In seconds, they had emerged through a layer of clouds into the black of night. A few minutes passed.

Avram spoke to Jon. "Let's give this a rest. Maybe after a few hours sleep, I can continue trying to configure a plan with you. But right now, I'm exhausted."

Jon replied. "Right. I also need a break." He terminated the call.

Another minute passed. The hum of the aircraft's engines suddenly went silent. Then the big plane tilted downward. Avram was instantly alert.

Avram thought, *something wrong here.*

Avram pulled his cell from his pocket. He punched in Ann's number. "Ann, it's Avram. We have a problem. Out aircraft is in a forty-five-degree angle of descent. I think the plane's been hacked."

* * *

Ann remembered her only other hack of an aircraft's flight control system. "Avram, I'll have to reboot the aircraft's systems. It should take just over a minute for it to come up clean. When the lights go out on the aircraft, tell the pilot to fly manually, using instruments, until the system completes rebooting."

Avram replied, "Okay. I'll do that now. Work quickly, Ann."

Ann pulled out her notebook and geolocated the aircraft using Avram's cellphone, then ran a program that was supposed to reboot the aircraft. But nothing happened. She tried again with the same result. She realized this had to be the work of the CypherGhost, and the other hacker had figured a way to close off the entry point into the system. It was that system address that Ann needed to use.

She'd need another way to hack the aircraft. If she was correct, anything she did now would be countered by the CypherGhost. *Except, perhaps, hacking the CypherGhost herself.*

Ann was sure that she wasn't prepared to battle the CypherGhost. *This is suicide. But as Spock from Star Trek once said, the lives of the many outweigh the lives of the few —or something like that. Here goes.* She focused on the aircraft and backtraced the location of the CypherGhost. Somewhere near Baltimore. She tried entering the other hacker's mindspace. And failed. Ann focused harder, concentrating so hard that she was straining every muscle in her body. This time, something happened. She saw the Cypher-Ghost from the other hacker's eyes. The CypherGhost sat in a dingy hotel room filled with dingy furniture She saw the other hacker's fingers on her notebook computer!

Ann concentrated on the CypherGhost's mindspace and saw her brain was filled with over one hundred active Bug-Loks. She felt her heart lurch in fear. She tried to turn one off. It worked! She turned off several more before the CypherGhost screamed.

She could hear the CypherGhost talking. "Ann! I've been expecting you. You've become more powerful. You must have taken a thousand of the little buggers for you to be able to do this. I have an offer: Be with me. I am power itself. Together, we can rule the entire planet. I have the codex of my daddy's contacts. Every one of them. I intend to run them all."

Ann kept working. She had turned off fourteen of the CypherGhost's Bug-Loks. "Your father? Cy DeSpain was your father?" She turned off three in under four seconds. It was working faster now. Ann relaxed for just a second and almost lost the connection. She clenched her fists and pushed her own mind back into her enemy's mindspace. Ann continued turning off the devices as fast as she could. She knew the plane would crash in under two minutes unless she could reboot the aircraft's systems.

The CypherGhost said, "Uh-huh. Daddy treated me and my mother like shit. I finally found a way to kill him."

"You know all your father's co-conspirators are going to die within a few days."

"No they won't. I can hack the orders Avram just sent, and call off their terminations."

"Fuck, no. And now, you're trying to kill my friends."

"They'll kill me if they can. I'm just doing what I must to survive."

"Well fuck you!" A few seconds passed while Ann continued destroying the Bug-Lok devices. Suddenly, she felt her hands burning. She opened her eyes. They were on fire! She ran to the bathroom, jumped fully clothed into the shower, and turned on the cold water. As she stood in the tub with water flowing over her burning fingers, she forced her mind back into the CypherGhost's mindspace. There were only seventeen Bug-Loks left within her enemy's skull. It would take just another few seconds more. She bore down and worked as fast as she could. And finally, *DONE!*

Now the flowing water drenched the flames and she could see her hands were badly burned.

Ann ran back to her notebook. Her hands were so terribly burned that when she tried to touch the keyboard, the pain from the burns was too much. She used her nose to key the last command. She watched the screen: "REBOOT-ING. American Flight Technology, Inc. REBOOTING ACCOMPLISHED."

Ann took a deep breath. She was sure the aircraft would recover. Now, she had to reenter the CypherGhost's mind-space one final time. A space with no Bug-Loks. Was that even possible? She clenched her lips. *Time to find out.* Inside the other hacker's brain she found multiple lesions along the CypherGhost's medulla oblongata where the Bug-Loks had been embedded. They were pulsating and seeping blood into the hacker's skull. Ann took a deep breath.

"CypherGhost, you are dying. I can see the damage."

"Well. Fuck you, too. I know you have a copy of Daddy's files from his cellphone. Too bad all of Daddy's files were encrypted by a PGP key. With me gone, you won't be able to decipher them."

Ann searched through the CypherGhost's brainspace, looking for anything useful. She could feel her enemy convulsing as more blood leaked into her brain. Time was running out.

She worked as fast as she could, knowing she had little time left before CypherGhost stopped breathing and her consciousness blinked out. She scanned the other's most recent memories.

And there it was. DeSpain's codex and his PGP cypher key to the files she'd already copied. She applied DeSpain's key and located everything in one of the CypherGhost's recent memories, a full list of names, titles, corporations, contact information, and a checklist of projects DeSpain had directed his team to work on.

The ones relating to the plot of the coup d'état were all there. Ann copied the decrypted information into one of her four functioning Bug-Loks, and then sent the copy to the Drafts folder of the Swiftshadow Group's website.

Exhausted, Ann felt herself fall into unconsciousness.

* * *

The CypherGhost knew that she was dying. She could feel a growing pressure in her head where her brain was swelling, slowly filling with blood. Over a hundred tiny holes in her medulla oblongata were oozing away her life. The pain was beyond anything she could have imagined. She knew with certainty she wouldn't survive the swelling of her brain, even if she sought medical attention. She tried to move but she couldn't feel her legs.

She sought out the Bug-Lok devices. No, they were all gone from her now, every last one. She was unable to move her hands.

She tried to emerge from the alternate mindspace but she was trapped there, between the real world and the wrecked world of the alternate consciousness that the Bug-Loks had created before they were all ripped out from her brain.

She tried to scream, but she couldn't even do that.

The CypherGhost knew she was seconds away from death. Had it been worth the ride? She decided it had been. For a short time, she had been someone important. *What should my final thought be?* She had fallen in love with Ann, and wondered if Ann had truly loved her. *Doesn't matter.* She decided to leave Ann one final gift. She had very little energy left, but she focused intently on Ann's mindspace and pushed her new-found talent into Ann. *Did it work? Would Ann even notice? If Ann could project flames like I had been able, what will she use this new talent for?* She tried to smile, but she felt her heart stop beating. Time stopped for her and she felt her consciousness swirl away.

* * *

Cassie returned from the office and found Ann lying on the floor in the kitchen, her hands blistered and severely burned. "Baby, can you hear me?"

Ann was unresponsive. Cassie carried her to the elevator, then out onto the street. She hailed a cab and took Ann to the nearest hospital. "Her hands!"

The ER nurse examined Ann's hands and yelled for a doctor.

* * *

Four days had passed since Ann and the CypherGhost had fought. Ann remained unconscious and Cassie worried.

She had read the memos Ann had sent her. She knew Ann and the CypherGhost had battled, and that her daughter had murdered the CypherGhost.

Cassie couldn't sleep and had cried so much her eyes hurt. She sat in Ann's private room with her husband, Lee Ainsley. He sat next to her, holding her hand.

"Don't worry, Cassie. I'm sure she'll recover."

"Maybe. Maybe. But so far, the doctors don't know why

she's still unconscious. And even if she wakes, look at her hands! They're bandaged and scorched. The doctors say they'll be scarred. They aren't even sure if she'll ever be able to use them again."

"At least the doctors didn't need to amputate them." Lee turned away.

* * *

Ann could feel each person in the room as if she were inside their consciousness. She heard what they said, and she could sense their thoughts before they spoke. But she wasn't conscious, and couldn't tell if this was just some elaborate dream. She could sense the green walls of her hospital room. Cassie sat across from her bed, crying. Ann wanted so much to comfort her mom. She reached out with her mind, but "it" was no longer working.

No matter. She would just have try harder to push herself into consciousness.

She tried to open her eyes. Nothing worked. So, she kept trying. It took a few more attempts, but she was able to force her eyes open, just a bit. The walls weren't green. They were taupe. She smiled.

Cassie said, "Ohmigod. You're awake!"

Ann's hands felt awkward. She couldn't move her fingers, so she looked and saw layers of bandages covering her hands, making her fingers stiff. She tried to bend her fingers and found she could, but just a little.

Cassie yelled at Ann. "What were you thinking, going after that rogue hacker all by yourself? You knew it was too dangerous!"

Ann smiled and forced her fingers to give Cassie the middle finger salute. Her lips felt like plastic as she tried to form words. "I just played my part, Mom. But, I do love you and dad." Her voice was slurred. *Maybe some damage here.*

Cassie rushed to Ann and gave her a hug. "Well, I'm so glad you are going to be okay."

Ann hugged Cassie, her hands behind Cassie's back. Ann felt her fingers grow hot. She moved her hand to where she could see it. Her fingers were white hot but she felt no pain. *What the fuck?* She calmed herself and the glow emanating from her fingers disappeared.

Ann wondered what would happen if she told anyone, even her mom, what she'd become. *I will tell no one. I don't even know if I could repeat what I've done. So, now, this remains my most closely guarded secret, even more than my hack of the Russians last year. But now, I'm not just a hacker anymore.*

CHAPTER 2

Ten Months Later

**Ann Sashakovich's apartment,
#211, 3950 Louis Road, Palo Alto, CA**

September 11, 3:34 p.m.

Ann lugged her book bag up the stairs at one of the Student Cooperative apartments. A group of parents of Stanford University students had bought several apartment buildings on streets east of the university grounds. When parents bought a share, their child had the right to use one of the apartments. The buildings were basic for such an upscale area, but they were kept neat. Cassandra and Lee had invested, and Ann's unit was on the second floor of the building on Louis Road. Ann had accepted a roommate to help cover the expenses.

She exited the stairway at the top of the second landing and walked the hallway, looking for the unit the cooperative had assigned her. This was the start of her sophomore year. She had missed half a semester of her freshman year while recovering from her battle with the CypherGhost. Her grades, as a result, had suffered. Now she would have to ace her entire course load to get off probation.

Her fingers hurt. The burns had healed into scars, but

she always felt any pressure on her hands as a wall of pain. Six surgeries hadn't helped much. *Mom was right. I should have stayed out of danger*.

Apartment 212. She opened the door and saw a room almost exactly like the one she'd lived in a year ago. *Looks like a room at a convent.* There were two beds, and two identical dressers old enough to be antiques. The two desks looked like they had been used during one of the world wars. The colors of the furniture and walls were monochromatic gray. *Depressing.* She sighed and dropped the book bag on one of the beds. Whoever her roommate was, the girl was going to be late to the party. *First one in chooses whichever bed she wants.*

She selected the bed on the left side. Its dresser and desk were in the shade, so she wouldn't have constant sun on her hands.

She unpacked her book bag and took the stairs back to her car to retrieve her suitcase. The brown-gold Toyota Corolla was nearly five years old.

By the time she had completed her third trip and emptied her car, her hands felt like she had destroyed them. She took a painkiller and rubbed lotion into the spots where the skin on her fingers had cracked open.

* * *

Laura D. Hunter thought, *it feels so good to be back at school.* She wore a shit-eating grin. She was finally out of her grandparents' house. They always tried to micromanage her. Stanford was the only place where they couldn't reach into her life and force her to live as they wanted her to. She climbed the stairs, looking for room 212. She prayed her roommate wouldn't be a slob, like the one she'd had during her freshman year.

The door was closed. She took the key she'd been mailed

and pushed it into the lock. When she opened the door, she saw another woman on one of the beds. But she was in luck: the other woman had left the sunny side of the room for her. The other woman seemed to be asleep, so Laura made as little noise as possible, pushing her two suitcases in and closing the door as quietly as she could. Apparently, not without a sound though.

Her roommate stirred and her eyes opened. She tried to hide her hands, but Laura couldn't help staring at the extensive burns on her roommate's fingers. "How?" she said, pointing at the scars.

Ann frowned. "I fought and won." She stared at her fingers. "But this was the cost."

Laura stood without replying. Finally, she said, "Does it hurt?"

"All the time. Especially when I carry something. Hi, I'm Ann Sashakovich."

"Oh, sorry. I'm Laura D. Hunter. Most people call me Laura D. I see you chose the dark side of the room. Bad joke."

Ann smiled. "Yeah, I'm the virtual essence of the dark side. I'm majoring in computer forensics, so I guess 'dark side' is where I should be."

"I'm majoring in art technology."

CHAPTER 3

**Sashakovich-Ainsley home,
220 East Kirke Street, Chevy Chase, MD**

September 11, 7:21 p.m.

The brick house sat in the middle of a high-walled compound and the walls were topped with razor wire. Cassandra Sashakovich had long ago stolen nearly a billion dollars from the United States government. She had hacked funds that were being used illegally to support a terrorist network sponsored in secret by the government. That was six years ago, before she married Lee Ainsley and adopted Ann Silbey Sashakovich. Now, she worked with Lee and Avram Shimmel for the United Nations Paramilitary Force, headquartered in Manhattan.

Cassie cooked dinner for herself and Lee. It was a small dim sum feast she had learned to prepare when she was a management consultant nearly a decade ago. She and Lee sat at the kitchen table. Cassie could barely hear the guards walking their rounds outside.

She reached into her pants pocket when her cellphone buzzed. The phone's screen lit the entire kitchen of the huge home even brighter. She read the screen and smiled. "Lee, I just got a text from Ann. She says she likes this roommate better than the party girl she shared with last year."

Lee Ainsley rose from his seat and rounded the table. He popped his head over his wife's shoulder and read the text. "That's one worry gone. I hope Ann can use her fingers to type now. That dictation software she tried was nasty."

Cassie frowned. "Well, there is that."

Lee still stared at the screen. "Ann says her name is Laura D. Hunter." He turned and started up the stairs.

"Lee, what are you going to do?"

He spoke over his shoulder. "Let's see who she is. No surprises for Ann this semester."

* * *

It was nearly one hour later when Lee appeared in the compound's laundry room where Cassie folded newly cleaned clothing. He said, "I googled Laura D. Hunter and filtered by age. This woman isn't totally normal."

Cassie looked up. "What makes you say that?"

Lee read the notes he'd typed onto his cellphone's screen: "Her father murdered her mother for an affair the mother was having. He's in prison now. Turns out, they were both bank robbers. Not hackers, but the old type of bank robbers. Guns and getaway cars. Laura was twelve when her dad murdered her mother. After that, she was raised by her grandparents."

Cassie scratched her chin. "Should we tell Ann?"

Lee shrugged. "Yeah. But if she knows we're snooping after her roommate, she might be angry with us. She already thinks we're 'helicopter parents.' Especially what happened last year with the CypherGhost. I think we should encourage her to do her own research. She's competent enough. It will take her less time than I needed."

Cassie stopped folding. "Okay, then. Let me draft a text." She pulled her phone from her pocket and her fingers tapped away for a few seconds. "Before I send this, you should read it. Here." She showed him the screen.

> Ann—what do you know about your roommate? Is she really safer than that woman you were paired with last year? Please let us know.

Lee shook his head. "No. Way too obvious."
Cassie edited her message. "How about this?"

> Ann—Glad your new roommate isn't the monster you barely survived last year. Thanks for the message.

Lee nodded. "Yeah. Send that."

* * *

Ann read her mom's text and frowned. She was sure that she had correctly interpreted what the message really meant. She thought, *Mom's right. Knowing is better.*

She waited until Laura left the room to get lunch. Ann figured she would be alone for at least a half hour. But it took her only half of that time to do a routine search. As the half hour passed, she completed hacking into Laura's school records, then visited the site of her hometown newspaper. Laura's different addresses pointed the way. She'd lived at one address for the first twelve years of her life, and the move to the second address was concurrent with a series of news headlines regarding a murder case. Ann read eight articles about how Laura's dad dealt with her mom's affair with—of all the possibilities—the mailman. The trial of her father filled six of the pieces. Not until the final one did it mention that the twelve-year-old Laura had ended up with her grandparents.

So, there was more to Laura than she had told Ann. Now

Ann had to decide what to do with her new-found knowledge. *Damn Mom for hinting I should look into Laura's back-ground*. It took only a few seconds for Ann to decide she wanted to help Laura adjust.

* * *

Laura Hunter went to the student cafeteria and bought an egg-salad sandwich. She sat in a secluded corner and nibbled at it. She wasn't really hungry. She was never hungry. But she knew she had to eat in order to live. She tried to focus on the vast opportunities that attending Stanford offered her. *With just a bit of luck, I might carve out a future in academia.* Then the word "carve" brought her past back. She heard her parents arguing as if they were right in front of her and it was happening now. She cringed at the memory of the foul lang-uage they used, yelling at each other until she remembered hearing her mother scream.

She shivered, remembering how she had emerged from her bedroom and walked to theirs. Her mother, still alive, was covered in blood, with more pulsing from her neck as she gasped. Blood spurted from her neck, covering the floor. The coppery smell filled Laura's lungs and made her heave up her breakfast. She saw the dead body of a man in the corner of the room, his throat sliced open. Her father stood facing away from Laura, holding a blood-drenched knife. He sobbed.

Laura remembered how she had backed away and fled to her own room. She stayed there for a long time. *Some-times*, she thought, *I think my soul is still trapped there.*

* * *

Frank Lucessi yawned as he opened the office door of his cas-ita. He could hear the buzz of the jungle. The afternoon in Areguá, forty-five minutes southeast of Asunción, Paraguay, was more humid than usual for autumn. He wiped perspiration from his face using the sleeve of his Oxford button-down shirt.

He'd been expecting a call from an associate on a pressing business matter. He pulled the collar from his thick neck and tugged its front buttons from his barrel-chested torso in a failed attempt to cool himself off. When that didn't work, he walked back into the room and closed the door. He sat at his desk. His Rolex told him it was 7:57 a.m. *Any minute now.*

The landline chirped. "Lucessi."

"Santos here. We have several problems."

"Crap. You told me this would be easy."

"The FBI and Interpol are working together. It will be much more difficult to deliver the goods."

Frank mumbled a curse word under his breath. "What do you need? More men? More baksheesh? More time?"

"Señor Lucessi, I cannot tell you as yet. Let me work a plan and I'll call you back. Figure about two days."

"Okay then. You have two days to come up with a tactical plan." Frank slammed the phone down on its receiver. "Fuck!" He brushed a lock of black hair away from his eyes.

* * *

Robert Randall felt the buzzing in his pants pocket. He pulled his cell out and read the screen. "Randall."

"Robert, it's Don." Don was an independent contractor Randall sometimes used. "We picked up on that guns-and-drugs guy you asked us to follow. Seems he's up to his neck in a deal with one of the smaller cartels."

Randall rose from his desk at the CIA and walked to the window facing the parking garage. He ignored his reflection, because at nearly fifty years of age, he looked much older. He hated how thin he looked, and being bald didn't help. "Is he still in Budapest or has he traveled?"

"He's been at his villa in Paraguay for the last two days."

Randall thought for a few seconds. "So, this is drugs, not guns."

"You're as sharp as a pencil, Robert. What are you going to do?"

"I'm heading to my apartment. I'll pack a bag and I'll see if I can find him at his villa. Make him an offer he can't refuse." Randall terminated the call. He smiled. He was sure he could turn Lucessi into an "off the books" asset. Things were going his way.

* * *

As she left her first class of the fall semester, Ann found her mind filled with questions. Most of them were about how she could ever read all the books on the list for this one class when she had four other classes that would also assign reading. Another was how to cope with her anger at Cassie for pushing thoughts about her roommate into her head. The most confusing and compulsive question was how she could start a conversation with the cute boy who sat next to her in class. Ann didn't think of herself as attractive or sexy. She had no specific quality that could draw a guy. She was about five-foot-six and one hundred twenty pounds, just a bit heavier than last year. But their seats were so close she could read his name—Glen Sarkov—on his book bag, which she assumed held his assigned-reading handout notes and his notebook computer.

She tried to push his image from her mind, but she couldn't. As she hurried to her next class along the brick-and-plaster walls of the quadrangle's cloister, all she could see were his golden curls and his snarky lips. She found her interest in him interfering with her ability to walk. She sat on a bench in the campus quadrangle. *Damn him!* But what followed was, *how do I meet him?*

She felt the bench bounce a bit with the weight of another person and looked to her left. She gulped and the smile dropped off her face.

"Are you okay? You were stagger-stepping and I worried you might trip."

He had a slight Russian accent that she hadn't expected. But, before she could muster a word, he smiled at her and her heart melted.

"I'm Glen, Glen Sarkov. We're both in Dr. Kallberg's class on software economics."

She tried again to speak. Her lips moved but the only sound she could produce was "Ahhhh."

He laughed. "I see I've rendered you speechless. That's never happened before."

She recovered and smiled back. "Just surprised. I'm Ann Sashakovich. Were you following me?"

"No. Just on my way to my next class. Computer language development with Abrams."

She was on her way to that very class. So, he was also a computer science major. They might easily have the same professors for many of the same courses. She rose from the bench and found herself once again steady on her feet. "Me too. We can walk together."

He followed her for a few steps, then drew even with her. "What made you choose Stanford?"

"My mom went here, got her PhD in economics. She wanted me here. What about you?"

"Parents emigrated from old Russia. I was born in Moscow. My parents weren't oligarchs. We moved here for a better life. And Stanford is the best."

She nodded as they walked. *So now I've met him.*

* * *

The sign on the door in one of Washington DC's older, dilapidated buildings read "Skorkin Consulting." The offices within that corner of the building were either empty or threadbare, and Alan Skorkin's tiny office appeared to discourage any client he might have from entering. Alan had purposefully set it up that way. Skorkin's real purpose for the office was its usefulness as a mail drop.

He was built like a linebacker, but still needed to take a deep breath after climbing the three flights of stairs to reach his office. In his early fifties, he kept in shape, but still, that was more in terms of martial arts than physical stamina.

To better his odds of physical security, he'd spent months searching for an office building without an elevator. This building, in a run-down section of the nation's capital, was particularly uninviting.

He popped the door open and picked up the envelopes lying near the door. As he rifled through them he saw one that caught his eye. No return address, and on the back was the single letter "K," scribbled in pencil.

He opened the envelope and found a slip of paper small enough to fit inside a fortune cookie. It had what he knew was the address of a website, but without the "https://" prefix. He pulled his cellphone from his pocket and entered the address, which led him to a spot where he could enter his private key. He tapped the key into his cell and a plain-text message downloaded onto his cell. It made entertaining reading:

Clean up needed: 679 Excelsior Drive, Sunnyvale, CA. Dispose of 2 occupants and clean premises.

Clean up needed: 94287 Argonaut Avenue, Mountain View, CA. Dispose of 6 occupants plus any visitors, and clean premises.

50% of payment sent, 50% of payment on completion.

Skorkin smiled. He headed back to his apartment to pack a suitcase. He loved visiting California.

A friend of his in the government had funded a Silicon Valley tech startup. When the company no longer depended on its initial personnel for further development of its product, Skorkin sometimes was called upon to make the cofounders disappear for good. He wasn't sure why his friend wanted them dead, but the pay was good and he enjoyed killing people.

* * *

Ann couldn't focus on the lecture and was glad she'd decided to record it using the mike in her notebook computer. They sat in adjacent desks at the class. When the class ended, Glen asked her if she'd like to grab coffee with him. She focused her sight on his heart-shaped face. All she could do was nod.

As they walked to the cafeteria, he spoke but she just smiled at him. The wind blew his blond hair into swirls. She resisted the urge to pat them back into place. Was this love at first sight? *No way*, she said to herself. *No, I just like him.*

They sat across from each other, sipping cappuccinos. "I noticed your hands. Looks like serious burns." He reached out and touched her scarred fingers. "You had multiple surgeries."

It took all her willpower not to pull her hand away from him. "Yes, an accident."

He nodded. "Still hurts?"

"No. The only thing still there is the scar on my mind from what I did to let this happen." She hoped her fake bravado covered her lie.

"If you want to tell me, I promise not to say something stupid."

"Maybe some other time." She waited for his next comment, not sure if she was interested in pursuing him further. *My hands. The scars. I'll be deformed forever.*

"So, listen, there's a party off campus tomorrow night. Would you be interested in being my date for the evening?"

She thought again about him. She remembered Charles, her boyfriend in high school, and how he'd dropped her once he entered Harvard. She saw the face of Charlette, the CypherGhost she had murdered six months ago to keep her from murdering her mother and her friends. Ann sighed and forced herself to smile. "Sure, but don't expect too much from me."

He nodded. "Just a date then."

* * *

Laura walked from her last class of the day. Late into the afternoon, it was still warm and bright, and she soaked in the sunlight as she crossed the quadrangle. Midway across, she slowed and stopped. Without understanding why, she burst into tears. At the other side of the quad, she saw a bench and she staggered over to it. As she sat, she dropped her book bag and her head fell into her hands.

She hated herself but wasn't sure why. It had something to do with her parents. She could hear them screaming inside her head. She knew this wasn't normal. The words she heard them say to each other were the same ones she always heard:

Ingrid:	You should leave now. I hate you.
Frederick:	I can't leave. Someone has to watch you. You aren't normal. Laura isn't safe with you around.
Ingrid:	I'll kill you if I get the chance.
Frederick:	That's why I can't leave. You're dangerous.

She heard them get louder. Then she saw her father holding a knife and slash it across her mother's neck. The sound made Laura sick. She remembered screaming.

She sat on the bench for nearly an hour. The sun set and it grew dark before she could once again rise and walk to the apartment.

* * *

Ann felt hunger pangs and looked at the school library's clock. *Want dinner now.* She packed her notebook into her book bag and rose. University Avenue had hundreds of restaurants of every description, less than a mile away. She needed the exercise after sitting for several hours. There was an autumn chill in the air outside. She decided to take a shortcut through the woods. No streetlights, but she felt confident she would only be in darkness for a few hundred yards. Less than three minutes.

About halfway across the wooded field separating the quad from Palo Alto city streets, someone hit her from behind and took her down. She rolled onto her back, ready to defend herself. Her attacker was a young male, possibly her own age. He wore a hoodie and landed atop her.

"Don't resist or I'll cut you." He restrained her hands with one of his, using the other to drop his pants. He held a knife with his free hand and prepared to cut her jeans.

Ann concentrated on his penis and thought, *FIRE!* Her hands tingled, fingers glowing with heat. Then, as she watched, the man's penis caught fire.

He howled and jumped away, using his hands to beat off the flames. Then he rose from her body and stared at her, turned, and fled

Ann, rose off the ground and aimed at his retreating bare ass. Once more, she thought *FIRE!* As he ran away from her, the bare skin on his backside burst into flame. She smiled as he continued running across the field.

Her hands cooled quickly and she saw no evidence on her fingers of the flames she had created.

She was sure her special ability had been given her by the CypherGhost, but had no idea how or why. All she was sure of was that using this skill had made her famished. *Now, I must have food.*

* * *

Ann sat rigid in the dining room of the Dynasty restaurant in Palo Alto. She tensed, waiting for it to happen. *Any second now.* She opened the menu and told the waiter, "mapo, hot and sour soup." As the waiter turned away and headed off to the kitchen, Ann began to shiver. From the bottom of her spine up through the top of her skull, a freezing chill engulfed her. She watched her hands as they turned blue, then gray. Seconds passed before the chill faded. This always happened when she used her little trick. Setting her attempted rapist on fire tonight was the first time in over two months she'd attempted it.

She hadn't any idea how she had developed this new "talent" but it happened just after she murdered the Cypher-Ghost. Less than a month later, she decided the only people she could trust with this knowledge about her capabilities were William Wing and Betsy Brown, fellow hackers and friends. William had helped her learn about how to control it, and deal with its aftereffects. She had found that this chill would happen about a half hour after she used her hands to ignite anything. It wasn't getting any worse, but the experience wasn't any easier to tolerate

She rubbed her shoulders as the waiter placed a tureen of hot and sour soup in front of her. She eyed the brown, steaming liquid with its shredded pork, bean curd, and wood ear slices, and sniffed its sesame aroma. She placed the napkin on her lap and picked up the soup spoon. After several mouthfuls, the heat from the soup transferred its spicy warmth into her body. She quickly consumed the entire tureen. *Back to normal.*

As she recovered, she turned and saw that many of the restaurant's other patrons were now watching her. The waiter approached, his look of concern etched on his face. "Are you okay?"

Ann nodded. "Sometimes, my blood pressure crashes. It's called a 'vasovagal syncope.'"

The waiter nodded as the look of concern disappeared off his face. He turned and disappeared.

Ann thought about her situation. Would her attacker go to the police? No, he might even get himself arrested if he tried. Would he tell others what had happened? No, no one would believe him. What about the burns she'd inflicted on him? He'd surely need medical attention. She had already determined that the heat hitting him was in excess of six hundred degrees Fahrenheit. She winced, knowing how much pain she had caused him. Even though he'd attempted to rape her, she felt remorse for what his life would become.

Where would he go? Stanford Hospital? It was the closest hospital with an emergency room. *What lie would he tell them?* She was sure it would be obvious. And that might open an investigation. *Careful. Don't do this again except in self-defense.*

The waiter returned with the mapo tofu. She plucked up a chili pepper with her chopsticks and chewed the fiery delight. *I'll have to figure out what to do if I ever am called out for this.*

* * *

Laura was at the desk in the living room of their apartment

when she heard the front door open. She looked up. "Ann, what are you up to?"

"Just ate dinner out at Dynasty. Got my Asian fix." Ann sat at her own desk. She pulled out her notebook and logged herself in. Then she sneaked a peek at Laura. Laura's eyes were bloodshot and the skin around her eyes was pink.

Laura sat still, not reading the open book in front of her. The look on her face was living proof she was preoccupied with something.

Ann reached across the gulf separating the two desks and touched Laura's arm. "What's bothering you? If you don't want to talk, I'll leave it be. But if you need someone to talk to, I'm here."

Laura's lips quivered before she began to wail. Ann waited for several minutes until Laura was once again in control of herself. Laura looked like she'd been through hell. "I've never told anyone. Not sure I should ever tell another person. We aren't even really friends."

"Yeah. As I said, if you're not comfortable telling me, that's okay. But it looks to me like you need to tell somebody what's upsetting you."

Laura looked away. "My secret. I was very young. My father and mother argued constantly. Angry, violent with each other. She often hit him. When she did, he'd hit her back. Then, one day, I saw him cut her neck open with a knife. My mom fell to the ground. There was blood everywhere. There was also a strange man on the floor with his neck sliced open. I ran to my own room and bolted the door. The police, when they arrived, they found... they found my mom and the strange man both dead."

"That's awful. What happened to your father?"

"They arrested him. There was a trial. He was sentenced to death. He's been on death row for fifteen years now."

"What happened to you?"

"I went to live with my grandparents. My mom's parents. They took care of me. I got an art scholarship to attend Stanford."

"You paint?"

Laura nodded.

"Can I see some of what you've done?"

The paintings Laura showed Ann were nightmarish depictions of brutal crimes and battle scenes. None of the figures had a face. The colors were smears on the canvasses. Ann was mesmerized. "Wow. These look like they should be in museums."

Laura stared at the one she was holding. "These are what I see in my dreams when I try to sleep. Every night, another battle, another mugging, another killer. Every night without fail."

Something didn't feel right about what Laura said. It sounded rehearsed. Ann realized she feared for Laura. But more than that, she feared Laura.

CHAPTER 4

906 Simpson Street, Sunnyvale, CA

September 12, 6:02 a.m.

Alan Skorkin found a parking space for his late model rental sedan six blocks from where he was to complete the first leg of his contract. After locking the car, he walked to within visual range of 679 Excelsior Drive and saw that it was totally residential. No stores for him to use as perch sites to develop profiles beyond what he'd already gathered off the internet while he was on the flight here. The two occupants were co-founders of a company named Redoit Write. Their company made an AI software product that could read software manuals in digital format and reword them to be under-standable in seven languages. InTelQ had funded them from a seed round eight months ago until now, with their product having completed its first beta round. Skorkin had figured out the "why" to killing the cofounders: his government friend was a greedy man who wanted to take profits from their products as soon as possible now that his cofounders were no longer necessary for further development of their product.

Death would be their exit strategy.

He stood in the shade of a cypress tree, sure the shadows shielded him from view. He could see activity within the house through its windows. He heard the sound of a conversation, two voices, one male, one female. *Lucky me.* He waited for the inevitable. Soon, one or both would leave for work, and he could complete the research he needed to do within their empty house. If both left, he could set the house to look like a probable robbery-homicide had gone wrong and wait inside for them both to return. *If only one leaves, I can murder the other occupant and set up the other as the murderer. Either way, they'll no longer have a claim on the startup my client funded. And, I read the docs on their standard funding agreement at one of my previous side-jobs. Too bad they agreed to not let any heirs have claims on their stock.*

Soon, one of the occupants left the house and entered the auto parked curbside.

She looked to be in her mid-thirties, brunette and trim. He recognized her from the photo his client had included within the link. Then the garage door opened. The man who exited on a bicycle wore a helmet, obscuring his face. He rode off as the door closed automatically. Skorkin checked his watch and noted how long they'd been together,

Skorkin walked down the street looking like he belonged there. He took the paved walkway around the house to its backyard. *Time to work.*

* * *

Robert Randall had driven his car far away from his office, all the way to Baltimore. It was time to call Frank Lucessi, and he'd need to do that on a pay phone. So few remained, but he knew of one near the Baltimore Orioles baseball stadium. The phone was right outside the main exit, in plain sight, and the street was busy with passersby. *But*, he thought, *it'll have to do.*

He'd committed Lucessi's phone number to memory,

along with a script, to make this fast and easy. Randall dialed Lucessi's number in Paraguay and paid for the first three minutes with pocket change. Lots of pocket change.

"Frank Lucessi here."

"Mr. Lucessi, I'm interested in being one of your customers. I have a business proposition I think you'll like."

"Not interested." The line went dead.

Randall cursed. *I need a new cutout to replace the guy I had killed last week. The idiot found out too much about what I'm doing and wanted a cut.* He repeated his process. This time when he heard Lucessi answer, he said, "Don't hang up again unless you want me as your most powerful enemy."

He heard Lucessi laugh. "Then you're a jackass. But, okay, I'll play along. I'll give you thirty seconds."

Randall smiled. "I want you to act as a venture capitalist to several startup companies. I'll give you what we want you to send to them in funding, dollar for dollar. The minimum for any of our investments is a half a million, USD. If you can sign a deal with them on our behalf, you'll need to attend board meeting with the cofounders for maybe a year. Then you'll receive your share of the proceeds, equal to what you gave them. If they become successful, you get to do another for us, and soon you get to do two at a time. In two years, that's at least three million for you, and it would take maybe a total of twenty days across each year. I know you don't like to travel to the United States, but you can demand they travel to wherever you want the board meetings to take place. Interested?"

"I can travel to the United States if you make it easy for me to go there without being arrested. Do that and double the money and you have a deal."

Randall smiled so hard he felt like he was glowing. "Okay. I'll send what you need to your office. Sign the papers and return them to me in the enclosed envelope." Of course, the names on the agreement would not be his.

He terminated the call. The money would be recoverable when Lucessi died of mysterious causes in two years. Easy for him to arrange.

* * *

Alan Skorkin had completed the setup for his termination of the first two names on the contract. First, he took note of the locations of the four security cams mounted around the house's exterior. He approached them from an angle that would not let them capture his image. He disabled each with a can of blue spray paint.

Once within the house, he found several more cams and did the same with those. But he couldn't find the disk storage device they transmitted to. *Probably offsite. Crap!*

He sat on the couch in their living room, watching their 65-inch high-end television set. CNN was reporting on the latest news, a story about America's dumbest presidential candidate, who was threatening a kinetic war with China. The idiot mentioned his friendly relations with Russia. The man couldn't see that Russia wanted China weak, and no matter who won the war, Russia would then be stronger than their southern neighbor, and China would be ripe for invasion. America would soften them up. He shook his head and smothered a laugh. He heard the garage door open and turned off the television set. He rose and walked to the doorway, a loaded syringe in his right hand.

The doorknob clicked as it unlocked, and then twisted, and the door opened. Skorkin waited as the door swung open, hiding him behind it. A twenty-something man entered alone and closed the door.

"Who the fuck are you? What are you doing here?"

Skorkin smiled. "I'm the locksmith. Your door was open

and one of your neighbors called me to fix the lock. I'll need you to pay me for my work."

The young man frowned, trying to understand the situation.

Skorkin didn't wait. He reached out and pulled the man closer. Before the young man could react, Skorkin plunged the syringe into his neck and injected its contents. He counted off the seconds as his target's hands reached for the spot where the syringe had just been. Skorkin reached "eight" and the man's knees buckled. Skorkin caught his target and dragged the now-unconscious man to the living-room couch.

The man would remain unconscious for at least an hour. Skorkin entered their garage and found a full set of tools he could use. Not that he needed them. But, they had made it so convenient for him. He smiled, took what he thought he might like to use, and returned to the living room where he set to work on the man's slumbering body. The injected solution was mostly a customized form of fentanyl, one that was difficult to detect in autopsy. He used the plastic tablecloth he'd brought with him to keep blood splatter from staining his expensive business suit. He pulled the trigger of the .22-caliber pistol he'd bought on the street in East Palo Alto earlier. The round entered the man's head just below his ear and didn't exit. He left the man's corpse on the floor at the point where the kitchen and living room joined without any hallway.

When his other target returned, he would complete his work on both of them.

* * *

Ann woke from a vivid nightmare. It was dark in their room and it took her several seconds to adjust to consciousness. She always kept a pad and a pen by her bedside. She jotted down her thoughts: *Laura's paintings could be taken from real events in her conscious life. In her paintings, Laura committed horrific acts. Maybe she killed her mother and let her father go to prison to keep her from being sent away?*

She shook herself. *Why am I thinking the worst of her?* She closed her eyes and tried to go back to sleep. But the thoughts remained playing out in her head and nothing she tried quieted her mind.

* * *

Skorkin heard footsteps approach on the walkway to the house. He tiptoed to the door and waited behind the bulk of it where it would hide him as it opened. When it closed with the home's other occupant inside, Skorkin covered the woman's face with a rag doused in ether.

Time to finish up. He sat her down at the couch adjacent to the dead man's corpse on the floor between the kitchen and the living room.

He pulled the photo sent by his client and identified her as his second target. After binding her hands and feet with duct tape and tying a gag across her mouth, he placed smelling salts under her nose to wake her.

She gagged.

"You're probably wondering who I am and why this is happening. So, as a kindness, before I kill you, I'll answer these." He always did this, to reduce the guilt he felt. If he explained before he murdered, he'd found it made him feel better.

She struggled against the duct tape.

"I'm good at my job. Don't bother. Pay attention." He grabbed her chin and slapped her face. "That's better. You two had a startup funded by my client. You should have done better research on whose money you took. They fund about twenty startups a year, and the money isn't sourced from private investors as they led you to believe. No, it's government funds. They look for startups whose products can be weaponized in some way. Like yours. When something with real potential comes along—like yours—they do what they need to keep the public from investing in the tech. An IPO would put you in public scrutiny. Your imminent deaths will cause a minor struggle for those you've named in your last will and testaments, but my guess is either you didn't closely read the investment docs or you didn't understand them. With your deaths, the government will end up with total ownership of your work." He shook his head. "Sorry for you."

The woman was now furiously shaking her head.

"Again, I'm sorry. But I have to kill you now. I'll give you a few minutes to make your peace. I promise your death will be relatively painless. And everyone dies, sooner or later. Your time is now." He sat next to her looking at his watch. Then, he smiled at her. "Okay then." He took the knife and plunged it into her neck. He waited until her pulse had vanished.

He carefully placed the knife into the dead man's hand. As he stood up, the dead bodies stared back at him. He took a deep breath to keep their ghosts from causing him to regret what he'd done for money.

He had placed the plastic tablecloth he'd brought with him between him and each victim when he killed them. Now he washed the tablecloth in their kitchen sink along with his plastic gloves, then scrubbed the kitchen down with bleach and water. After packing his tools, Alan Skorkin sneaked out the back door and made his way back to his car. It would be a rather short drive to Mountain View for his appointment with the others he'd been assigned to terminate. He sighed happily, knowing he'd given his latest victim time to digest the reasons for his visit.

* * *

Frederico Santos drove his late-model Subaru past the entrance to Chapultepec Park into the Zona Rosa. He looked into the rear-view mirror and smiled when he was sure he wasn't followed. His visage stared back. Nearing his thirtieth birthday, he still looked like he was barely twelve. His dark curly hair held its form. Good. *Mr. Lucessi likes me to not look like a hood.*

Lucessi would be meeting him outside one of the upscale bodegas in twelve minutes. The man had told him he was dissatisfied with how Santos was handling the drug distribution operation and he might only have one chance to explain what had caused the problems.

The man was always prompt and complained if Santos was late. The idea was to make their meeting look casual and as brief as possible. Santos suspected there might be Federales trailing either or both of them. He parked the car illegally half a block away and trotted down the street to the alleyway fronting the bodega. Lucessi wasn't waiting. Santos scanned his wristwatch and frowned. The message had stated "3 p.m." He stood still and tried to decide what to do. *Look casual,* he thought. But then he saw them. Two of them, staring right at him. He turned to walk away and saw the other two coming at him from the other side. He was sure Lucessi hadn't sent them, but they didn't look like Federales either.

No. These were either here to take him or kill him. He had a handgun in his pocket, but one of them was smiling and shaking his head. He tried to draw the handgun anyway, but the shot from one of the ones behind him was the last sound he ever heard.

* * *

Robert Randall ended the call from his Mexican "consultant." *So, Frederico Santos is not working for Lucessi anymore.*

He's being buried. He chuckled. It was time to call Lucessi again.

This time, he was sure that Lucessi wouldn't hang up. He was pretty sure Lucessi wouldn't try to backtrace the call, since they had already established that Lucessi would work with Randall. He punched in Lucessi's number.

"Yeah. What now?"

"Mr. Lucessi, I've just heard that your friend Frederico Santos has retired. Did you know this?"

"Huh? Where'd you find this out?"

"I have sources. You must realize that if this is true, I'm now your only source of income. I believe this should cement our business relationship. Yes?"

The silence went on and on, but Randall was willing to wait much longer. Finally, Lucessi replied. "Yeah."

"Good. I have a client in Los Altos, California. They're looking for venture funding for a startup that plans to manufacture a product I would love to be able to purchase. Owning a chunk of the company would be even better. I know you love to negotiate deals. I'm prepared to offer them six million for one-third ownership as a seed round. I'll send you documents and a reading list on how the process works. You have six days to call me back when you have learned how to do this. Oh, and remember, it is vital that they know you aren't a United States citizen and that you live in Paraguay."

"But I am a United States citizen."

"Lie. You're good at that. It's one of the reasons I chose you."

Randall terminated the call, ready to watch the process from afar. If Lucessi performed to spec, there were fifty more prospective deals he had ready to cook.

CHAPTER 5

**Stanford University Student Union,
Palo Alto, CA**

September 12, 10:40 a.m.

Glen Sarkov smiled as he read the email. Then he rose from his seat in the student cafeteria and did a little happy dance. Other students nearby gave him just a glance, then went back to their own notebook computers. Glen read the email from the venture capitalist several times more, looking to see if there was an escape clause that might make this moment less joyous, but, no, there was no caveat. The VC was making an outright offer to fund his startup company.

His first date with Ann Sashakovich had been much more than pleasant. But last night when they met for dinner and a movie, he was just another student with big plans. Now, this very second, he'd become someone who might become a serious player in the startup world.

In short, his life was suddenly wonderful. He wanted to share the moment with someone. He punched Ann's phone number into his cell and waited.

"Sashakovich here."

"It's Glen. I just got an email from a venture capitalist. I got an offer of a seed round."

"Glen? You got what? Wow. Congrats. Want to celebrate?"

"Oh, yeah. How about after class at your favorite restaurant."

"Mmm. Okay. Either Yucca De Lac or Dynasty. You make the call. My last class ends at 5 p.m."

"Okay. I'll meet you at the cafeteria."

Now Glen felt doubly happy. He read the email yet again, preparing himself for the next step in the process. The VC stated that his interest was dependent on a meeting with Glen, where, if all went as hoped, they would sign papers. The seed round would cost Glen one-third of his company. The amount the company would net was six million dollars, and Glen and his cofounders would have to produce a prototype before they had spent one million of the cash. Hard, but certainly possible. Glen called his cofounders on a conference call and relayed the news to them.

The first step would be finding them an office that had access to a next-door laboratory. He guessed that either an incubator or a private space of at least five hundred square feet would be the minimum that would work. He'd seen a few spaces in Sunnyvale that were big enough.

* * *

"So, tell me how this all happened." Ann sat back into to plush chair in the main dining room of Yucca De Lac, a Hong Kong–style restaurant.

Glen grinned back, obviously enjoying his opportunity to share such good fortune. "We had an assignment in the startup business management course I'm taking. We were told to find and convince an angel or venture capitalist to meet face-to-face about funding our final project for the course. We were given a list of twenty people who might be more willing to meet, having a formal relationship with Stanford. But I decided on several others who are totally independent from the university, since those seemed to be more interested in nanotech medicine projects."

Ann frowned. "So how did you get their interest without even meeting face-to-face?"

"I sent them the first page of the business plan's executive summary plus a summary page of the projected financials. I was hoping for interest in a face-to-face. That's all. You can't imagine how surprised I am."

"Do you have a copy of the email with you? Can I see it?"

Glen reached into his jacket pocket and produced a printed copy of the email he'd received. He carefully unfolded it and passed it to Ann.

She took it in her hands with the reverence one might show for a newly discovered ancient religious manuscript. She scanned the words, looking for hidden meanings. "My mom was once very rich. She was a member of an angel group at NYU's Stern Graduate School of Business. I've seen letters like this in her files at our home in Washington DC. This reads like one of the ones she'd sent to a couple of cancer cure companies."

The waiter arrived with their food.

Ann sniffed the aroma wafting from the roast duck sliders she'd ordered for them. "Yum. This smells like heaven." She passed the letter back to Glen and picked up one of the sliders.

Glen used his chopsticks to hoist a xiao long bao to his mouth. He gently sucked the soupy mix from the dumpling, then tasted a corner of the Shanghai dumpling and smiled. "Nothing beats soul food for a celebration."

They ate in silence, passing smiles between them.

Glen leaned across the table, bringing their faces just a few inches away. He kissed her briefly, no more than the brushing of their lips for a moment. "Now that we've kissed, there won't be that awkward moment later on." He smiled, and to his joy, Ann smiled back.

The waiter returned with a tureen of hot and sour soup.

"So, what will you do if you get funded? Won't you have to leave Stanford?"

Glen shrugged. "I might be able to take classes at night, but it'll take me longer if I'm not attending full time. I'm really not yet sure."

Ann's eyes stared at the table, away from Glen.

His jaw dropped a bit. "Are you really worrying about me?"

"Maybe."

Glen couldn't hide the smile that flashed and then disappeared. "I'll still want to see you. Even if I'm not a student anymore."

Ann nodded, her head filling with questions for which there was no answer. *If he's going to be a startup guy, will that make him more arrogant? How will it affect the demands on his time? Will I have to compete with the startup for his time?* The questions were endless.

CHAPTER 6

Supermax Prison,
16 miles southwest of Las Vegas, NV

September 12, 4:10 p.m.

Frederick Hunter sat in a corner of his tiny cell, trying to stanch the blood seeping from him. He'd collapsed after one of the prisoners shivved him in the gut in the exercise yard. He suspected that if he'd let one of the guards see the wound, they'd have finished the job. His attackers would try again. And even uninjured, he was short and not in good shape.

Hunter had been a doctor in his pre-lockup days. His medical practice ended when he'd operated on a patient while drunk. To make their lives possible, his wife had encouraged him to help her rob the local savings and loan. Yes, he'd been a drunkard, a fact that the prosecution had used to make his conviction on a charge of murder a slam dunk. He remembered that day, a day filled with lies and blood. His wife's blood.

When he'd arrived home, he heard loud voices coming from the bedroom. He thought it was his wife arguing with their daughter. Ingrid was an alcoholic. The two of them, Ingrid and Frederick were a matched pair, he thought. Laura, their daughter might also end up an alcoholic with two drunkard parents. He remembered sighing as he walked through the front door and headed toward the bedroom. And as he entered, he saw the scene that would forever end his life as a free man. Another man lay next to his wife, naked. His wife was also naked, but she lay on the floor, her neck pulsing blood. Laura held a blood-covered shard of glass in her hand, and she was plunging it repeatedly into the dead man.

Frederick grabbed Laura and tried to calm her. He talked to her. "Please, Laura. Let me have that sharp piece of glass before you cut yourself." She seemed to suddenly become aware of what she was doing. She dropped the glass.

"Good." He made his decision. "Go to your room. Right now, go. Take off your dress and wash yourself in the shower. Then dry yourself and get dressed. Don't come out of your room until I tell you it's safe."

She walked down the hall. He heard her bedroom door close, and then a minute later, he heard the shower come on.

He examined the room. He could imagine a story where he had murdered them both after finding them in bed. Frederick modified the bodies to fit this new story, and then washed Laura's fingerprints off the glass shard. He dipped the shard in each corpse's blood, then wiped some of each body's blood on his clothing. He cut into his palm with the shard, so it would appear he had injured himself while stabbing each of the cheating lovers.

"Oh, Ingrid. I suspected you were having an affair. I could still love you and hope to earn back your love. I'm so sorry." He picked up the telephone with his bloody hand and dialed 911. When the operator asked what his emergency was, he said, "I want to report two murders. I just killed my wife and her lover, in my house. I'm calling from there."

There was no way he could let Laura's life go down the drain. As he waited for the police to arrive, his thoughts focused on his daughter.

Now, nine years later, he was sure he'd made the correct decision.

* * *

Frank Lucessi passed through customs at San Francisco Airport with no problems. His business partner had done what he'd promised. He first rented a car and then drove south into Silicon Valley. He'd heard of it, of course, but had never actually been there. Robert Randall had sent him a blind text, indicating the clients he would meet with, the hotels he would stay at, and everything else Frank would need to know to complete his tasks.

The Best Western in Mountain View was unremarkable in every way. Frank rolled his suitcase through the door of his tiny room and looked around. *Supposed to be a rich venture capitalist, and this is what they give me?*

He pulled his handwritten notes from his pocket. Randall had told him to commit everything to memory and then delete the text he'd sent. Frank had tried memorizing everything but the text was over eight thousand words, much too long. Frank had handwritten crib notes onto paper so he could spend more time trying to cram it all into his memory. He reread instructions on the questions he should ask the entrepreneurs, and how to respond to their questions. Fifteen more minutes with the papers and he folded them, then walked to his rental car. According to Randall, the first person on his list was a thirty-two-year-old tech cofounder working at an internet security startup. Then, later in the afternoon, he'd meet with a Stanford University student whose company was looking for a seed round. Over the next three days he was to meet seven entrepreneurs and hand out checks for roughly twelve million dollars.

Frank started the engine and drove out from the parking lot. *Easy work*, but he'd need to file reports with Randall and he'd worried about this. He decided to use his cellphone to tape each meeting, then write the reports from his recordings before he erased them. *What could go wrong?*

* * *

Laura Hunter hurried from her last class of the day. Medieval Art History was the driest course on her schedule and the two cups of coffee she'd downed in the Student Union cafeteria before class had worn off. She had a paper to write and headed back for more coffee. All the tables were filled, some partially and most totally. She found a table where only one other seat was taken. She took the seat farthest from him. He appeared to be much older than the other students on the campus. Short, dark, curly hair, slightly chubby, a vintage gray pinstripe business suit, but no necktie. *Faculty or administration*, she wondered.

He was also drinking coffee and reviewing some hand-written notes. She could tell that he wasn't aware of her presence. She decided not to draw him into a conversation.

When he finally looked up and saw her, he seemed to be surprised. His eyes bugged, then narrowed. "Uh, sorry. I just needed a place to sit while I review some notes."

She smiled and nodded. "You aren't a student."

"Uh, yes. I—"

She reexamined him. His posture was too aggressive to be one of the Stanford elite. "You're not faculty or admin either."

He sat in silence for a few seconds. She waited. Then he said, "I'm not associated with the university in any way. I'm here to meet with a student about a business deal. I'm Frank Lucessi."

"Laura Hunter. Pleased to meet you. And, yes, I'm a student. What's your business?"

"I'm a venture capitalist."

Laura's nose twitched. "You do tech stuff."

"Pretty much."

"Which firm?"

"Ah, it's InTelQ. We're from Paraguay."

She sat still, thinking for a few seconds. "Well, I'm an art history major. So, I'll let you get ready for your meeting. But, if you don't mind, I'd like to sit here since there aren't many unfilled seats this time of day."

"Yes, sure." With that last sentence, he went back to reading his scribbled notes.

Soon, a male student that Laura had seen with Ann walked into the cafeteria, looked at the tables as if he was searching for someone specific, and walked over to their table. He nodded at Laura, then walked one more step and smiled at the venture capitalist. "Are you Frank Lucessi?"

Lucessi nodded. "Yes. I'm with InTelQ. We can talk here if you like."

"I'm Glen Sarkov." He extended his hand and Frank extended his. They shook.

Laura looked at her coffee cup. Empty now. She had noted Glen's exotic accent. Sounded Russian. She said to both of them, "Well, I've got to go. Nice meeting you, Mr. Lucessi. Nice seeing you again, Glen."

She got up and left them at the table. It was time for her to get to the student library where she could write her paper.

* * *

Frank Lucessi had been successful at three deals for Robert Randall so far. Three deals in two days. *I'm one deal ahead of schedule.* His standing orders were to close the deals while looking like he needed to be convinced by the entrepreneur that the startup in question was worth his own firm's cash and consideration.

He examined Glen Sarkov. The student wore upscale

business casual clothing and spoke with a noticeable Russian accent. Frank imagined he must be related to some of the oligarchs who had migrated from Moscow to San Francisco in the Gorbachev–Yeltsin era. "Tell me about your startup. Why should we at InTelQ be interested? And, who are your team members?"

Glen smiled before he spoke. Then he said, "I'm in the nanodevices program. I have a major in particle physics and I've discovered that new medical technology is too easily hacked. My team has developed a nano firewall that is physical in nature. It can be programmed to let only 'desired' telecomm signals pass between users and their 'friends.' The physical device can be inserted between the user and any comm signal. And, best of all, it can be set up to protect the physical body as well as the computer devices of a person."

Frank seemed to be confused. "How can a physical device act as a human shield?"

Glen smiled again. "Ever hear of shear thickening fluid? STF? Invented by the US Army? Well, that was last generation. This new generation can be painted on human skin."

Frank had no idea what Glen was speaking of, but he smiled back. "Aha. So how does this work?"

"The molecules can be controlled by a computer device to set the STF to harden against certain signals, biohazards, or communication signals. That way, the STF itself cannot be hacked. The STF nanofield is programmed, then painted on the skin. It makes the user literally bulletproof, and any medical devices they wear become hack proof." Glen waited, as if he had anticipated a question that Frank knew he should be asking.

But, Frank hadn't any idea what he should say. An awkward silence surrounded him. "Ah, sounds expensive.

How much funding does your company need to produce a working prototype?"

"Oh, almost nothing for that. We've already produced a prototype. We're set to prove the tech to buyers. Our first target is the Department of Defense. We'll need the investment round to go from prototype to final design, then manufacture and market. We're asking for six million for a thirty-three percent ownership."

Frank's mind went blank. He couldn't remember how much to write the check for, but the percentage ownership seemed too low and the amount of cash seemed too high. He decided to trust his instincts. None of these deals was supposed to earn a minority share. "I can give you three million for fifty-five percent ownership."

Glen shook his head. "But we agreed to my amounts. I'll need to talk your revised offer over with my cofounders."

Frank felt like this deal was slipping away. But he'd no idea what Randall had agreed to in his email messages with Sarkov. "Okay then. Speak with your team. Call me tomorrow morning. We can talk then."

Sarkov rose from his chair, a worried look on his face. He extended his hand, and they shook. In seconds he was gone, leaving Frank to search his notes to see how big an error he'd made.

There it was: Glen Sarkov, MindField Technology, six million for fifty-point-one percent. He shook his head and left the cafeteria.

CHAPTER 7

**Stanford University campus,
Palo Alto, CA**

September 13, 8:22 a.m.

When Laura saw the out-of-place man in the cafeteria the next morning, she smiled and said hello.

His face brightened. "Oh, hi." He lifted his coffee cup and smiled at her.

"Whatcha doing here?" She placed her tray at his table and sat across from him.

"I have another meeting here today with the student I met yesterday."

"You mean Glen? He's my roommate's boyfriend."

"Really? Well he has a bright future. I want to fund his startup."

What's this man's name? She frowned into her coffee cup. Finally, she knew she'd have to ask. "I forgot your name."

"Frank. Frank Lucessi."

"Where are you from, Mr. Frank Lucessi?"

He seemed to take a rather long time before being ready to speak again. "Actually, I'm from Paraguay. But business takes me to America frequently."

"I've never been to Paraguay." She wrinkled her brow. "What's it like?"

73

Again, he took even longer this time. "Um, it's just another place. A little like northern California, but hotter and more humid."

Laura decided to do a little research on Paraguay. She finished her coffee, tossed her wrapped sandwich into her book bag and rose again. "It's been a pleasure making your acquaintance."

Frank thought about Laura and realized he found her desirable. She reminded him of all the women he'd wanted to date before he became wealthy. When he was just a street hustler. Before he had anything to offer. "Wait. Please."

She remained standing. "Yes?"

"I'll be spending another week here. I'm alone. May I take you to dinner?"

Laura thought for a few seconds before replying. She'd never had anyone express interest in her before. "Sure."

He passed her a business card. She scribbled her name and phone number on its back and exchanged that card for a fresh one of his. He smiled. "I'll call you tomorrow afternoon. Think of a place where you'd like to go for dinner tomorrow."

"Sure." She pocketed the card and walked toward the exit.

* * *

Glen Sarkov would be arriving in a few minutes. Frank Lucessi reviewed his notes one more time, so as to be sure not to make another mistake. He'd felt lonely since he left his base of operations in Paraguay, He closed his eyes for just a second, enjoying the afterglow of meeting a young woman. He was at least fifteen years older than her, but he was certain he could make the difference in years seem like a non-issue.

His eyes were still closed, a smile on his lips, when he

heard a male voice with a Russian accent: "Mr. Lucessi. Have you rethought your bid on MindField?"

Frank's eyes popped open. "Yes. Please accept my apologies. It was jet lag. The original offer stands. Six million for one-third ownership."

Glen smiled back. "Do you have the contracts?" He pulled his pen from his jacket pocket.

* * *

At the Student Union cafeteria, Ann and Glen sat across a table from each other. "No, not really. But, I mean, what's the difference if I didn't do any research about Lucessi's venture capital firm? Sure we took shortcuts. From what I've seen in Silicon Valley, everyone does. No one has time for product testing anymore. We all let our beta customers do the real grunt work. And in this environment where everyone needs to be first to market, who has time to research investors? They've got the money and they want to invest. Isn't that enough?"

Ann felt like Glen was setting himself up for a big disappointment. He was taking big chances with his tiny, vulnerable startup. She decided to get a better view of what had happened at the meeting with the venture capitalist before she offered advice. "What happened next?"

Glen smiled. "So, then he says, do you want to show these to your attorney before you sign them?" Glen leaned across the cafeteria table, bringing his face closer to Ann's.

She stifled the impulse to move back when he penetrated her personal space. "So, do you have the papers?" She frowned slightly. "You didn't sign them without showing them to one of the startup attorneys, did you?"

Glen reached into the oversized pocket of his sport jacket and pulled the papers out. "Do you know any of them?"

She nodded. "My mom uses a guy from the Corporate

Law Group. Paul Marotta in Burlingame. He might take a percentage of ownership in lieu of a corporate check. Did you incorporate yet?"

"Yes, we each put in three hundred in cash, so we have all that done."

Ann wondered who Glen had used for a corporate attorney. "So you have an attorney?"

"Not exactly. We read some Google webpages and incorporated ourselves."

Ann restrained the urge to reach across the table and throttle him. She was sure that not having a real attorney to do the work would bite him. She wondered if Glen would listen to her advice. "Not good. Really not good." She looked at the contracts. There were several paragraphs that looked nasty on the first page. She scanned the remaining pages. "Glen, this is bad. We'll have to fix this."

He looked like a child caught stealing cookies. "How bad is it?"

CHAPTER 8

**Stanford University campus,
Palo Alto, CA**

September 13, 9:32 a.m.

Laura read the text off her cellphone:

> Tomorrow night at 6:30. Where shall we go and
> where can I pick you up?
> Frank.

She grinned. *What's the most exclusive local place to
eat?* She searched her phone for "high end restaurants, Palo
Alto, CA."

A long list popped up onto the screen:

Evvia Estiatorio (Greek)
Pampas (Brazilian)
Saint Michael's Alley (Californian)
Zola Restaurant (French)
Tamarine Restaurant & Gallery (Vietnamese)
Sundance The Steakhouse
Baumé (French)
The Sea by Alexander's Steakhouse
Bird Dog (Californian)

Crepevine (Creperie

She examined all the photographs on the listing page. All looked attractive, and so did the descriptions of the food. Then she wondered what Frank would like. She decided on Pampas, since it was South American, and that was close to Frank's home base. An easy choice.

She looked at her wristwatch. *Time for class*. There was still some of the coffee in her cup. She gulped it down as she exited the cafeteria.

* * *

Daniel Strumler stood on the stage and tapped the microphone. He scanned the audience of over seven thousand people and suppressed his smile, making him appear more angry than pleased. "Welcome to the Indianapolis City Stadium."

He had to stop for nearly thirty seconds as the crowd applauded, drowning out his voice. As the cheering finally died off, he spoke again. "Thank you all. Remember that it all works only if you vote in the first week of November."

Once again the audience applauded. While he waited to speak, his thought drifted for a moment about what he would do if he really was elected president. And, he thought, winning the election would depend on the skills of the Russian intelligence group that was his special hacking team. *How good are they?* Then, as he remembered that the Russian president held a set of highly embarrassing and criminal videos of Strumler during his last trip to Moscow, his demeanor changed from merely angry to a state of palpable rage. "I promise that if I'm elected, my first act in office will be to roll back every one of the executive actions that Hernandez had signed into law. He deserves to be locked up!"

More cheering, followed by the crowd screaming, "Lock him up! Lock the fool up!"

This time Strumler smiled for real. Carl Hernandes had lost control of the Congress, the Senate, and many of the governors' mansions across the center of the country. His popularity was rising, but not high enough to affect the upcoming election. As a result, Strumler's popularity was finally rising from under thirty percent to nearly fifty-two percent. And with only six weeks until the election, it was finally looking good for Strumler.

* * *

Glen Sarkov sat at the head of the table in the Student Union's common area. Samantha Trout, MindField's chief financial officer, Harvey Kalinsky, the chief technical officer, and Ford Bane, the senior vice president of sales and marketing, were all displeased and showing it.

Sam spoke first. "Glen, my bank account is empty. If I'm to buy textbooks for this semester, I can't invest any more. Where the fuck am I going to find six hundred dollars more?"

Harvey and Ford both nodded.

Ford asked, "Same here. Is there any other way?"

Glen frowned and shook his head. "'Fraid not. We need to hire an attorney, and in addition to stock, they'll want us to pay the incorporation fees. Seems we bolloxed it up the first time. We're going to need a total of at least fifteen hundred total, but to resolve all the issues, twenty-five hundred would be safer."

Harvey said, in a voice just above a whisper, said, "I may have a way. I have to find out if it's legal. So, give me a day."

Everyone nodded at Harvey. Glen knew Harvey was the master of shortcuts.

Each rose from the table and left the common area.

* * *

Ann's cell buzzed in her pocket and she plucked it out. She scanned the screen and smiled. Avram Shimmel was her god-father. "Hello, big guy. It's been months. How are you?" She remembered how each had saved the other's life multiple times. Her successful attempt to thwart the CypherGhost by hack his aircraft's flight control system many months ago had been just one of the many times she'd helped him.

"Ach, good. And you?"

"Classes are my life. Right now, I'm on my way to advanced calculus. I assume this isn't just a call to touch base. How can I help?"

"Ann, I may need a hacker for an op we're planning. You won't be in any danger. And, I'll ask your mother's permission before I give you more details. Interested?"

Ann frowned. Avram had been one of Cassie's partners before he took a job heading the United Nations Paramilitary Force, a tactical "peacekeeping" squad with fewer than two thousand soldiers. He was nearly a giant, six-foot-seven or -eight, and huge in every other way. He had saved Cassie's life a few years back.

"Only if it won't take me away from school."

Shimmel remained silent for several seconds. "Okay. Jon Sommers will be contacting you if Cassie lets me borrow you."

Ann said, "I'll be looking forward to working with Jon. Bye." She wondered what Avram would want from her. Jon was someone she liked and respected, so that soothed her thought of the inherent dangers in all of Avram's military ops.

CHAPTER 9

Twenty-ninth floor,
United Nations Secretariat Building,
330 East 44th Street, New York, NY

September 13, 1:48 p.m.

Avram Shimmel ended the conversation with Cassandra.

When he assured her that Ann would be working under non-official cover with the United Nations, Cassie had objected. "If you want to borrow her, you'll need to provide her with official cover. None of this black-ops shit. She's just over eighteen years old. Can you do that?"

Avram sighed. "Okay. Consider it done. Send me electronic copies of her high-school and college transcripts, a copy of her birth certificate, and a copy of her driver's license. Thanks, Cassie."

He terminated the call and looked at the wall clock. Jon Sommers had the office next to his but Jon's office hours started later and went further into the evening. Avram fetched a cup of coffee and walked to the video conference room.

He flicked a switch and nearly one hundred screens depicting ongoing operations from around the globe buzzed to life.

Jon knocked on Avram's office door. Avram smiled and

motioned him to enter. He beckoned Sommers to sit in a chair adjoining his. Jon grinned at his friend. "So, what is it this time?" Jon scribbled text into his notebook.

Avram shrugged. He touched the screen of his own notebook and one of the screens on the wall changed its view to an overhead view of terrain. "We recorded this two days ago. A suspect entered our safe house in Sunnyvale. When he left, two of our operatives had been murdered. Samuel Meyer asked me to look into this."

"What, exactly is 'this'?" Jon looked at his friend.

"The Mossad's captive venture capital firm, the Ness Ziona, noticed that a new weapons tech they had developed appeared on InTelQ's website. InTelQ is the CIA's captive venture capital firm. The Mossad sent a team out to determine if the specifications of the InTelQ weapon had originated with the Ness Ziona, but two things happened. First, the team couldn't find any trace of the American entrepreneurs who supposedly received the funding to develop the tech. The cofounding team had simply disappeared. So, they took the next step, backstopping two coverts into American entrepreneurs and renting a house for them in Sunnyvale, California. The covert operatives pitched InTelQ for funding. They received the cash and provided InTelQ with a product— a product the Ness Ziona had developed and lent the Mossad. Two days later, they were set up as a murder-suicide. The video we're watching is the outside of the house. After it finishes, we'll see the video from inside the house. Seems their murderer managed to loop the video cam on the inside, although he wasn't able to defeat the offsite backup recording. I fear that an American venture capital firm is killing the entrepreneurs after they provide funding for product development. The cofounders are murdered, as soon as they have produced a product."

Jon pulled his chair closer to the screen. "What do you intend to do if an American VC is actually doing this?"

Avram scratched his chin. "We need proof first. I think this will call for a setup of our own. We'll need an entrepreneur who can interest them enough that they offer funding, and then we'll need to catch them in the act."

"Dangerous ground. Do you have an operative who can perform to spec?"

"No. We'll need a pretender."

"I assume that you're showing me these videos for a good reason. What's my role?"

Avram nodded. "You're the spymaster on this one if you want it. Most of the action will take place in Northern California, in Silicon Valley. If you need a hacker, use Ann Sashakovich."

Jon smiled. "I've been dormant too long. Count me in.

* * *

Glen sat in his apartment in Palo Alto, phone in hand, waiting to be taken off hold. He listened to elevator music and the repeating message about how important his call was.

Finally, he heard a voice. "Paul Marotta here." The voice sounded friendly.

"My name is Glen Sarkov. We have a mutual friend, Ann Sashakovich. She suggested I call you about a startup company that I'm the CEO of. We need legal representation. Are you interested?"

"Maybe. Tell me more. What's the intended industry and product?"

Glen smiled to himself. Maybe things would work out for MindField after all.

* * *

It was long after sunset, but the streets were bright from

neon signs and streetlights. Laura looked around the restaurant as she entered. Frank had held the door for her, a perfect gentleman. Pampas was precisely what she'd hoped it would be. Casual to the nines, with stained polished wooden walls, tablecloths, and the smell of roasting meat.

They were led to a table by a black-gowned woman, and Frank pulled Laura's chair out so she could be seated first.

She opened her menu and picked something that wasn't too cheap or too expensive. When she looked across the table, Frank caught her eye and smiled. "You have excellent taste."

Now it was her choice to smile. "Thanks. Tell me about where you live. I've never been outside this country.

Frank's smile dropped off his face in a flash. It took him nearly thirty seconds to finally speak. "Well, um, it's just a small country with some small cities and a large number of ranches in its countryside." He smiled again, but this time she could tell he felt uncomfortable.

Laura smiled back at him to try to put him at ease. *Why is he being so vague?*

* * *

Paul Marotta sat behind a large oak desk. The walls were covered with stock certificates from now-defunct corporations. He scanned the documents Glen had sent to him as email attachments. One of the documents in particular troubled him. It specified that in the event of the deaths or incapacity of all the cofounders, ownership of the patents and copyrights would be transferred immediately to the venture capital firm. He'd seen venture capitalists try to do this before. But there was also a "buyers' remorse" clause that gave Glen and his cofounders forty-eight hours to renege on the contract. He read the time off his wristwatch and then shifted to the time field on the signatures page. There were still two hours left before the contracts were cast into stone.

Paul called Glen's cellphone and hoped Glen would answer. It went directly to Glen's voicemail.

* * *

Harvey Kalinsky examined the screen on his notebook and frowned. If he hit the Return key, he'd be breaking multiple laws, committing felonies. But if he did nothing, he wouldn't have enough to protect his interest in MindField. He hesitated, but only for just a second.

The screen changed from the InTelQ server's landing page to a white screen with black lines of source code. He read through page after page of code. He noted that the server appeared to be owned by the federal government. *What the hell?* He'd have to tell Glen and his team about this.

He found several lines that were his targets, and edited them to point to a new location, then accessed that location and changed the result to one that had InTelQ awaiting a decision from MindField's cofounders on the offer they had extended. He then deleted the electronic copies of the contracts Glen and the others had signed. But, he had no access to the paper documents. Harvey wondered where the paper copies were being held, and if it was even possible to somehow snatch and destroy them.

His work finished, he wiped all traces of his presence and his activities off the server and signed off from his internet connection.

* * *

Glen received an encrypted text from Harvey Kalinsky and read the message. His brow knotted. *Not what I'd expected. Looks like InTelQ is a government-funded organization. Would that even be legal? Would it make any difference for the future of my startup?* His cellphone buzzed and he looked at the screen. Then he answered the call.

"Mr. Marotta! Thanks for calling. What have you discovered?"

"You signed a terrible contract. We need to get you out of it, but we have less than two hours remaining before that isn't possible. Interested?"

"Hell, yeah. What do I have to do?"

"You have to send an email to Frank Lucessi stating these exact words. Open your email app and tell me when you're ready."

"Ready now. What do you want me to say?"

* * *

Cassie and Lee sat at the kitchen table of their house in the compound. Cassie leaned forward. "I got an email from Avram today."

Lee looked up from his dinner plate. "How is he doing?"

"He wants to use Ann as a backup resource for an op. That is, only if we agree, and only if the op requires a hacker."

Lee shook his head. "Absolutely not."

"Lee, Avram says she'll be kept out of any direct contact with the op. Hacking only."

Lee frowned. "Last op she was involved in left her hands burned and almost killed her. And remember, she wasn't anywhere dangerous. The CypherGhost set her hands on fire from hundreds of miles away, through the cellphone towers."

Cassie thought about this. "She'll end up doing what she wants, no matter what we tell her."

Lee paced the room. "If she's going to do any work for Avram, we need to be there to act as a security force for her. Does she know anything about this yet?"

Cassie nodded. "Yes. She's already agreed but only if we approve. So, I'll text Avram and approve her use as an asset if we can act as her protection. We'll need to travel out west."

Lee nodded. "Have you been in contact with Ann?"

"Yes. I received an email from her this morning, just before this mess bloomed. She said she was worried about her roommate. She's even more worried about her new boyfriend."

Lee was silent for a few seconds. "If we go there, we may make more trouble than we solve. I hate for us to be helicopter parents."

Cassie nodded. "There is that. How many days can you take off from work?"

"Right now, a week. I have over six weeks saved in paid time off, but there's a new project starting in less than two weeks. I can try to find a substitute while we're travelling."

Cassie pulled her phone from her pocket and opened a travel app. "I'll set us up for a week visit."

Lee's expression showed he wasn't sure this was a good idea.

"Oh, come on, Lee. She's our daughter."

Lee shrugged. "All right. One week."

* * *

Glen knocked on the door of Ann's apartment just as she ended the phone call with her parents. She answered the door and let Glen in. Laura was leaving their room to get dinner.

Glen's excitement was palpable on his face. Ann, on the other hand, felt subdued.

Earlier, when Cassie called Ann, she had warned her daughter about the dangers inherent in any hacker's life, and had harangued her on what had happened the last time Ann had worked a hack. "You were in danger in Moscow," Cassie had stated, "and you were there as my child without my permission. Last year, you ignored my demand that you let more experienced operatives take on the CypherGhost, and you almost lost your life. So, I'm giving my permission this time, but only if you involve me in every step of the op. Every step! I'll be at your apartment tomorrow, with Lee. We'll help you to stay safe."

The browbeating hurt, and having her mother with her would complicate her school life more than it would keep her safe, but Ann knew it was too late to change her mother's stubborn mind.

Glen's expression fell into a frown. "What's wrong?"

"My parents are visiting. They'll be here tomorrow."

Glen's mouth formed an "O." He wore a dead serious expression now and said nothing for a few seconds. "Do you want me to meet them?"

She frowned. "Probably not. It's too soon for us to know where this is going."

Her cell buzzed. She drew it from her pocket and looked at its screen. "Hi, dad. Where are you guys?"

She listened as Lee answered. "Okay. I'll expect you here in an hour."

Glen's brows rose. "So?"

"They're a day early. I think you should leave for a few hours. I'll call you when I have a bit of privacy."

"Wait. Can I have a few minutes with you now to give you an update on what's happening with MindField?"

She examined his expression. A bit of desperation mixed with hope and fear. "Okay. Whatcha got?"

"Marotta found an escape clause from the contract and I exercised it. A 'buyer's remorse' clause. He dictated a letter that I printed, signed, and sent to him via FedEx. He also sent me an email containing the text I should read over the phone to Lucessi, detailing what I wanted him to include and exclude from the contracts we originally signed. Thanks, Ann. You saved our asses."

She nodded. Then she moved in for a kiss and finally, she told him, "Okay now, out with you."

* * *

Lee Ainsley huddled close to Cassie as they walked through one of San Francisco Airport's terminals toward the exit. He said, as calmly as he could, "Cass, don't argue with her. She's a full-fledged adult, and she has her own mind."

Cassie stared back with a look designed to kill her enemies. "She's still too young to be seeking dangerous situations, which is what she has done before. She's shown little regard for her safety. Not once but multiple times."

"If you come at her that way, she and you will spend the entire time you're together designing battle tactics to use against each other. Remember, we're here to help her. We're her to watch her back."

Cassie stopped dead in her tracks. "Oh, crap. Lee. You're right. I'll be respectful of her." She walked more slowly now as they crossed to the terminal exit and found the limo waiting for them.

* * *

Ann tried to complete one of her papers, due in another day. She had typed and then deleted the same sentence three times. She finally gave up and sat at her desk, her mind flying in several directions without settling. *Crap!* She pulled a candy bar from her desk drawer and took a bite.

The doorbell of her apartment rang while she furiously chewed and swallowed. "Coming." She opened the door.

Cassie smiled and entered, then hugged her. "Hi, sweetie."

Lee carried their bags into her room. "We're not staying with you. We'll be checking into the Stanford Park after dinner. Can we leave our bags here until after that?"

Ann nodded. "I still don't understand why you're here."

Cassie nodded back. "Over dinner. We'll tell you everything. Where do you want to go?"

Ann frowned. "Dunno. What are you in the mood for? There's everything you could want to eat down on University Drive. Five minute walk, ten if you want the scenic route."

Cassie smiled. "Let's go somewhere it's quiet so we can talk at the table."

Ann's brows furrowed, but she said, "Okay. I know somewhere we won't need a reservation."

Cassie frowned slightly. "Wait. I have an idea. When I was a student at Stanford, I had a favorite sushi bar in San Mateo. Sushi Sam's Edomata. It'll be well worth the half-hour car ride. I know it's still there, on Third Avenue near B Street. Let's go there."

Ann said okay, but she was sure that Cassie wanted to start their marathon conversation in the car. She sighed and nodded. *This is going to be torture for sure.*

* * *

Ann noted the large black limo with a chauffeur holding the door open. "So much for being inconspicuous. I thought you guys were spies."

Cassie said, "This is a vacation for Lee and me."

She climbed into the back between Lee and Cassie, even more sure now that any conversation would turn into an argument. She vowed to say nothing.

As the limo headed down Camino Real, north toward San Mateo, Cassie asked Ann about her studies.

"I'm doing well. I anticipate mostly good grades since I already have a head start on my work in computer tech, but the economics class and the psychology class you convinced me to take are much more difficult than the others. And that political science class is a first-class nightmare. Twelve textbooks for just the poli sci. I wish there were CliffsNotes for those three classes."

Cassie nodded and smiled. "I remember having the same problem. But I'm sure you will conquer it, just as I did."

The car was quiet for a while, Ann's discomfort and expectation of Cassie asking an embarrassing question grew. Lee shifted in his seat, still quiet.

Then Cassie asked, "Did Avram contact you?"

Ann sighed. "You already know he did."

"What did he tell you about the assignment?"

Ann took a deep breath, giving her time to organize her thoughts. "General Shimmel"—she pronounced "general" with a hard "g"—"ordered me to assist covert operative Sommers when he needs hacker support. I'm not to insert myself into any kinetic operation, and I am not to take time away from my studies if my grades might suffer."

Cassie nodded. "Good. Good. And we'll be here if this becomes a time burden for you or if there are kinetic consequences."

Ann stared at Cassie. "Right." She was about to say something more, but she hesitated.

The limo slowed and stopped. Cassie looked out the window. "Wow, how San Mateo has changed. Well, we're here. It's five-oh-two, so Sushi Sam's Edomata has been open for less than two minutes. We won't have to wait to be seated. Let's get inside."

Ann followed her mom and dad into a moderately large and aging sushi bar. The owner, Sam, was a man in his early fifties. He stood with two younger men beside him behind the counter in the nearly empty restaurant. They all wore white robes with black ties around their waists, and black ties around their foreheads, and they were all cutting and assembling sushi pieces. Sam looked up and said something in Japanese to Cassie, Lee, and Ann. A waiter guided them to a table.

Cassie and Lee sat on either side of Ann. Cassie asked, "Do you have a boyfriend as yet?"

Ann felt her face widen in shock. It took a tiny amount of time to freeze her face, but she was sure Cassie saw her expression.

Lee coughed. "Girls, before talking let's order some food."

Ann smiled at Lee. He always acted like her friend and helper. Her mother, on the other hand...

Lee beckoned to their waiter. "I want one of your famous chili dogs. And an uni. And a scallop in mayonnaise. And nama ebi. Oh, and a 'California Special.' Girls?"

Cassie ordered first, and then Ann. The waiter placed a pot of green tea on their table and left with their order,

"Mom, how'd you find this place?"

Cassie beamed. "Sam's is legendary. He's been here for over thirty years. There's a story that when Bill Clinton was president, one of his intelligence agencies let it slip how good this place is, and Bill came here for lunch along with a Secret Service detail. Not sure if that's true. I found out from one of the folks in my economics study group. Sam's sushi is simply addictive."

The remainder of their dinner was quiet and especially tasty, and by the time they finished, Ann considered Cassie's presence a mixed blessing.

But on the return drive in the limo, Cassie began asking questions once more. "So, no boyfriend? I'm assuming no girlfriend, either. Is that right?"

Ann turned her head to the window and looked out in silence. But, she caught her own reflection and saw the rage that was evident on her face. Her eyes rolled as she thought about a way to end her mother's incessant interrogation. She smothered a grin. "Nope. He dumped me when I told him I missed a period."

Cassie's eyes popped wide until she realized Ann was trying to silence her. She took a deep breath and said nothing more.

This visit will be trouble, thought Ann. *She's gonna bug me to death.*

CHAPTER 10

Jon Sommers ended his cellphone conversation with Avram Shimmel. He was seated in the middle section of a commercial flight to SJC. The flight was about to taxi down the runway. Just enough time left to call Ann and assure her that the assignment wouldn't compromise her studies. He punched in her cell number and she picked it up on the first ring.

"Ann, it's Jon Sommers. Do you have a minute?"

"Hello Jon, I'm in a limo with my mom and dad. Whatcha got?"

"I'm on a jet to SJC right now. Taking off in about three minutes. So I'll arrive too late for anything tonight, but can we meet tomorrow? When will it be convenient and not take time away from your classes?"

"Call me tomorrow in the early afternoon, after your lunch. We can meet on campus. How about the Student Union building after 2 p.m.?"

"Consider it done." Jon terminated the call and put his phone away as the aircraft taxied down the runway, increasing its speed by the second.

After the aircraft lifted off the runway, he removed his notebook computer from its case and opened his scheduling software. First he keyed a series of tasks he'd need to accomplish to start the mission:

- Find a suitable startup company and offer funding in return for using them as the sacrificial goat.

- Have them contact the alleged "venture capitalist" responsible for the deaths of the covert Mossad team.

- Send proof of complicity to Avram.

He connected to the aircraft's internet service and used Google to search for internet startups seeking funding. To his surprise, over three thousand venture capital company names dropped out in a neat, ordered list, subcategorized by their preferred market segments and funding stage preference. But he became even more unhappy when he Googled "California Venture Capital Funds" and found well over three hundred entries just in the early stage and seed market. There were even more in the late-stage market. He couldn't even count them all. *This market is a free for all*, he thought.

* * *

The next morning just after dawn, Ann's alarm on her cellphone buzzed. She'd been dreaming about her last violent encounter with the CypherGhost, but in her dream, their fates were reversed and Ann was dying when the alarm buzzed.

Time to get up, she thought, but her phone's time was set at 7:12 a.m., eighteen minutes before the alarm was set to pound her into consciousness. It was an incoming call, not her wake-up alarm. She punched in the Accept button and put the phone to her ear.

"Ann, it's Jon. Sorry, but I need your help." Jon explained the huge number of startups seeking funding.

"Jon, give me a few seconds." Ann walked to her tiny pantry and spooned instant coffee into a mug, then topped off the mug with hot water from the tap. She gulped it down. Then she scanned the rooms to make sure Laura was still sound asleep. "Okay. I'm alone. Is this part of the op? What is the op? How do startups play a role?"

As Jon explained, Ann's eyes grew wide. "Wait. Let's see if I've got this straight. This is a Mossad op, not a United Nations op. And the Mossad sent some operatives looking to investigate a venture capitalist they think has been killing entrepreneurs for the rights to their products. By any chance, is the name of the VC Frank Lucessi?"

Jon was silent for a few seconds. "I'm not quite sure. We have a video of the murders, in Sunnyvale about a week ago. The product the Mossad gave them the specs for was a nanodevice with military weaponization potential. That's all I have right now."

Ann would have to call Glen to see if his startup's product fit the bill. "I'll call you back soon. Bye, Jon."

* * *

Daniel Strumler watched the television screen and found the polling result difficult to believe. *How can I be so far behind in the polls?* He shook his head in denial. He picked up a pad of paper and began listing the issues he had yet to comment on during the previous two weeks of his campaign. The intelligence agencies and their recent failures were perhaps the most important of the ones he hadn't publicly spoken about. He sketched out a series of steps he could take to enrage the public over the misdeeds he was sure the intel community had made, even though most of the facts were drawn solely from his imagination.

- They've hidden the true facts of President Carl Hernandes's illegal surveillance of the alt-right.

- They've falsely accused me of lying about the sources of my wealth.

- They've falsely attacked me for lying about my connections with the Chinese, but they failed to investigate the threat of China's and Russia's involvement in that rumored invasion attempt.

The list was over twenty items long when he was finished. What to do about the CIA, the DIA, the other intelligence organizations, and the IRS that all hated him? *Get rid of them! As soon as I take office.*

* * *

Once again, Glen Sarkov sat at the head of the table in the Student Union common area. Harvey Kalinsky seemed angry. Glen looked directly at him. "Harvey, what's bothering you? You look like you want to start a fight."

Harvey scanned the others at the table. Samantha Trout and Ford Bane both looked as if they were pleased at Glen's report. So Harvey was the only one disturbed that Paul Marotta, their new corporate attorney, had saved their asses. "Yeah. Glen, I broke the law for us by hacking into that venture capitalist's website and deleting all the references to his agreement with us. If he gets to looking around, it'll be my ass on the line. Why didn't you tell me you and the attorney already had the problem solved?"

Glen frowned back. "I had no idea you were considering hacking their site, since you told us to not ask you questions. What you said to us was you were going to need just one day to fix the problem. Shit, man. Now we're involved in illegal activities."

Harvey looked daggers at Glen. "As the movie *Cool Hand Luke* says, what we have here is a failure to communicate."

Glen turned away and tried calming himself but it wasn't working. "Okay. Sorry. So, I sent an email and a certified letter to Lucessi's firm. I think we'll hear back from him soon.

Samantha raised her head. "What if we don't hear from them?"

* * *

Frank Lucessi had packed his suitcase. The next "client" expected him in less than two hours. He decided to check on his email before leaving to visit the next startup in San Francisco.

And what he saw wasn't an email from the next client. It was from the client he'd just finished with:

> Dear Mr. Lucessi,
> My cofounders and I have decided to rescind our agreement with you, offering us funding. The terms, specifically those related to ownership of our products in the event of our deaths, were too risky to our loved ones.
> Should you decide to continue to negotiate with us, we will be happy to meet with you once again.

Frank could feel the heat in his face. *Fuck! Fuck!* He needed that client for him to reach his quota. He sat on the hotel bed and took several deep breaths. *Calm down!* Then he pulled his cellphone from his pocket and punched in Glen's number. But when the call rolled into voicemail, it took nearly ten seconds for him to calm himself yet again. "Glen Sarkov, this is Frank Lucessi, I'd welcome another meeting, and I hope we can reconcile our differences. Please call me back at your earliest convenience."

Frank grabbed his suitcase and walked to his rental car. He headed north for his next meeting.

* * *

Jon Sommers checked into the Four Seasons Hotel Silicon Valley in Palo Alto. Avram told him that Cassie and Lee were staying at the Stanford Park Hotel in Palo Alto a few miles away. Jon figured he'd be less likely to draw attention to them if they stayed in different places.

He dragged his rolling suitcase through the door into his room and set up a security system of measures and counter-measures. Some of it consisted of Cold War–era tricks like a thread placed into the doorjamb. Opening the door would drop the thread, and Jon would see if an intruder had entered his room from outside, before he opened the door. Others were more modern tech toys. He unscrewed an outlet box and placed a video cam behind the plate cover, then tested it and adjusted it to ensure it had a wide-angle view of the room. He installed a temperature sensor in the doorjamb to activate the video cam when the room's temperature increased by one-fiftieth of a degree in under three minutes, and connected the video signal to his cellphone. He placed a canister of gas into the desk light and set it to go off if he transmitted a signal to the room using his cell.

Then he took a brief nap to keep his body from experiencing jet lag.

He was asleep when his cell buzzed against his belt. He saw it was from Cassie and answered the call. "Sommers."

"Hello, Jon. We're at the Stanford Park a few miles from Ann's apartment. Where are you?"

"Four Seasons. What can I do for you?"

"Please, a sitrep."

"Well, I'm at the very start of this mission. There are over three hundred venture capitalists on Sand Hill Road funding seed- and early-stage startups. And over three thousand potential "pretenders" for this project. I'll be busy for at least a week vetting the turf."

"Lee and I can help. Would you like that?"

"What do you want in return?"

"Keep my daughter out of harm's way."

Jon frowned. That would be harder than he'd originally thought. He knew Ann very well. She was always sporting for a fight. "I'll try." But he knew Cassie would realize he was lying.

CHAPTER 11

**Four Seasons Hotel Silicon Valley,
2050 University Avenue, East Palo Alto, CA**

September 15, 8:12 a.m.

Jon Sommers heard his hotel room's doorbell ring and put down his razor. He scanned the door with an app from his cellphone and saw the ID's for Cassie and Lee. He opened the door, still holding a towel in his other hand. "Hello. Been almost a year. How are you two?"

Cassie smiled. "Okay. We've been trying to civilize Evan but he's resistant. A handful. Who knew a four-year-old could run your life."

Lee nodded. They both entered and closed the door behind them.

Jon thought about his own parents. He'd been treated by them as if he was a prodigy, but they died when he was twelve. "Is Judy Hernandez watching him while you travel?"

Cassie smiled. "Evan is now in a military preschool. I didn't even know there was such a thing, but Lee's father is former military and he advised we do it. When I declined, he went on a full-fledged campaign to have his way. Lee was useless in the argument. In fact, his father used Lee as the example of how the resulting person is more responsible."

She stared at Lee and he threw his hands into the air.

"Dad's right," Lee said. "I learned to focus in military schools from 'pre' through West Point and Naval Post-Grad. Cassie and I talked it over and decided the school would provide better parenting than retired spies could. So, no. Judy is working for Avram on a special assignment right now." He asked, "Need help with your selection for startups?"

Jon nodded. "Well, make yourselves at home. Back in a minute" He walked back into the bathroom and continued getting ready to face the day.

Cassie looked around the room. "Jon's a very tidy man."

Lee nodded. "The Mossad trained him to not leave anything in place that could identify him or compromise his mission. Good to see he still maintains that discipline."

Jon opened the bathroom door and walked into the living room of his suite, dressed in a dark blue conservative suit and a white shirt, but no necktie. "So, here's a pile of printed pages that have a description of each startup." He unlocked the safe in the room and placed about five hundred pages of text on the desk.

Cassie breezed through a handful of the pages. "Jon, what does Ann know about your mission?"

"Nearly nothing. Just that in the case where the mission goes south, I may need her to expunge all traces of my visit by hacking me off every vidcam and every place I may have signed a credit card receipt."

Cassie breathed deeply in relief. "Good. What do you want us to do, exactly?"

"Go through the records of each startup. Pick those that have a decent founding team and haven't received offers as yet. When we have a population of five, we'll try to see if we can convince them to act as "pretenders" for the Mossad. We'll need them to accept the plans for a weapon and claim the plans are their own. We'll target the three venture capitalists that we think might have stolen Mossad plans for an espionage tech toy, especially InTelQ. We'll need to provide round-the-clock protection for each startup team. If we can determine who stole from the Mossad, I'll take them out. Then, in return for the risk the startup cofounders endured, the Ness Ziona will fund their real project. That's the plan."

Cassie thought for several seconds. "It's full of holes. Do you have a whiteboard?"

Jon shook his head. "Ben-Levy's board is back in my condo in Manhattan. Sorry. We can call down to the main desk and they'll send one up. Whatcha thinking?"

Cassie sat on the desk's chair. "First, if one or more of the startups rejects your offer, word will spread of your planned takedown. Silicon Valley is boiling over with gossip. VCs talk to each other. Startup teams also cross-pollinate just in case their current project tanks. No way to contain the gossip. We need to 'buy' a team or create our own. Second, the amount of cash required to nudge a team into accepting what they will see as a dangerous project is well past trivial. Just normal seed rounds these days will draw tight the Mossad's purse strings. Once again, we might need to coerce a team, not just attract them."

Jon turned away and stared out the window. "Yes, of course. You're correct. Avram's plan won't work. Let's try to find some weak teams with a single star and try to separate them from their team. Think that might work?"

Cassie looked to Lee, but he just shrugged. "Don't know. But let's try that."

Jon nodded, but he was beginning to assume his lack of experience with the Silicon Valley startup world might doom the mission.

CHAPTER 12

**Stanford University quadrangle,
Palo Alto, CA**

September 15, 10:46 a.m.

Ann found a sunny spot where there was an empty bench at a corner of the quad. She dreaded her next class: economics. It would be starting soon. The sunshine and warmth of the day brightened her as she pulled her notebook computer from her book bag and reviewed the notes for today's assignment. She'd need about an hour to research and then write the project. Between that and her other classes, her day would be full.

She checked her email and saw a note from Jon:

Ann—
Your parents arrived and we're starting on the
mission Avram assigned me. I have your parents'
permission to outline what we'll all be doing, so
you'll know what to expect. If things go south, there
are three potential times when the use of your
talent would be life-saving. When can we meet?
I'll only need a half hour.
—Jon

Ann frowned. More time than she actually had. Something else would have to be postponed. She called Jon's cell.

"Jon here."

"Hello, hero. I'm pretty much filled to capacity today. Can we do this over the phone?"

"No. Absolutely not. Phones aren't secure. When can I steal a few minutes? I'm less than a mile away."

Ann thought that if she visited Jon in his hotel room, she might see her parents, possibly turning a half-hour meeting into an all-day excursion. "My apartment." She gave Jon the address. "How about right after lunch? Figure 12:30? I have a class at 1:00. Okay?"

"Yes. See you then."

Ann knew Laura's class schedule. Laura had a class starting at 12:30 and it would go for at least ninety minutes. Jon and Ann could speak privately. The apartment would do quite well.

She opened her internet browser and Microsoft Word, and took notes for the assignment today, comparing the latest VPN software to the product it would likely displace.

* * *

Laura Hunter touched the canvas and the sensation of old oil paint took her breath away. The painting was nearly four hundred years old and in need of restoration. She knew the university wouldn't let a sophomore do the work, but being assigned as an assistant to the restorer would be a high point in her credentials. She'd have to compete with three other students, and from what she knew of them, it was possible she might be picked.

"Who can tell me what the elements are in the pigment used in the blue sky?" The restorer scanned the four faces.

Laura didn't know the answer. She thought hard in the

growing silence. One of the other students raised his hand to respond.

By the time the class had ended, Laura had been able to answer only three of the twenty questions the art restorer asked. Each of her competitors had done much better.

She left the classroom knowing she had blown a chance at being the bright young star of the class. It was 1:35. Perhaps this was the end of her ambition to be a rising young painting restorer. She headed back to her dorm room, her lack of knowledge like a storm cloud following her.

* * *

On Howard Street in downtown San Francisco, Frank Lucessi shook hands with each of the biochemistry startup members in the UCSF cafeteria and packed away the signed contracts in his French-edge leather attaché case. He smiled, more to himself than to the others, and headed to the elevator.

His car was waiting for him in the parking garage. If he could manage it, this would be the time to set an appointment with Glen Sarkov and the rest of the MindField cofounders and finally get that piece of business put to bed.

He punched in the number of Glen's cell and heard it ring once. "Sarkov."

Frank took a deep breath. "It's Frank Lucessi. Have you received the changes you want made to the contracts from your corporate attorney?"

"Uh, yeah. They're in my hand."

"I'm in San Francisco right now. Please read them to me."

He listened as Glen read less than one hundred words.

"I'll need them included in new documents, so give me to the end of today. When can we meet tomorrow?"

Glen said, "How about 10 a.m.?"

"Good. How about in the Stanford cafeteria again?"

When Glen agreed, Frank ended the call. He'd be stuck on the Peninsula again tonight. As a treat, he booked himself a room at the Four Seasons Hotel in East Palo Alto. Then he made another call. "Hello, Laura. It's Frank."

"Oh. I was wondering if I was going to hear from you again."

"Yeah. Well, I'm in town for what I'm thinking will be my last night this trip. I'd like to take you to dinner again. Are you interested?"

"Sure. Pick the place. I'll be ready at six. Meet you at the cafeteria then. Okay?"

Frank agreed as the elevator reached the lobby. If he was lucky, he might reach Palo Alto before the rush-hour traffic nightmare.

* * *

Glen waited in the cafeteria. One-by-one, his cofounders arrived. Each bought coffee or a snack and sat at the table with him. He turned his notebook computer so the others could all see the screen. "Ladies, gentlemen, here is the revised contract. Mr. Lucessi will meet with us tomorrow at 10 a.m. to sign them with us, or if you have a class at that time you can sign today. Lucessi agreed to the revision that Mr. Marotta crafted for us. So, we're good to go. Next week we should all schedule some time to open a corporate bank account and look for office space."

All of the others smiled back. Even Harvey, who was dour at the best of times.

* * *

Ann heard the doorbell ring. It was 1:40 p.m. Jon was late. She opened the door and saw Jon smiling at her.

Ann smiled back, "Okay, come on in. So now we can

talk, but probably only for a few minutes before my roommate returns. What's the project and where would I be useful?"

"The mission. Not just a project. Avram was told by Sam Meyer, the current director of the Mossad, to send a team to Northern California. The Mossad's analysis section believes that a venture capital firm has gone rogue and is signing contracts with startup teams, and when the team has completed product design and begun production, the team simply disappears and the product becomes the property of one of the world's intelligence services. I'm 'the team.' Just me. I've been asked to recruit a set of cofounders for a product that could easily be weaponized, and follow them closely as they attempt to secure venture funding, then review the contracts to see if there'd be an easy way to obtain the rights from the cofounders once they're gone. Dunno how many vultures there are in the community, but I'm thinking there are at least several."

He stared at Ann, and she nodded. "Good. So, if my cover gets blown, I'll need you to help me backstop one of my alternative identities on the fly so I can get away cleanly. Assuming we get to the next phase, I'll need to have a way to neutralize each of the guilty venture capitalists. Drain their bank accounts, set up each of their execs with arrest warrants, and possibly terminate a few if that's what Meyer wants. Finally, I'll need an alternate way of contacting Avram, and through him, Meyer. Something cryptographic and not easily cracked. I'm assuming you could help out with each of those, and without your getting into serious danger. Correct?" He placed his notebook computer on her kitchen table and turned it on. He entered the password and it booted to completion

Ann nodded again. "Right, then. If you think we need more time, I can spare another ten minutes. Make yourself at home. There's warm coffee in the pot."

Jon nodded. "I'll be back after I use the restroom." He walked into the bathroom and shut the door.

Ann smiled. He'd just given her a subtle invitation to see what was on his notebook computer. And, she hadn't even had to ask. She sat and pulled a thumb-drive from her pocket. She placed it into one of the USB ports on Jon's machine, and when the computer asked what to do with the drive, she keyed Run Program. The list of programs on the thumb drive was a single line: RatWorm. She highlighted it and hit Confirm. The program took less than two seconds to load. She pulled the thumb-drive from Jon's notebook and pocketed it.

A few seconds later, Jon reemerged. "Are we all ready?"

"Yes. I know what you want, and I'll be available when you text me. Send the word "Now," and I'll come back with "Sure." After that, you can send me instructions by text. Use the Signal app to make sure we're secure when we communicate. Okay?"

Jon nodded and smiled. "Well, that didn't take long. Welcome on board, and thanks."

Ann smiled back and Jon left her apartment. She walked to her desk and opened her own notebook computer. Rat-Worm had dropped a copy of all of Jon's files onto her notebook. She scanned Jon's notes on the mission. The plan, its background, and a note stating that any black ops which might be required were already acknowledged and approved.

As she read through the notes and the associated documents, she saw Glen's name was third from the top of the list of entrepreneurs Jon was considering as "pretenders."

"Fuck this," she muttered. *No possible way my boyfriend is gonna become target practice.*

PART II

One thing VC's never talk about is how screwed
founders get.
—Mark Suster, speech at DogPatch Labs,
April 5, 2011

CHAPTER 13

Stanford University Student Union cafeteria, Palo Alto, CA

September 15, 1:32 p.m.

Ann found a seat at a table that was emptying. She sat and looked at her wristwatch. *Glen will be here in less than five*, she thought. She closed her eyes, thinking of what she could say that might keep him safe and out of the mess that this mission might bring. *When I see him, what do I tell Glen?*

She sat motionless, eyes closed, trying to conjure something witty, like, *Hey, sweetie, how would you like to volunteer for a deadly assignment? Oh, wait, your venture capitalist may have already volunteered you! Oops!* No. This was going to be a nightmare. She could smell danger, and even though it was her imagination, she felt a chill and smelled something coppery, like the stench of blood.

She felt the breeze of the cafeteria door opening and shutting, then the noise of the chair next to hers scraping back. She opened her eyes and smiled. Ann struggled to keep her hands from shaking, or worse, from glowing with heat from her special "talent."

"Hi, Ann. I got your text. What did you want to talk to me about?" He seemed friendly, not annoyed at her violation of the two-day rule for new couples. It was a "thing" back in the days when she and Charles were dating, before he started college at Harvard and discarded her like a rotten piece of fruit. She wondered if there still was a two-day rule.

Ann let her eyes drift away, unfocused, so she could imagine some additional distance between them. She took a deep breath. "I kept some things about me from you. If I tell you my secrets, will you promise not to reveal them to anyone else?"

"Uh, sure. What's so serious I have to promise something?"

"Can we find some place more private?"

"Uh. Sure." He rose from his seat. "How about the quad? There are some seats no one ever seems to use there."

Ann followed him. They walked nearly half a mile. As Glen promised, there was no one visible close by from the vantage point of four metal benches grouped on the quad. She nodded as they sat. "Glen, I want to know if I can tell you things I've sworn never to reveal. See, I'm not who I appear to be."

Glen remained silent, his mouth opening just a bit more than usual, as if he was unsure of how to respond.

Ann took another breath. "I've been modified. I've—"

"You've what?"

Ann sighed. "I was modified with nanodevices about a year ago."

Glen sat back into the bench, then leaned forward. But he made no attempt to get up. "So, let's see if I understand. You were experimented on by... by who?"

"I'm a hacker. My mom used to work in an intelligence service. My dad also worked in the same service. It's how they met each other. The service closed, then was replaced by a private mercenary corporation, and that's where they work now. One of their projects was human testing of a nano-device, and I received one of the devices." This last statement,

Ann knew, was a lie. She'd actually volunteered to test the device. Her next lie was to omit that the CypherGhost had administered a thousand more of the nanodevices to her without telling her. But Glen would never know about the CypherGhost. And then she omitted that as the nanodevices began to fail, one-by-one, she learned to replicate their functions with her own brain. By the time the last one had failed, she was capable of striking someone with flames emanating from her fingertips. No, that would be too much. She couldn't ask him to believe that.

"Why are you telling me this today?" She could see disbelief in his expression. *Maybe I've already gone too far?*

It was now or never. "Because my mom's firm is investigating how a team of their operatives died while in the field. Their team was sent in to act as entrepreneurs after some military weapons secrets were stolen and showed up with a Silicon Valley startup. The startup's team disappeared after they completed development of their product. When the fake startup's cofounders were murdered, the product then ended up the sole property of the venture capital firm that funded them. Got this so far?"

Glen obviously did, and she could see his discomfort. "MindField's first product. It's our own. Our own design. Not hacked from some intelligence agency."

"Yes. I know. But what I fear is that your venture guy, Frank Lucessi, may not be what you think he is. And that his venture capital firm may not be acting in MindField's best interests, or, for that matter, your own." Ann sat back in her chair, not sure how Glen would react.

Glen sat, speechless, for nearly a minute, his eyes darting around like a cornered animal. "No venture capital firm has the cofounders' interest at heart. They're in it for the money." He was silent, thinking. "Okay. What do you want?"

Ann nodded. "That's what we need to talk about. Here. Now. Okay?"

Glen nodded back.

Ann said, "There's this guy I know who works with my parents. His name is Jon Sommers. He used to work for the Mossad, the Israeli intelligence service. Now he works for General Avram Shimmel, the director general of the United Nations Paramilitary Force. Both of these guys are friends of my parents, and my parents work for Avram. Jon needs people he can run as independent contractors to the United Nations for this investigation. They will be in danger for the duration of the investigation. If they survive, they'll be offered venture funding from an Israeli venture firm as a reward for their service. Please, please, please, do not do this. I just found out that you are on their recruitment list. Jon will tell you a bit but not all of what I just told you. He'll lie and embellish his story. Don't believe him, and don't offer your services. You might not survive the op."

Glen's eyes focused to the grass around the benches. "So, you're not just a hacker. You're also a spy. Right?"

Ann shook her head. "Not now. We can talk about this later. Just please, if Jon calls you, remember that he's dangerous. If I were you, I'd turn down any offer he makes. My guess is he'll call you within a day, if he can't find some-one else. Okay?"

But she could see that Glen was no longer paying attention. His eyes were drifting with thought.

* * *

The three spies sat in living-room section of Jon's hotel room.

Cassie focused on the screen of her notebook computer. Her fingers moved across the keyboard, driven by her need to find the ten best prospects for Jon's list of pretenders. The list now included four names, but she thought the one she was reviewing right now would make a decent fifth choice. So far, she had reviewed the credentials of over eight hundred of the one thousand names.

There were a total of nearly three thousand names Jon had arrived with. Jon himself was reviewing a thousand of the total.

Next to Cassie, Lee was also reviewing names. He'd found two out of the seventy-eight on his the list of over seven hundred.

Cassie looked at the screen of Jon's notebook, a few feet away. At this rate, it might take as long as two complete weeks to finish the list. She sighed to herself. This kind of work was frequently part of the front end of any mission. First research, then march, and then fight.

Jon got up and walked to the coffee pot. He poured a cup for himself then interrupted the others. "Anybody?" He pointed to the cup. Lee and Cassie both nodded back. Jon poured and delivered coffee. "Time for a status report. I found three names. How about you guys?"

"Two," said Lee.

"Five," said Cassie.

Jon shrugged. "Okay, take a breather. Five minutes, then back at the list."

Lee and Cassie rose and refilled their coffee cups.

* * *

It was all Daniel Strumler could do to contain his rage. "Please repeat the question."

Nikolai Puchenko smiled, but the expression seemed to reveal a nasty intention. "I asked if your campaign might be able to use some help."

"If I accept, you'll own me."

"If you don't accept, let me remind you that we already

have enough just in photos and videos to end your campaign. We also have signed contracts between your businesses and our oil companies. Not to mention—"

"Yeah, not to mention what we were just talking about. But, all of that is just gossip. If I agree to your 'help,' then you really own me."

"But if you do, your odds of winning go from slight to nearly a sure thing. Remember, we only back winners."

Strumler sat in silence for a few seconds. He wished he had the patience to see all the angles, every bad thing that could go wrong. But his mind simply wandered.

"Well? Mr. Strumler, do you wish to become president?"

Strumler could no longer control his rage. "You fuckin' piece of shit. Of course I do. But what you're asking me to do is treason!"

"It's survival of the fittest in regards to all political dealings. Do you have what it takes to be your country's leader?"

Strumler took a deep breath. His hands were shaking and he'd hidden them behind his back. He looked into Puchenko's calm face. The Russian's eyes were staring back at him, their focus bright and steadfast. Strumler knew he was cornered. He lowered his gaze. "What the fuck do you want from me now?"

* * *

As the afternoon drew into evening, Lee looked up from his notebook's screen. "That's the last one on my segment. I found a total of five out of seven hundred eighty-two that meet the requirements." He looked across at Cassie and Jon, seated in front of their own notebooks. "Well?"

Jon smiled. "I've found seven in my segment. Finished three minutes ago."

Cassie frowned. "I found eleven. That makes a total of twenty-three potential pretenders. Before we break for dinner,

we should sequence the names according to their potential effectiveness. Okay?"

Jon nodded. "Yes. I've already sequenced my pretenders. Let's see where both of your lists fit with mine."

They completed the task of combining their three lists into a single one in priority sequence. Cassie read the list aloud, then said, "Let's decide how to proceed with the list."

"Simple," Jon said. "We start with the top name and proceed downward. First, let's compile a more thorough record for the twenty-three candidates."

That took quite a while. It was nearly 7:30 when they finished.

Jon said, "Let's take the files for the short list with us. He looked at Cassie. "You went to school here, so why don't you choose the restaurant?"

Cassie nodded.

Jon smiled. "Let's eat somewhere special. Cassie, you lead the way."

CHAPTER 14

Chef Chu's,
1067 N San Antonio Road, Los Altos, CA

September 15, 7:52 p.m.

The small restaurant was situated at the busy intersection of El Camino Real and San Antonio Road, next door to Armadillo Willy's BBQ restaurant. Jon sniffed the smoke and pointed. "That sure smells good. Sure you want Asian, Cassie?"

Cassie frowned at Jon. "This place is the one we want to go to. Chinese food that tastes like heaven. We can do smoky ribs next time."

Jon, Cassie, and Lee entered the more elegant place and found the formally attired maître d'.

Jon asked for a quiet table. He opened the menu. "This is the kind of place William Wing would adore. There are dishes on this menu that read like taste adventures."

Cassie looked up from her menu. "I'd prefer if I could relive some of my favorites from college. Okay?" Both men nodded. "Good, good. Let's order the hot and sour soup, one of the very best I've ever had, the minced crystal prawns in lettuce cups, and the "vegetarian" goose, for starters. Then, uh," she gazed back at the menus and when her head bobbed up, she said, "for mains, how about the boneless tea-smoked duck, which I think is as good as their Beijing duck but tastes different, smoky. And, the classic dry-braised prawns, which I had at an amazing, famous restaurant the last time I was in Hong Kong. And then, either yu shang pork or mapo tofu?"

It took the others nearly two minutes just to catch up and read the descriptions. Jon voted for the tofu, and Lee wanted the pork, so they ordered both, along with everything Cassie recommended.

While they waited for the onslaught of food, Jon distributed the printed folders he had brought. The folders held complete records of each of the twenty-three in the short list. Each candidate had about four pages of notes, including everything found in public records for that person. By the time the food had come, they had narrowed the list to eight names.

While they ate, they caught up on social gossip.

Jon grinned. "Avram's wife Shula is fighting for her command at the bank's top position. She was running wire transfer and foreign exchange, but a consultant hired by the bank's CEO did a study and discovered that over half the bank's profit is from foreign exchange. It's a battle she neither sought nor wanted. Avram's furious. Thinks it might draw attention to her role as guardian of Israel's interests in counterterrorism."

"So Shula wants to remain hands-on?" Lee was obviously unconvinced, but Jon simply nodded.

Cassie asked, "What about your social life, Jon? Are you and Lily Lee on or off at present?"

Jon shrugged. After almost two years, I'm still confused about Lily. Sometimes I think she wants me, other times it looks like she just wants the comfort I offer her through her green card. I'm not at all sure about how I feel. So, when I'm at home in Manhattan, we fight a lot. When I'm away, she doesn't call much. I do most of the outward reach."

Cassie and Lee exchanged glances. "Doesn't sound promising to me," she said to Jon. She changed the subject by asking Jon about William Wing and Betsy Brown, the two directors of Avram's cybersecurity department within the UN Paramilitary Force.

"They are currently on assignment in Eastern Europe" Jon said. "I expect they'll be returning in a few months."

After dinner, they went back to the folders and cut the eight names down to three. The plan was to approach them in sequence, one at a time, until they received two acceptances. Jon would then send them out as cofounding teams.

Jon argued for those with the best tech, Lee for those who spoke fluent English. In the end, the sequence they arrived at was:

1. Kosh Vindar
2. Chin Wang
3. Glen Sarkov

Jon saved the file containing the names. He closed his notebook computer. "That's enough for today. Tomorrow we finalize the plan and begin taking steps. He smiled briefly.

Jon paid the bill and they rose as one from the table. They were soon gone from the restaurant.

CHAPTER 15

Stanford Park Hotel, Palo Alto, CA

September 16, 8:26 a.m.

Cassie opened the door and let Jon in. He held a tray containing three cups of coffee. "Where can I put these down? They're very hot."

Lee pointed to the desk. "On the corner." Then he darted from the living section of his room to the bedroom and dragged a whiteboard from the clothes closet. "I bought this at a box store." He pulled three different-colored dry-erase markers from the container attached to the side of the board. "Not as filled with memories as the one Ben-Levy bequeathed you, Jon, but it'll do in a pinch. Let's use this for drafts of the plan."

The three spent the morning brainstorming, with scant results. The whiteboard had three lines on it:

- Meet with all three candidates and assess their usefulness.

- Select numbers one and two and give them each a backstopped legend.

- Send them out to the suspect venture capital companies and wait to see what happens.

"If that's all we can come up with in an hour, Jon, your mission is doomed. It'll be next summer before we have a complete plan scoped out." Cassie frowned and sipped from her coffee cup.

Lee nodded. "Well, maybe you're right, but getting appointments with these three shouldn't take long. Maybe we should just do that, meet all three and see how they stack up against one another."

Jon scanned the three folders in front of him. "Why don't I just call the first one. Kosh Vindar."

Both Lee and Cassie shrugged.

Jon picked up his cell, turned on speakerphone, and punched in a number. It rang three times then rolled into voicemail.

"You have reached Kosh Vindar, CEO of Vindar Computing. I cannot talk with you now, but please be assured that your call is important to me and Vindar Consulting..." The message continued on, with a thick Indian accent.

Jon left a very brief message.

The three all bore amused looks. But when it happened again with the second name on the list, their expressions became borderline desperate.

Cassie said, "We're down to our last possibility, unless one of the first two returns your call. I guess we can always dip into the more complete list if Sarkov isn't available either."

Jon nodded. Then he put the phone on speaker again, dialed the cell, and waited.

"Sarkov."

Shocked at hearing a real person, none of the three spoke for a few seconds.

Then Jon finally recovered. "Mr. Sarkov, my name is Jon Sommers. I'd like to talk with you about an exciting opportunity for you and MindField. Do you have a few minutes?"

"I know who you are. Ann Sashakovich spoke to me about you. She warned me about working with you."

Jon's jaw dropped. "You... you know Ann? She warned you? How?"

"It really doesn't matter. I already have an offer of seed funding from InTelQ. But thanks anyway." He terminated the call.

Jon seemed to be shocked by this turn.

Lee used his hand to cover his earsplitting grin. "Ann just outed you!"

Cassie picked up her cell and was dialing Ann's cell. "That little stinker," she said, her voice just a whisper. This call also went into voicemail. "Ann, it's your mother. We just spoke with Glen Sarkov. You've been meddling in our op. Call me back as soon as possible." She ended her call.

Jon shook his head. "Too late, Cassie. Glen now knows too much."

Lee asked, "And what does that mean?"

Jon said, "It means we'll have to try and use him. Remember, our primary target is probably InTelQ. They're owned by your CIA."

CHAPTER 16

**Stanford University Student Union cafeteria,
Palo Alto, CA**

September 16, 10:57 a.m.

Ann had just completed her early morning class in computer auditing. She paid for a cup of coffee and sat at a table near the door. Her cellphone buzzed and she took a quick look at its screen. *Mom. Shit. I'm not ready to talk to her.* She left the call unanswered, and wasn't surprised when she found a voicemail in her inbox. *Later!*

Glen was becoming her best friend. But so far, it seemed that it wasn't going anywhere besides friendship. She sighed. And it didn't surprise her when he sat down next to her a few seconds later.

"Hello, Ann." She looked up and saw he wasn't smiling. In fact he seemed deeply worried.

"Hey. You seem bugged. Whazzup?"

"Your friend Jon called. He offered me some weird kind of 'exciting opportunity' if I volunteered to help him. I told him to fuck off."

Ann nodded. "Good, good. You'll be safer this way. But I'm also worried about your deal with Mr. Lucessi."

"How bad could it be? Every venture capital firm brings with its image a long list of nightmare stories. But I have to find funding somewhere or MindField will remain a school project and die a short painful death."

Ann nodded again. Glen was right. Everything involves some level of risk. "The key is to select the most prominent VC. The one with the most to lose if they cheat you."

"Wow. Ann, that's a lot more depressing than anything you've told me before."

She simply stared back, lost in thought about what to say to her mother.

* * *

The three spies sat together in the Stanford Student Union. "That little stinker," Cassie repeated. "When I get hold of her—"

"You'll do what?" said Lee. "Ann's our daughter and she's over eighteen. She has her own world and if I know what she'd thinking, it's that we're intruding. So, we should look for 'pretenders' elsewhere. For all you know, this Glen may end up being our son-in-law."

Cassie turned away, her anger still visible but now fading from her face.

Jon looked like he'd lost his best friend. Lee asked him, "What's wrong, Jon?"

"I just realized I don't know enough about venture capital to pull off this mission. I'll have a steep learning curve. I'm going to get a guest pass for Stanford's main library. I'll have to visit the campus bookstore, too. The research might take me a couple of days."

Cassie forced a smile. "I used to be an angel investor. It was about five years ago, but how much could things have changed?"

She knew Lee was a geek, and when he shook his head, she asked, "What?"

Lee said, "According to Moore's Law, everything associated with the changes in high tech itself changes every eighteen months. So no, your old knowledge might more likely be useless. I go with Jon. You should come with us to the bookstore. We'll all need a refresher."

They all rose from their table outside the cafeteria and left by the front exit.

* * *

Frank Lucessi read over his list of prospective deals. He'd completed eleven of twelve. One more and he could report back to Robert Randall. He still needed to get the signed contracts from MindField. According to Glen Sarkov, the contracts had been signed by him and all his cofounders and were ready to be picked up. While their first set of docs were letters of intent, these would stand up in a court of law, according to his handler.

He also wanted to see Laura Hunter again. Their date last night got him into bed with her. He wondered if he was in love. *No, that can't be. My first relationship of any kind in over fifteen years. But I'm unable to think of anything or anyone else right now, so maybe it's just lust.*

He parked the car in one of Stanford University's student parking lots and headed off to the Student Union cafeteria. *Soon, I'll finally have MindField complete.*

When he reached the cafeteria, he selected an empty table by the entrance, so he could see who was arriving before they saw him. He punched Laura's cell number into his phone and pressed the Call button. But it went to voicemail. "Hi, Laura, it's Frank. Are you free for dinner again? Call me."

He bought a cup of coffee and sat, waiting for Glen.

* * *

Cassie visited the Student Union bookstore and scanned its computer index, noting books she thought would deliver the venture capital knowledge Jon, Lee and she needed. There were so many. Given Jon's desire for some basic texts to start with, she compiled a short list from the bookstore's index before visiting the library for a list of current studies and articles.

- *Venture Deals: Be Smarter Than Your Lawyer and Venture Capitalist*, by Brad Feld and Jason Mendelson

- *The Business of Venture Capital: Insights from Leading Practitioners on the Art of Raising a Fund, Deal Structuring, Value Creation, and Exit Strategies*, by Mahendra Ramsinghani

- *The Entrepreneurial Bible to Venture Capital: Inside Secrets from the Leaders in the Startup Game*, by Andrew Romans

- *Mastering the VC Game: A Venture Capital Insider Reveals How to Get from Start-up to IPO on Your Terms*, by Jeffrey Bussgang

- *Venture Capital for Dummies*, by Nicole Gravagna and Peter K. Adams

- *Zero to One: Notes on Startups, or How to Build the Future*, by Peter Thiel and Blake Masters

- *Venture Capital 101*, by Bill Snow and Amber Cordova

- *Venture Capital Valuation, + Website: Case Studies and Methodology*, by Lorenzo Carver

- *Venture Capital Deal Terms: A Guide to Negotiating and Structuring Venture Capital*

Transactions, by Harm de Vries and Menno van Loon

- *Masters of Corporate Venture Capital: Collective Wisdom from 50 VCs, Best Practices for Corporate Venturing, How to Access Startup Innovation, and How to Get Funded,* by Andrew Romans and William Kilmer

- *The Masters of Private Equity and Venture Capital: Management Lessons from the Pioneers of Private Investing,* by Robert Finkel and David Greising

- *Venture Capital and the Finance of Innovation,* 2nd Edition, by Andrew Metrick and Ayako Yasuda

- *Venture Capital and Private Equity: A Casebook,* by Josh Lerner, Felda Hardymon, and Ann Leamon

- *The Little Book of Venture Capital Investing: Empowering Economic Growth and Investment Portfolios,* by Louis C. Gerken

- *Fundraising Field Guide: A Startup Founder's Handbook for Venture Capital,* by Carlos Espinal and Matthew Cobb

- *No Dead Monkeys: The Communications Survival Guide for Startups,* by Jonathan Englert and Jeremy Kirk

There were many more, but she had enough to get her the basic concepts. She then visited Amazon and bought a few of these as ebooks, so she wouldn't have to lug physical tomes around. She knew that as a computer forensics major with an economics minor, Ann might have read some of these and wondered if she should talk with her daughter about what she knew of venture capital and investing. But then she realized that until Ann and she had reached a more comfortable point, it might be better to wait.

* * *

Glen trotted down Palo Alto city streets from his apartment along the pathway to the Student Union cafeteria. He'd overslept and was running late for this, the final prefunding appointment with Lucessi. It was beginning to rain and he didn't want to stop, even to open an umbrella. As he reached the doorway to the Student Union cafeteria, Ann stepped into his path. He almost tripped over her.

"Stop, Glen. I need just a minute before you meet with Lucessi."

"Why? What's so important?"

"I just read the contracts he wants you to sign."

"How'd you do that?"

Ann looked away for just a second. She then seemed to muster her courage and stared back at Glen. "I'm a hacker, remember?" When Glen nodded, she continued. "There are still two clauses I think you need to understand. First, a majority of the accredited investors can vote to devalue the shares held by the unaccredited investors as a group. That means your venture capital group can vote to revalue your shares, which are owned as 'unaccredited,' to a thousandth of their current worth, and more or less take over total ownership of the company. Since most of your salary is being paid in stock shares, effectively, you'd be working for nothing. Got it?"

Glen nodded, his face showing surprise.

"Good, good. Also, Mr. Lucessi's firm has the right of first refusal on any other investor buying into your company. In effect, they can reject anyone else as an investor, so their vote to devalue would be fiat."

Glen nodded again. "How come your Mr. Marotta didn't tell me this?"

Ann took a few seconds before answering. "Mr. Marotta has seen these in almost every venture capital funding contract he's ever reviewed. I just wanted you to understand that your ownership after signing is tentative. It depends on your ability to perform according to their standards. Seller beware. Got it?"

Glen nodded. "Anything else?"

She shook her head. "Good luck, sweetie." She pecked him on the cheek, turned, and left him standing there.

Glen thought for a while about the things he'd missed and wondered, *Is there more? This is like Odysseus's trip. So much hidden under the waves.* He shook his head to clear it and entered the building. But as he walked toward the table where Frank Lucessi sat waiting, Glen felt increasingly unsure of himself.

* * *

Frank smiled at Glen as he extended his hand. "At last, we can conclude our business."

Glen shook Frank's hand, then sat across the table from Lucessi.

The expression on Glen's face left Frank feeling unsure of what might happen next. Frank cocked his head. "You still have misgivings?"

Glen shrugged. "I'm a beginner at this. We have a great product and it's just the start. I'm not very sure I understand your rights as a venture funder and oncoming member of our board of directors. Seems you can literally make us vanish any time you feel like it."

Frank's jaw opened a bit. He wasn't sure of a venture capitalist's rights, because he wasn't really a venture capitalist. He felt unsure of what to say.

Glen watched Frank's confidence evaporate, and it hit him like a bullet. The silence between them grew like a disease.

CHAPTER 17

**Stanford University Student Union cafeteria,
Palo Alto, CA**

September 16, 11:38 a.m.

Glen picked up his pen and steeled himself to all that he didn't know and couldn't find out. He had already signed the documents where Frank had placed a "SIGN HERE" sticker. Now he handed them back to Frank.

Glen faced him. "So, I'll schedule our first board meeting in three weeks. That will give us time to deposit your check, find offices, buy furniture, and refine the computer models of our first product."

Frank nodded as he placed the contracts in his attaché case and handed Glen the signed check.

Glen rose and extended his hand. "Thanks, Mr. Lucessi." After they shook hands, Glen left the cafeteria.

Frank remained behind.

* * *

As the rain continued falling in a steady stream, Laura Hunter approached the Student Union cafeteria. She pulled to a stop about ten feet from the door and thought furiously about what she was about to do. She and Frank had enjoyed the restaurant last night, with its glorious food. Then they had taken a walk and somehow ended up at Frank's hotel, where they sipped a few drinks in the bar. And then they enjoyed each other's bodies. She wasn't sure why she had gone so far with him.

But now she was certain he would want to take another step. She wasn't sure what it was, but she believed it could change her life forever. After her failure in the art restoration class, she feared she would ever amount to much in the art world. *Maybe this meeting today is a sign?*

Drenched, she stepped inside the cafeteria and saw Frank speaking with Glen. She couldn't hear what Frank was saying but decided not to interrupt. She sat at a nearby table and watched their conversation. Frank handed Glen two thin, clipped documents and Glen folded them and placed them in his book bag. One appeared to be a check. Then Frank flashed a smile. Glen didn't appear to be happy. He rose and extended his hand. After they shook, Glen walked from the cafeteria. When he passed Laura without noticing her, she could see he was uneasy.

Laura took a deep breath and walked to the table where Frank sat. She smiled and sat across from him. "Hi."

Frank smiled at her. "I was hoping I'd see you here. Last night took my breath away."

"Well, I came as I promised. Uh, no pun intended. I, ah, also enjoyed last night."

"Yeah. But I wasn't sure. Look, tonight is my last night here. I'll be traveling back to Paraguay. I'd like you to come with me."

Laura's mouth fell open. "What?"

"Come with me. Live with me. I think I'm in love with you."

She sat totally still, thoughts and emotions rushing through her head and her heart. "I need to think about this."

Frank nodded. "Yes, of course you do."

Laura abruptly rose and left the cafeteria. Frank remained, stunned at what had just happened. He hadn't intended to tell her he loved her. He wasn't even really sure he did. He was even more surprised she had just disappeared. And, now, what should he do? He hadn't any idea.

* * *

Laura could hear the noise of Ann's fingers typing before she even reached their apartment. She unlocked the door and entered. Ann looked up from her work and nodded. Then she went back to her work.

Laura smiled absently and sat on her bed. As she sat and thought, she broke into tears.

Ann looked up from her work. "Hey, what gives?"

Laura shrugged. "I need to make a decision. One that will change my life forever."

Ann rose and crossed the room. She sat at the edge of Laura's bed and touched Laura's shoulder. "You might as well tell me. Maybe I can help you figure it out, maybe not. But give me a try."

Laura nodded but remained silent. She grimaced. "This morning I realized that I'll never amount to much in the art world. I mean, maybe if I learn everything I can, well, maybe I can become mediocre. But I'll never produce work that makes people gawk and gasp. I just don't have that much talent. And I don't just want to sell art from other artists' galleries. Ugh, what a waste."

She saw Ann shake her head and begin to open her lips to speak. "No, Ann," said Laura. "Let me finish. I recently met a man who seems interested in me. I like him a lot. He's a venture capitalist and he's been talking to your friend Glen. His name's Frank. Tonight, he offered me the opportunity to move in with him. But not anywhere near here. He lives in Paraguay."

Ann's mouth opened slightly. She shook her head. "You can't be at all sure about your future. This all seems premature. It will short-circuit any chance you have of growing your talent. But there's something more. I don't think you understand who Frank really is."

"What? What do you mean, Ann? What do you know about Frank?"

"Glen has been trying to work a deal for funding from Frank Lucessi. His venture capital firm is called InTelQ. My mom and dad think his firm isn't what it seems. If they're right, neither is Frank. I've warned Glen about Frank and his business."

"What are you talking about?"

"A few weeks ago, two startup cofounders both died in the house where they lived. But the truth is they were really Mossad covert operatives, and their deaths weren't a murder-suicide as it appeared to the police. My mom, dad, and one of my friends think they were terminated so the venture capital firm that funded them could gain total ownership of the intellectual property of the startup. They aren't sure yet, but it looks to me like the venture capital firm funding the startup was InTelQ. If so, then Frank is a party to a double murder, and there may have been more startups whose execs suffered the same fate. The investigation is just beginning."

Laura moved away from Ann. "You're crazy. Stay away from me." She opened her dresser and packed clothing into a suitcase. "I'm out of here. Now." She slammed the suitcase shut and ran from the apartment while Ann sat on the bed, a shocked expression on her face.

CHAPTER 18

**Four Seasons Hotel Silicon Valley,
Palo Alto, CA**

September 16, 1:48 p.m.

Frank Lucessi was packing his suitcase when his cellphone buzzed. He scanned its screen and smiled. "Laura! I was hoping you'd call."

"I owe you an explanation and an answer." She paused and he thought the call was dropped. But then she spoke. "Well, here goes. I'm not sure whether what you proposed is workable, or even if I want it. But, I am willing to give it a try. At the university my professors hate my work. I'm so frustrated I can't stand it any longer. I doubt I'll ever achieve what I'd hoped. And it's too humiliating to keep trying after all their feedback over my first two years. So, my feeling is, I have nothing to lose. But don't get your hopes up. I might easily fail at the relationship you propose."

Frank stood and paced the room while he thought. "Okay. But give me a chance. I've been single my entire life. Never even thought I'd ever find someone I wanted as a mate. So, my desire to have you by my side is as much a surprise to me as it is to you."

This time her answer came immediately. "Where do you

want to meet? My suitcase is packed and I'm ready to leave right now."

"Sure. First, I'll buy you a ticket for the plane. Where's your apartment? I can drive my rental there in about a half hour."

"I'm no longer at the apartment. Why don't we meet in the student cafeteria?"

* * *

There was a knock at the door to Ann's apartment. She opened the door and saw Glen waiting outside. "Come in."

Glen scanned her face. "You look like something truly awful just happened."

Ann's voice was soft with the anguish she still felt. "My roommate, Laura, just left with her suitcase. I get the feeling she isn't coming back. She said I was crazy."

Glen stared at Ann. "What did you do?"

"I tried to talk her out of leaving school and moving out of the country with her sudden boyfriend. Your funding source. Frank Lucessi of InTelQ."

Glen sat at the edge of Ann's bed. It looked to Ann as if he were having trouble processing the information she'd just delivered. "Your roommate and my venture capitalist. Now, that is crazy."

Ann shook her head. "It makes no sense to me." She looked directly at his eyes. "Did you actually sign and deliver the contracts?"

Glen shrugged. "Yeah. So I'll also be leaving my dorm room."

"What are your first steps?"

"I'll be looking for an office site for MindField and an apartment for myself. So, I'll still be in the neighborhood."

Ann shook her head. "Yeah." *I guess, really, I'm the only sane one. So now it makes sense that she called me crazy.*

You can't let crazy people decide who's crazy and who's sane.

She turned away from Glen. *Maybe I should tell Mom about what's happened on my end.* She decided to call Cassie and give her a sitrep.

* * *

At the airport, after they had checked their suitcases, Frank's cell buzzed. He turned away from Laura and scanned the cell's screen: Robert Randall. "Lucessi."

"Frank, this is Robert Randall. Congratulations on completing your first assignment. I'll have another for you in a few days. Until then, you can have some time off to refresh. Oh, and I'd advise you to learn a bit more about the venture capital business. Seems you made a few mistakes with one of yours. MindField, I think it's called. I'll send you a reading list. For your completed work, I've wired your account a total of forty-eight thousand dollars. Enjoy your time off."

Frank hadn't had a chance to speak. He turned off his phone and shook his head.

Laura asked, "Who was that?"

"Just business." Frank sat in one of the seats at the gate and tried to think how his world had so completely changed in just three short weeks.

* * *

Jon Sommers completed reading the last of the ebooks on venture capital that Cassie had sent to his cellphone. He'd written a set of cheat sheets, just in case. Now he was ready to call the first of the nineteen remaining names that Lee, Cassie, and he had thought might be most likely to help them snare the venture capitalist responsible for the carnage of the Mossad operatives.

He practiced his speech for nearly an hour before

pulling his phone from his pocket. He took a deep breath to calm himself and smiled in an attempt to push a friendly demeanor into his consciousness. Then he called candidate number four, Daniel Tremain, CEO of StarClaims.com. "Hello, Daniel. My name is Jon Sommers. You don't know me, but I'm interested in helping you and your startup, StarClaims."

"Well, I've never heard of you. Be brief, I'm on my way to a meeting."

Jon read from his script: "I represent Abah Investments, an Israeli venture capital aggregator. I've read your firm's profile and it looks like you're developing an AI product that might have military applications. If you're interested, I'd like to pursue finding investors for your startup. We at Abah represent several angel capital firms, some corporations, and a few government entities."

"Angels? An aggregator? What's an aggregator? How do you approach the process?"

Jon smiled. The hook was set. "So, I assume you haven't yet obtained a seed round. Do you have a current business plan?"

"Yes. We're looking for funding to produce proof of concept."

Jon read the next portion of his script. "How much would be necessary for you to produce a viable product?"

"A half mil."

Jon thought. "So what's your estimated pre-money?"

"One hundred twenty mil."

Jon did his own set of calculations. "So you're assuming that you can retain about fifty percent ownership after funding your seed round."

"No. I'm assuming we'll continue to hold seventy percent."

Jon tried the calculations again. They didn't add up. "Are you firm on holding that percentage?"

"Mr.... uh, Sommers, is it? Well, as you know, every deal has negotiable parameters. What would you like to see?"

"I can offer you a set of investors for fifty-one percent ownership. The shares will be held by Abah on behalf of its member investors. I can offer the half mil. Of course, we'll have to read your business plan, meet to kick the tires, and then, if it all looks good, we could arrange to have you sign papers in less than a week. Are you interested?"

"Yes. Send me your contact details and I'll email a current copy of the business plan."

Jon sent a text of the email address for "Sommers at Abah." He smiled as he terminated the call.

He looked at his list of prospects and read the description of the fifth name on his list. Once again, he entered the phone number and started his next call. By the time the afternoon ended, Jon had signed up four of the remaining fifteen from their list of nineteen candidates. He wasn't sure if this would be enough to discover who had murdered the Mossad team, but it would have to do.

CHAPTER 19

**Sultana Restaurant,
1149 El Camino Real, Menlo Park, CA**

September 16, 7:54 p.m.

The restaurant Glen had chosen claimed to offer "a tasty menu of authentic Turkish cuisine." It was decorated to look like the inside of a tent, with images of roses on the wallpaper.

Ann tapped her fingers on the table where she sat waiting for Glen. *Is he my boyfriend? We've only kissed and it didn't light me up. Why am I so protective? He's more like a best friend, or maybe even a brother. Worse, he's a distraction from my studies. Damn, I need to figure this out.* The door opened and Glen entered, looking around for her, and smiling when he caught her eyes.

Glen sat across the table from her. He reached across and took her hand in his. "What a long day. I found suitable office space. Tomorrow the team and I will begin moving in. I bought secondhand office furniture from a local place, computers from Fry's, and office supplies from OfficeMax. By the end of tomorrow, we'll be productive." He gleamed back. "How was your day, Ann?"

"Okay I guess. Order the lahmacun. It's like a Turkish version of pizza. Delicious." She stared at him, trying to decide if this was the right time for "the relationship" discussion. "Glen, I like you. A lot. But I'm not sure about what we expect from each other, and I'd like to talk about that. With you. Now."

Glen's expression showed he felt surprise. "Um, okay."

"Who are we to each other? How do you feel about me?"

Glen took a deep breath. "I'm not sure. I mean, I like you a lot, too."

The waiter arrived and handed them menus. Before he examined the menu, Glen said, "lahmacun" to the waiter.

Ann said, "The same, for me. We'll decide on entrées in a few minutes."

The waiter nodded and turned, then walked away. Soon, he returned with round slices of flat-baked dough topped with minced lamb, parsley, onion, and tomatoes, served with fresh tomatoes on the side.

Glen sniffed the lahmacun. He nodded. "Should we decide on what we're eating before having so serious a conversation?"

She sighed. "Whatever."

Silence reigned, with them each staring at the other.

The waiter returned and Ann ordered the imam bayildi, made of roasted eggplant stuffed with tomatoes and onions, and served with rice.

Glen went with the lamb divan, consisting of ground lamb and beef kebab rolled in lavash bread, topped with melted mozzarella cheese, and served with sautéed spinach and garlic yogurt.

As they ate, Ann returned to the relationship discussion with a single word: "Well?"

Glen looked at the food in front of him. "Delicious."

"No. Not the food. Us. Is there an 'us'?"

Glen remained silent for a few seconds. Ann wondered

what he was thinking. Finally, he said, "I'd like there to be an 'us.'"

Ann nodded. "So, Glen, when will we kiss again?"

He reached across the table and touched her lips with his. "After dinner. My apartment."

Ann nodded. "Okay then."

* * *

At the airport, Frank asked for her passport and examined it. He handed her a visa, and said, "This is for you. I have a friend in the government who can do almost anything."

When the aircraft took off on the first leg of its journey to Paraguay, Frank placed his arm around Laura's shoulder. She felt the pressure as the aircraft lifted off the runway at SFO as a comforting gesture. She still wasn't sure if she had made the right decision, leaving her old life behind. She didn't know if she was prepared to face an unknown future.

But his hand, compressed by the pressure of the aircraft climbing into the sky, quickly became an annoyance for her. She shifted in her seat, but his arm remained firmly across her back. "Frank, this is uncomfortable. Please remove your hand."

"Huh? Yeah. Okay."

* * *

Ann lay in Glen's bed. He was gently snoring. She graded his performance in bed as *"in need of improvement. Lots of improvement." He took very little time to come to climax. Not long enough for me. Not enough foreplay, not enough time of intercourse. He moved too fast.* After, she tried to calm herself. *He'll need lessons. Most men I've had sex with do. But now, he is my problem.* She closed her eyes and focused on the dregs of yesterday. Soon, she was drifting into sleep.

When Glen's cellphone buzzed, she opened her eyes and forced herself from his bed. At first she thought it was an incoming call, but then as it buzzed on, she realized it was his wake-up alarm.

He rolled over, nearly slamming one of his arms into her face.

She flinched. "Hey! Watch it."

His eyes popped open. "Oh. Sorry."

She moved further away. Her clothes. Where were they? She scanned the room and saw they weren't anywhere in his bedroom. She found her bra and panties on the floor in his living room. Her blouse and skirt were on the dresser. She grabbed the pieces as she found them and dressed. Then she walked into the hallway leading to the bathroom. She found him in the bathroom, so she waited outside until the sink was free. Neither spoke. She wondered if he felt as dissatisfied with their close encounter as she felt. *I'll have to talk to him about this soon. But when?*

* * *

Robert Randall read the email and frowned. He'd drawn the short straw. The Director of National Intelligence had just added a new assignment to his portfolio. Randall would be in charge of delivering the daily intelligence threat assessment to one of the candidates running for president. He'd never met Daniel Strumler before, but had seen a few of the debates. Strumler was a rich, pompous idiot who had never run for office before. According to the latest polls, there was no chance he could win. Randall decided any time spent with Strumler was a waste of time, and he had more important things to do. But this assignment, from the DNI, was an order. Randall always obeyed orders.

He sighed and called the DNI's secretary. He asked for Daniel Strumler's cell number, then called Strumler's line and was connected. "Hello." The voice was a female—either that or Strumler's voice hadn't changed yet. "Roxy Mills, assistant to Mr. Strumler."

"I'm Robert Randall, case officer at the CIA. The DNI assigned me to give Mr. Strumler his daily intelligence threat assessments. I'd like to schedule the first one for the day after tomorrow."

"Mr. Strumler is at a campaign event. He doesn't have time for an assessment. Everyone already knows how intelligent he is."

Randall's grin split his face. It was all he could do to keep from howling with laughter. "No, sweety. Spies. You know, the American version of James Bond. As I told you, I'm with the CIA. Again, I need to schedule Mr. Strumler's first daily intelligence briefing. He needs to know what's happening in the world. You know. Threats."

Apparently, Roxy was a dud. He waited. Finally: "I'll give him your message. Is this the phone number you want him to dial?"

"Yeah. Please have him return this call ASAP." Randall ended the call. *The DNI gave me a turd.*

* * *

Sitting in his hotel room, Jon called Cassie on his cell. "Can you guys drop by the Stanford Student Union's cafeteria? I need you both with me to discuss the strategy we'll use when recruiting our entrepreneurs to work with us."

"Sure. Give me ten minutes to get Lee and find an Uber."

Jon retrieved his notebook from the hotel room's safe and headed out the door to the elevator. Jon wondered if he should ask both Lee and Cassie to accompany him to all meetings with potential entrepreneurs. That way, he would have a better idea if he was succeeding or failing in his attempt to explain how what he needed was different from what a venture capitalist would expect at the point of making an investment.

* * *

Glen hadn't even had a chance to say good morning to Ann before she hurried from his apartment. What was wrong? Hadn't he been attentive and happy as they enjoyed each other's bodies?

He passed by the wall clock and realized he was late for his first class. Since he had paid for the semester, he felt he might as well attend every class he could, and take all his exams. If he remained in school through the end of the semester, he'd graduate with his MS in information systems. As he rushed through washing and dressing, his mind continued to wander. He thought about the rental office spaces he'd seen and the one he'd chosen for MindField. Then his thoughts returned to last night with Ann. *Should I talk to her about what happened last night? What should I do?*

He trotted across campus to his class. As he entered the auditorium, he could see that all the best seats were already taken. Glen found a seat where he'd not be seen by the professor at the lectern. He opened his notebook and logged into the class so he could record the lecture, and located the webpage where he could see the professor's slides as the lecture progressed. One glance at his watch. He had little time before the professor would arrive. He sent a text to his cofounders listing the address of the property he'd selected yesterday and the move-in details. Instantly, all of them had replied. Three sent "K" emojis. Harvey said he'd visit the property today and examine the CAT-5e that the owner had preinstalled, before the end of the workday.

As the professor stepped to the front of the room, Glen wondered again, *what went wrong last night?*

* * *

Before beginning his new post, Robert Randall had a few loose ends to attend to. He knew he couldn't handle Strumler and still run InTelQ. He'd have to wind InTelQ down. And, since InTelQ was not really a CIA operation but his own private side business, his only problem would be to keep it totally off the books and hidden from his CIA employers. There was no way he could sell the stock he'd placed in Child Industries Associated, the corporation he'd formed for the op. He'd have to find another way to move the shares. He was sure he could sell them anonymously using Bitcoin.

He reviewed his notes on each of the entrepreneurs in his startups, both the living and the dead. InTelQ now controlled fifty-seven companies with living cofounders, and eleven that had borne strategic fruit. The cofounders of those eleven were now deceased, courtesy of Alan Skorkin and "Skorkin Consulting." He'd need to get the status of the remaining fifty-seven and determine if any of them had made an unnoticed discovery worth the effort of sending Skorkin to remove them from this earth. For that information, he needed Frank Lucessi to attend each company's next round of board of directors' meetings. He crafted a spreadsheet table in his notebook showing each one's next board meeting and sequenced it into a schedule. He sent this table, named "Your_schedule_of_assignments.xls" to Lucessi's cellphone.

When Randall checked his email, there was a reply from Roxy Mills:

Dear Mr. Randall,
Mr. Strumler can see you next week on his private aircraft when it lands in Cleveland, Ohio, at 12:30 p.m on Thursday.
Sincerely,
Roxy Mills, Assistant to Mr. Strumler

Randall frowned. He'd need more time to finish winding down his InTelQ operation before assuming his new presidential-advisor function.

CHAPTER 20

**Lucessi compound, Areguá,
45 minutes from Asunción, Paraguay**

September 17, 4:16 p.m.

Laura Hunter clutched her visa and passport to her and dragged her rolling suitcase through the terminal. She met Pedro, her driver, at the Ascunción International Airport ticket counter, just as Frank told her. He said he'd be along soon, but had some business to complete in the city. Her driver escorted Laura to a black Hummer in the parking pavilion and drove them from the airport. She continued to look out the window of the Hummer at the forested land and one-lane road for about forty-five minutes until the driver took a slow turn over scattered potholes into Areguá, which appeared to her to be a laid-back town with a nice church and lake.

The driver spoke. "Señorita Hunter, Areguá is home to many artists and writers who have set up nice galleries and museums. Outdoor street market selling colorful ceramics. You can visit the Museo del Mueble, Centro Cultural del Lago, and El Cantaro Almacén de Arte, The town is less than fifteen minutes from Señor Lucessi's compound. I can drive you whenever you wish."

She felt a wave of discomfort rattle her stomach. *What*

the hell am I doing? She rubbed her belly and grimaced. "Thank you, Pedro."

She could see his smile reflected in the rear-view mirror. Remote from the town, the compound looked like a prison, complete with barbed wire topping the masonry walls that surrounded two tile-roofed structures. As Pedro approached the gate, it opened for him. The Hummer passed through, and the gate closed. Laura saw uniformed guards carrying automatic weapons on the top of the walls. She was unprepared for life inside an armed compound. Her jaw dropped but just for a moment.

Pedro opened the Hummer's rear door and nodded for her to exit. She followed him on a brief tour of the main house. It was large and modestly decorated. She examined paintings on the wall of the living room. Old, but probably copies. The originals, she hoped, were on the walls of museums.

There were five bedrooms. One was obviously Frank's. No clothing was visible, so she assumed Frank must have had a housekeeping staff neatening up the house. The other bedrooms were smaller, and contained at least a bed and a dresser. She asked Pedro, "Where will I be staying?"

Pedro looked confused. After nearly a minute, he said, "With Mr. Lucessi, I assume. When he returns, you may ask him."

As she continued touring her new home, she wondered if she was committing to Frank too easily. *What am I missing?*

* * *

Frank Lucessi read the short text from Randall and then opened the attachment and cursed. The calendar schedule of board meetings covered almost every day for the next two months starting tomorrow, crisscrossing the United States nearly three times. Fifty-seven meetings in eleven cities. And his first meeting was in Akron, Ohio, at eight in the morning.

He cursed in four languages. *I'll have to call Laura and apologize.* He trotted to the ticket counter and picked up the envelope with his name on it. Within, he found his ticket on the flight out and a voucher for a Best Western in Akron. He picked up his suitcase and ran for the gate where the aircraft was now boarding.

He was the final passenger to board and as he entered, the flight attendant closed and locked the door. He plucked his cellphone from his pocket. But before he could punch in Laura's number, the flight attendant instructed all passengers to place their phones on Airplane Mode. He'd have to wait nearly six hours until the plane landed at its first stop in Chicago. That would be after midnight in Paraguay. *She'll be pissed.*

* * *

Jon nodded at Lee's advice. "So I should tell them everything?"

Cassie shook her head. "Absolutely not! You'll scare the bejesus out of them. Weren't you taught by the Mossad to lie? Well, if there is one situation where lying best serves everyone, it's this. Tell them a story about how their field is so competitive, and sometimes people lie in order to succeed. Be a bit vague,"

Lee's jaw fell. "No, no, no. Tell the truth."

Jon sat in silence. Then he shook his head. "Well, that confuses the issue. Tell you what. Let's play out both approaches. First, the 'truth' approach. What could go wrong?" He looked from Lee to Cassie but both were silent.

Jon waited until he was sure they wouldn't answer. "So, the risks here are at the very front end and at the back end. At the front end, we tell them about the danger they'll accept if they take our offer. Many will just tell us to go to hell. So, of the few we have on our short list, there's the risk that we'll have no pretenders to send out into the venture capital world. But the risk at the end is that they'll decide to tell the world our secrets. The result would be catastrophic. If the world discovers that intelligence agencies own and operate venture capital companies and terminate cofounders of their start-ups, there will be no trust in the venture capital industry. Worse, the idea will be compelling and contagious to every country's spy agencies. We'd have fed the monster we're trying to kill."

Lee nodded. "Each is a killer risk."

Jon looked at Cassie but she just nodded for him to continue.

Jon took a breath. "Right, then. Now, let's look at the 'lie' scenario. Here the risks run high throughout the exploit. At the beginning, we lie when we don't tell them about the danger they're exposing themselves to. Then as they perform, we must provide them with more protection than we'd have to if we told them the truth and gave them a mini-course on countersurveillance. And when we reach the end, if they're still alive, we get them what we promised: the funding for their enterprise. Less, maybe even no risk at the end. Which is a better approach?"

There was a long silence, Finally Cassie spoke. "Uh, I hadn't thought of the risks. I just thought we wanted to keep both the Mossad and the United Nations out of the exploit."

Lee shook his head. "Easier to keep your story straight and simple if you tell the truth."

Cassie's mouth opened slightly. "But, lying is what they taught you in your training for intelligence work. You prob-ably can keep your story straight."

Jon shook his head. "Not really. It's a decision that has

profound, unintended consequences. We'll need to decide this before we design our talking script."

They argued for hours. In the end, "lying" won out.

Jon grinned. "After all, lying is what spies do best."

* * *

It was after midnight when Frank's flight landed in Chicago. He disembarked and pulled his spinner suitcase through the labyrinthine airport terminal. At the terminal gate for the flight to Akron, he checked in and sat, waiting for the flight to board. Then he pulled his cellphone from his pocket and punched in Laura's number.

He could tell from her voice he'd woken her. "Hello?"

"It's Frank. Sorry to not be with you. That business issue I spoke about when we landed, well, it's become something more than an issue. I've been called away, and I'll be travelling for the next two months. I'm so sorry for this, but I didn't know before it happened."

"Two months? Frank, I don't know anyone here. I haven't any idea what to do for two months. Not fair."

"Yeah, I know. Look, I'll find a way to make it up to you. Give me a chance. Please."

Laura was silent for a while. "Oh, fuck this." She terminated the call.

Frank blamed Randall for this. He spent the half hour before boarding thinking of ways to get even. He could simply fail and force Randall to fire him. Or he could let it slip that InTelQ was a CIA operation. But, in the end, he found his seat and stared out the window.

CHAPTER 21

Lucessi compound, Areguá, Paraguay

September 18, 8:16 a.m.

Laura Hunter sat in the opulent living room and thought about her future. She could have Pedro drive her back to the airport and simply return to Stanford. But she'd have to find the cash to buy an air ticket. She was conflicted in how she felt about Frank. If she was truly falling for him, she could just wait for his return, but what could she do for two months that might please her?

She scouted out websites that might give her something interesting to do if she waited for Frank to return. She brooded about how he'd abandoned her in a place where she knew no one and couldn't speak either of the two languages—Paraguayan Spanish or Guaraní—that locals spoke. If she was going to wait for him, she'd need to learn to speak the local languages. She cursed Frank and herself for agreeing to travel to Paraguay.

There was nothing interesting in Areguá, but the capital city, Asunción, was less than an hour away by limo, and it was home to over a half million people. According to the websites she'd researched, there were a few sites worth visiting in Asunción. She made a list:

- Godoi Museum

- Museo Nacional de Bellas Artes (containing old paintings from the nineteenth century)

- Church of La Encarnación

- Metropolitan Cathedral and the National Pantheon of the Heroes, a smaller version of Les Invalides in Paris, where some of the nation's heroes were entombed.

Not enough to occupy her for two entire months. In desperation, she searched harder. She considered several other places. At first, she wasn't sure if they were worth her time, but her list was so short. In the end, she made a note to visit the Calle Palma, the main street downtown, where several historical buildings, plazas, shops, restaurants, and cafés were located.

The Manzana de la Rivera, located in front of the Presidential Palace, was a series of old traditional homes that had been restored and served as a museum showcasing the architectural evolution of the city. It might appeal to the art history major still living in her bones.

Asunción also had shopping malls. While she waited for Frank to return, she could spend his money there. But first she'd have to find where he hid it.

Asunción might not have many conventional tourist attractions, but if she were willing to be her own tour guide, Asunción was worth at least one entire day. She reminded herself that a full day would have to include midday siesta, when just about everything in the city was closed.

She decided to ask Pedro to suggest who might teach her the languages of the locals and to set up meetings with several possible teachers.

She felt a sense of panic rise inside her. *What will I do with myself for two entire months?*

She looked at another website for additional places of interest. The Municipal Museum and the Center of Visual Arts looked good, but she was afraid the Fine Arts Museum might be fairly unimpressive.

Finally, she stumbled across the Museo del Barro, which claimed to be Asunción's most interesting and underrated attraction. Years ago, this museum started as a private circulating collection and seven years later acquired a permanent location. It included three separate divisions devoted respectively to pottery, indigenous art, and contemporary art.

The list was so short. Soon, she would have nothing to do but sit and wait. She cried while she sat alone.

* * *

Frank Lucessi rose at dawn the next morning and drove his rental to his first-ever board of directors meeting for a startup called XXY Dimensions. He arrived at a run-down building that must have originally been a factory before the startup moved in. As he approached the building, he sniffed the air and smelled industrial lubricant. *What the fuck do they do here?* He searched for the door but the only one was locked. He looked in vain for a doorbell.

A voice rattled through a hidden speaker. "Can I help you?"

He couldn't find a microphone so he just opened his mouth and spoke. "Yes. I'm Frank Lucessi. I'm here for your board of directors meeting."

"Are you on the list?"

"I'm from InTelQ."

The door popped open and Frank entered. He found himself in a blind—a small room between the door he'd entered and another three feet away. The disembodied voice spoke. "Place everything metal on the tray." He looked around and watched as a tray emerged from the wall perpendicular to the doors. This area stank even more of industrial lubricant. He dumped most of what was in his pockets on the tray, then carefully pulled his notebook computer from his attaché case and placed it on the tray. He heard a slight, very low-pitched noise. The voice said, "Okay. Please take your things and enter." He reloaded his pockets and his attaché case, then walked to the inner door, which sprang open as he neared it.

The inside area was spacious. He could hear factory noises. Machines grinding and pounding. He turned and inspected the area for more details. The walls were a light green and the floor was concrete and painted gray. He waited for someone to tell him or show him where to go next.

Someone wearing a business suit emerged from around a corner. "Hi. I'm Josh Taggert, the CFO." The man extended his hand and Frank shook it. "Welcome to XXY Dimensions."

From the notes Randall had sent him, Frank had been able to research the business. According to the scant news they'd generated, XXY Dimensions, Inc., was a genetic modification startup, whatever that was. "What exactly happens in this building, Mr. Taggert?"

"Well, we're just getting started. This was the largest vacant building we could find. We're setting it up to house genetic modifiers using a CRISPR. Ever hear of the term?"

Frank nodded his head. He already knew that the acronym stood for "clustered regularly interspaced short palindromic repeats." Some saw the gene-editing tool as the future of medicine. Others saw it as a Pandora's box. "How far along are you and what are your intended applications?"

"We're in the process of designing a super soldier. As it states in our business plan, this project was designed to get us the seed capital. Today's board meeting will decide if we've made enough progress to seek a second round of funding."

Frank scanned the area. "Where's the meeting to be?"

"The other board members have arrived and are in the conference room. We have coffee and doughnuts. Please follow me."

Frank walked the halls of the warren around several corners and then up a short flight of stairs. Taggert placed a plastic card bearing his photo against the doorknob and the door swung open. This room was much brighter. His eyes took time to adjust. He saw a wooden oval table with six plush black leather chairs, four occupied. Taggert sat in one and motioned Frank to take his seat at the other.

As soon as he sat, the man at the head of the table smiled and said, "I'm Willy Hangshaw, CEO of XXY. I hereby open the second board of directors meeting. First, a summary of our progress since the first meeting." A screen dropped from the ceiling behind him and a movie soundtrack rattled through the conference room's sound system.

* * *

The Stanford cafeteria was noisy when Jon, Cassie, and Lee entered. There were no open tables, so they waited. Jon scanned the room for a vacant table. There was no movement. He held a manila folder in one hand and a cup of hot black coffee in his other. He brushed the forelock of his hair off his forehead with the back of a hand, then realized it was a sign of being unsettled. His head swiveled toward the door to the lobby as it opened. He saw a tall, dark-skinned male enter. The man's face matched the photo in the file he held. And, as if on cue, four seats at a nearby table opened. Jon smiled, approached the man, and held out his hand. "Daniel Tremain? I'm Jon Sommers of Abah Investments. We spoke on the phone a few days ago. My partners are Cassandra Sashakovich and Lee Ainsley."

Tremain stopped short and examined Jon. "You look much younger than you sounded over the phone."

They shook hands and Jon led Cassie, Lee, and Tremaim to the now-empty table.

Jon opened the folder. "As I told you, Abah invests on behalf of angel investors, corporations, and governments."

"Yeah, I remember. But when I tried researching you, nothing came up. Not a bit, not a byte."

"We're new, and by that I mean we haven't yet announced our existence. We'll do that as soon as we have signed agreements with at least three startups."

Tremain nodded. "So, what do you propose?"

Jon scanned the first sheet in his folder. "We ask for you to sign an agreement that outlines the terms of Abah's investment in StarClaims. This won't commit you to anything. It just allows us to work with you toward becoming a fungible startup. You can terminate at any time, but if you do, we'll stop issuing payments. As the payments progress, we vest shares of preferred stock." He handed a stack of paper from the file to Tremain.

Tremain nodded and scanned through the stack as Jon sipped his coffee. After Tremain read the final page, he looked up and nodded. "I'll need to have our attorney read through these and then present them to my cofounders. Figure two days."

Jon nodded. "Fine. Tell me more about StarClaims proposed products, your market, and your management team."

Tremain pulled a notebook computer from his attaché case and opened it up. "What's your email? I can send you a copy of the appendices to our business plan and then answer your questions."

Jon opened his own attaché case and pulled out his

notebook. "I'm sommersj@Abah.com." He'd set up the website and the email with Cassie and Lee earlier in the day.

Tremain punched in Jon's email address and pressed the Send button.

Jon smiled as he opened the first appendix to the Star-Claims business plan. *First step done successfully. Now onto setting the hook.*

CHAPTER 22

Lucessi compound, Areguá, Paraguay

September 19, 10:16 a.m.

Laura awakened from a nightmare. In her dream, she was seven years younger than now, and heard her mother and father arguing upstairs. She climbed the stairs, shivering with each step although the air in the house was warm. As she approached the door to her parents' bedroom, she heard a something heavy hit the floor and then—silence. She woke knowing her father had murdered her mother. The sheets Laura lay on were wet with her perspiration. She rose and paced the bedroom. This nightmare was familiar territory for her, but this was the first time the dream had ended before she opened the bedroom's door and seen the mess that had been her mother's neck, lying on the floor next to the bloody body of a naked male stranger.

She opened the window shades of the house within the compound. Outside, she saw bright sunshine. She decided to don her bathrobe and head downstairs for coffee. As if a cup of hot coffee could cure the deep depression she had felt from yet another dream of her mother's violent death.

* * *

At their next meeting, Jon smiled at Daniel Tremain as he

watched the young man review the documents. This time, Jon was alone, having earned the trust of Cassie and Lee. While Jon might be the head operative for the assignment, Cassie had at least as much experience in covert ops.

Tremain reminded Jon of himself a decade in the past when he had just been awarded his MBA from the University of London.

Tremain looked up and stared back at Jon. "Mr. Sommers, what does this mean? It says, 'In the event that any members of the startup team encounter a physically threatening situation, Abah Investments will deploy a team to ensure the personal safety of the team and their family members.' If my team lets you invest in StarClaims, how would that put any of us in danger?"

Jon's eyes widened. This language was from the original agreement that Cassie, Lee, and Jon had crafted before they made their choice to lie and obfuscate. Jon shifted in his seat and read the sentence himself. *Ouch. We did this to ourselves.* He would have to improvise something. "Ah, at one time we invested in a startup that had a running feud with another startup, and we wanted to ensure the continuation of our investment. It really shouldn't apply to StarClaims."

"Why would another startup threaten violence?"

Jon had enough time to think before he heard this question, and he'd already imagined an answer. "Cancer cure. Big Pharma. They're almost always sore losers."

Tremain continued to stare at Jon. Jon could tell he wasn't convinced that this was true. But the best tactic Jon could muster was silence and a nodding head.

He wondered if Tremain and his cofounders would sign the documents.

"Mr. Sommers, I'm getting the impression that there's more here and you aren't able or willing to tell me what it is."

Jon was now sure Tremain would detect any lie he heard.

Nothing less than the truth—the full truth—would pass muster with Tremain and his cofounders. He opened both empty hands, an ancient gesture showing he held no weapon. "Daniel, there is something more. Abah Investments is owned by a paramilitary force of the United Nations. Recently, the plans for a weaponized product had been stolen from one of the more prominent member nations. Their startup team members were murdered. The nation in question sent a team posing as cofounders of a startup out to investigate and to determine which corporation or which government was guilty of the theft and murders, but they, too, were murdered. I was sent out with the assignment of recruiting a team of startup executives and running them to see who had caused the theft and murders. In return for helping us, we will fund your team all the way through its IPO."

Jon took a deep breath and sank deep into his seat.

Daniel Tremain shook his head. He handed Jon back the documents and rose from his seat. "We're not into doing any dangerous stuff. Sorry. Good luck finding someone crazy enough to help you." Tremain walked away, through the doorway and out into the quad.

Jon's jaw had opened but he could speak no words.

* * *

Laura visited every site on her list in one day. Most of her visits were brief. She found she couldn't concentrate for very long. Still, she didn't think any of them was worth a second visit, although the Calle Palma's shops, restaurants, and cafés were enough to amuse her for most of the afternoon before siesta started.

But now, as sunset brought on a starry night, she felt terribly alone. She had the cook make her a light dinner and selected a book to read. Frank had accumulated a sizable library and it was entirely in English. She decided to read one of DS Kane's novels, *Swiftshadow*, a story about a female spy who was fired after her cover was blown by a mole from her own intelligence agency.

She stopped reading at one of the more violent passages and saw the clock on the wall of her room. It was after midnight. Reluctantly, she put the book on her nightstand, open to the page where she'd stopped reading. It was a page where the protagonist was tortured.

Laura turned out the light and drew the covers to her chin. When sleep came, it brought another nightmare.

She was once again in the kitchen of the house where she grew up. As before, it was the night her mother died. But this time, she opened the silverware drawer and picked up a long-bladed chef's knife. The house was silent as she walked up the stairs. Her father was down the hall in the bathroom. Laura opened the bedroom door and saw her mother in front of the mirror that was mounted on the closet door. Her mother was naked, standing next to a naked strange man. Laura sneaked up behind her mother and plunged the knife into her neck. Blood spurted from her mother as she turned around to face her daughter. Laura held onto the knife and thrust it into her mother's gut, then into her mother's chest. As her mother's body slumped to the floor, she cornered and gutted the strange man. Just then, her father walked into the bedroom and she could see the shock on his face.

She woke sodden with perspiration. Somehow, this dream seemed more vivid than any of the others that she had ever had.

She lay awake wondering if it was she and not her father who had murdered her mother.

CHAPTER 23

Sturgess Technology, Atlanta, GA

September 20, 9:46 a.m.

Frank Lucessi arrived early for his board meeting with the cofounders of Sturgess Technology. He sat in his rental car in the parking lot as the rain pounded down outside. About a hundred feet away was the office park that housed over fifty small companies. He stared at the modern building as he drew his cellphone from his pocket. *Time to call Laura.*

He called her number and waited. One, two, three rings, then voicemail. His face scrunched. "Hi, sweet, it's Frank. I'm in Atlanta this morning. Another board meeting. I miss you. I'll try again later."

This was the third straight call he'd made to her that went to voicemail. *Was something wrong with her cellphone?* His next thought sent a shiver down his spine. *Is she angry with me for traveling while she waits alone for me?*

The alarm he'd set on his watch buzzed, reminding him he needed to hurry to his appointment.

He pulled his umbrella from the back seat, opened the car door, and walked toward the sleek, black, glass-front building that housed Sturgess. The lobby contained modern furnishings and a digital directory. Sturgess was on the fifth floor. He took the elevator up to the fifth and exited. The color scheme was monochromatic: black floor, gray walls, white ceiling. He swiveled his head to see where the suite housing Sturgess was located. He turned left, away from the elevator bank, and saw the door to the public men's room. Frank entered. After drawing his comb through his hair, he left the restroom and walked to the entrance to the Sturgess office. The entrance's black glass door led him into an almost empty, professional-looking seating area, more like those for a doctor's office than a startup. There was a single desk with a young woman seated behind.

Frank announced himself. She told him to take a seat and offered him coffee, but he declined.

He thought about Laura but his vision of her was interrupted by a man wearing a sharp business suit. The man had a crew cut and wore a smile. "I'm Richard Stein. You're Frank Lucessi?"

Frank nodded and rose from his seat. He extended his hand, but Richard had already turned and was walking away. Frank followed him down the hallway to an elegant conference room filled with impressive equipment and a group of older men.

Richard told Frank, "Have a seat." Richard took one of the two empty seats. That left only one seat open seat at the large oval Beachwood table, and Frank took it.

Richard spoke in a whisper to another of those seated. The other flipped a switch at the tabletop and three very large wall monitors came to life, each showing one face.

Richard spoke to the monitors. "We're all assembled and ready to begin. This is the first board of directors meeting for Sturgess Technology. Present are myself, Richard Stein, our CTO and EVP of technology development. Please, can the others seated also introduce themselves?"

In all, seven people sitting around the conference room table spoke briefly, saying their names and titles. Frank knew he'd never remember them. He typed furiously fast. He'd correct the misspellings when he was alone.

Then the faces on the monitors introduced themselves. Frank was surprised to see that two of them were the heads of major venture capital firms that he'd read about, and the third monitor showed the face of a member of the Pentagon's Joint Chiefs.

This startup is already beyond Robert Randall's control. He said nothing else for the hour until the meeting ended.

* * *

The rising sun had lightened Jon's room at the Four Seasons Hotel Silicon Valley in East Palo Alto. International. Cassie tapped her foot with nervousness as she listened to Jon's tale of failure. She felt her face hot with anger. "You told him the truth? What the fuck, Jon! We're screwed."

Jon shrugged. "I was caught. I tried to think of a convincing lie, but nothing came to me. Sorry. We still have four others."

She shook her head. In a much calmer voice, she said, "Let me try. I can do the rest of them." She pulled the paper list from Jon's hands. "So, the next is Robert Nachez and his startup is HeadCloud." She turned to her notebook screen and brought up HeadCloud's webpage. It seemed that HeadCloud was a well-encrypted data cloud capable of defending itself from DDOS attacks and other hacks. They weren't looking for much cash. Just a small seed round of a half million USD. She copied the phone number and other data into her cell and left Jon's room.

She'd cooled enough to sound human by the time she reached her and Lee's room at the Stanford Park Hotel. He wasn't there. Probably out for his morning run. She sat at the desk and punched in HeadCloud's phone number.

She heard a genderless voice answer with "HeadCloud. Safety in the wilderness. How can I help you?"

"My name is Cassandra Sashakovich. I'm an angel funder, and I've read about you. Are you still raising a round of capital?"

"One second. I'll route your call to our CFO."

Cassie smiled. *Time to hunt.*

* * *

As the sun reached its daily zenith, Laura dragged herself from her bed. She searched for her cellphone, then realized it was gone. She stood thinking about what had happened since the last time she had touched it. Eventually, she remembered the stranger who bumped into her the day before, while she was touring the last art gallery in Asunción. *Was that when it was stolen?* It was a mediocre gallery, and it hadn't made either of the first two lists she'd made. She was sure he must have stolen her cellphone while she was occupied with buying a blue vase at the museum shop.

She walked to the bathroom and pushed herself through the act of washing up before she took the stairs down to the kitchen to get coffee and breakfast.

She wondered if Frank had tried calling her. Probably not. Most of the staff didn't speak English, but Pedro did. She decided to ask him if Frank had called the compound. Then she thought Frank was probably fucking another young woman. *What did I do wrong? Why wasn't I enough?* She wanted to kill him.

* * *

Robert Randall waited in the reception room outside Daniel Strumler's hotel room. He'd arrived on time and an hour had passed. He heard the door to the inner sanctum open and a suited man emerged, one wired ear containing a pigtail earbud wired to a radio, a definite sign the man was Secret Service. Randall rose. The suited man nodded and pointed his head back at the door.

Inside, Strumler sat at the desk, wearing his bathrobe. "Hi. You're Randall, right?"

Richard nodded. "Sir, I'm here to update you on the current threats to America."

Strumler shook his head. "Yeah, yeah. Threats, blah-blah. Okay, I can give you, ah..."—he looked at his watch—"three minutes. Starting right now." He waved Randall to the single chair exactly four feet away.

Randall sat. "First let me remind you that everything I tell you in this briefing is classified." He stared at Strumler, and Strumler nodded. "Okay then. I'll start with North Korea, then update you on the Middle East." Randall opened the folder he'd brought with him and handed a small stack of pages to Strumler. "North Korea is currently completing the final stages of testing a thermonuclear-carrying ballistic missile system. Each missile will be able to carry a multi-megaton warhead all the way to Washington DC."

"What have we done to keep them from completing this?"

Randall had memorized the notes that he'd received. He said, "We've sent a team from the agency to see if we can terminate their leader. That was several months ago. So far, we've heard nothing from the team. We've concluded that they were neutralized, and if so, then the North Koreans know our intentions. We've summoned members of Congress who are friendly and they have introduced a bill to slap further sanctions on trade in and out of their country. So far, that hasn't worked to slow them down."

Strumler shook his head. "If I'm elected, I'll nuke them the day after I take office. Would it help to spread that as a news item?"

"Sir, that might make them accelerate their development of the missile system."

Strumler sat silent for a few seconds. "What about China? Can they help us?"

"Sir, you've already accused China of currency manipulation and a few other nasty things. China is helping North Korea because it will take the pressure off them."

Strumler's lips trembled. "Fuck this. Okay, we're done for today. Tell me about the Middle East the next time we meet. Next week."

Randall's jaw dropped just a bit. "Sir, these threat assessments are supposed to happen daily."

"Yeah, well, that isn't gonna happen. I can make a few minutes next Tuesday when I'm back in New York."

"But—"

"Go. Now. I have a tight schedule." Strumler pressed a button on the desk and the door to the suite opened.

The Secret Service man entered and touched Randall on the shoulder. "Please follow me."

Randall left the room and the door closed behind him. *Yes, the Director has handed me a turd.* He brightened when he realized Strumler might actually be useful to him. He needed to make a plan.

CHAPTER 24

Stanford University library,
Palo Alto, CA

September 24, 2:16 p.m.

Sitting in a carrel in the Stanford library, Cassandra Sasha-kovich touched her chin with her left hand as she scanned the list of "pretenders." She had closed deals with eight of ten. One remained unsigned, and there was the one that Jon failed to close. She drew her notebook computer from her briefcase and sipped coffee while she waited for Arthur Creeg, CEO of Underwire Software to appear for their second and final meeting. While she waited, she tried to meditate.

Time passed while she considered her role and what attitude would best suit her for this last startup CEO. Creeg was the oldest of the startup cofounders, and had completed two advanced degrees. One of his master's was in computer science and the other was in business administration. Cassie had earned her MBA at Stanford in finance, but that was twelve years ago. Creeg had been involved in two prior startups, one as the chief tech officer and the other as the head of IP operations. Both had failed. He'd been looking for a seed investor for two months. The business plan he had sent Cassie was for an artificial intelligence product that a business could use to run a factory. She noted that the software could easily be modified to produce any product, including weapons.

She wasn't sure how much time had passed when her phone buzzed in her suit pocket. She looked at its screen. Creeg was at the library's front door and so, now it was time for them to meet. She examined her reflection in the glass of the nearby window. Her navy blue suit and white shirt were wrinkle free. The bow tie she had donned needed straightening and she attended to it before heading from the carrel to the lobby of the library. She had no picture of Creeg, but the single person waiting in the lobby had to be him. He was at least six inches taller than Cassie, and would be staring down at her. This was one advantage she would have to counter for this meeting to yield the results she hoped for. She modified her attitude for the meeting. *I'll have him sit with the sun in his eyes and my face in shade.*

"Mr. Creeg?"

"Ah, yes. You must be Ms. Sashakovich."

"Let's find a place to sit where we can discuss my offer and its terms." She led him to the back of the library, away from the tables and the carrels. Adjacent to the entrance to the cafeteria was a formal meeting room with a conference table and rolling chairs. The room was dark but she opened the window shades and shut the door to diminish the outside noise of students hurrying to and from their classes. She left the room's lights off, then pointed to a chair facing the windows, directly across the table from where she sat with her back to the windows. "I have reviewed your business plan. I also read the bios of your cofounders. It appears you need five hundred thousand. But your pre-money valuation is just over one mil. How far do you expect to get on product development with that little cash?"

"We, ah, we're hoping to complete the prototype with that much cash. Of course it won't be enough for a truly robust model, but we think it will be enough to interest investors for a second round."

Cassie turned her focus inward. She needed to appear to be considering the risk of the investment. In reality, she was trying to find a way to inspire Creeg to worry about what he'd been led to believe was a sure thing. She could smell the fear she was sure he was feeling. He had a nervous tic in the side of his cheek. She pushed her chair back, as if she was preparing to rise from her seat. "What if it takes longer?" She saw him gulp.

"I, ah, we're sure we can make sufficient progress on the prototype to earn a first full round. If not, we'll see if we can convince our investors to extend a small amount of additional cash as a convertible loan."

Cassie noted perspiration forming under his eyes. "Would the terms of that loan be negotiable?" She stared into his eyes.

"I'm sure we could come to an agreement. That is, if you're still interested in the product we hope ultimately to develop."

It was now time to give him back just a tiny bit of the confidence she had just robbed from him. She drew the contracts from her attaché case. "Good. In a startup, flexibility is necessary. Please note, we will seek additional investors if and when we find them. And we have right of first refusal on any other investors that you find or have independently come to you. It's in the contracts on page three, paragraph thirteen. Agreed?"

When he nodded, she handed him the stack of paper.

"Initial every page and sign where the yellow tapes indicate."

Arthur Creeg did as he was ordered.

* * *

Frank Lucessi shook hands with the CEO of yet another start-up and walked to his car in the parking lot. It was his twenty-third board meeting in three weeks. There had been so many that his notes were the only thing differentiating them in his mind. He sat in the driver's seat of his car and, once again, typed an update for Robert Randall. The startup he'd just met with had already attained advanced status as far as Frank was concerned. Their product would be one of the stars of the portfolio Randall had given him.

As he finished his note and started the engine, his thoughts drifted to Randall. Frank wondered if the man was a CIA case officer. If so, didn't that mean InTelQ was a CIA front? What he wasn't sure of was what the CIA wanted from the companies. Did they want perpetual sole ownership of the companies he'd met with? What other reason could they have had for buying the startups' stock? What other reason would Randall have for ensuring that InTelQ was the sole investor?

Frank thought once more of Laura. He'd called the staff at his Paraguay compound and asked them what she was doing. They thought she was flighty and had kept out of her way. He asked Pedro to have Laura call him.

Pedro had said, "Okay, señor." Now Frank would wait to see if Laura called him.

* * *

Laura woke that morning from another nightmare. She dreamed that her mother was still alive and had traveled to Paraguay to kill her. As she washed herself at the sink, she was sure someone was watching her. In the mirror, she thought she saw someone in the shower, and, alarmed, she ran to the shower, but it was empty. She finished washing and then dressed for the day. As she returned to the bedroom to dress, she admired the blue vase she had bought in the art gallery a few days ago. It looked like one her mother bought many years ago for her family's home. While she sipped a cup of coffee in the kitchen, she was sure there was someone watching her. But she scoured the room, searching for a place where someone could hide from her, but she found nothing.

She told Pedro to drive her to town. There, she strolled down the sidewalk alleyway into the gallery where she had bought the vase. There was nothing else there that she wanted to purchase. She decided to shop the rest of the stores on the street, but as she left, she once again thought someone was following her.

She ran to the limo and ordered the driver to take her home.

Once again in the house, she was sure that someone was watching her.

She felt sure she was no longer safe.

* * *

Ann finished moving the last box from her apartment into Glen's, at 137 Homer, south of downtown Palo Alto. There along his living-room wall were twenty large cartons, waiting for her to unpack them. She still had doubts regarding the wisdom of this decision. All her "relationship" decisions in the past had been bad judgments. From Charles in high school to Charlette last year. *No, not merely errors.* All her relationships before Glen were disasters. She was drawn to him, but something felt wrong. But she decided to give it a try.

She set about unpacking the first box: towels, pillow-cases, and sheets. Glen was gone from his apartment, setting up the new offices of MindField with his cofounders.

After she had unpacked seven of the boxes, she felt winded and her back hurt. She sat on his couch and looked around, trying to see if there were any bachelor amenities she would need to change into something more feminine. Atop his desk in the living room she saw a folder labelled "investors." She touched the folder, then without consciously intending it, she felt her fingers lifting its cover. Inside, she saw his notes on the meetings he'd had with possible investors.

She stared at the folder for a while, to convince herself not to intrude on his privacy. But, she didn't move away. After nearly a minute her hand seemed to have a mind of its own and she inched the open folder she held closer to her eyes. She hadn't intended reading his notes. But she did. They were stored in chronological sequence, each set corresponding to one meeting. She read the oldest first and then traveled on to the present. The oldest ones were short meetings with negative outcomes as he learned how to present MindField with more enthusiasm and could anticipate the questions that an investor might ask. By the time Frank Lucessi of InTelQ appeared in the file, Glen seemed to know what he was doing as a negotiator.

As she finished reading the last note and rescanned the agreements he and his team had signed, something nasty occurred in her thought process. While Glen was masterful in his negotiating, he had ignored hints Frank made about the things Frank was not telling him.

From Glen's notes, Ann was sure that there was a hole in Frank's knowledge of his own business. It was almost as if Frank was the go-between for someone who was handling him. Ann scratched her chin. She rose from the couch and paced the living room, considering what kind of person might behave this way. The most probable answer was that Frank was brought in to do the work of an organization that wanted to remain in the shadows. Who was he a cutout for? She pulled her notebook computer from her backpack and began searching for evidence of what InTelQ really was and who owned them.

After she reviewed the scant facts she had discovered online about Frank Lucessi, she became convinced that InTelQ was a front for an intelligence agency. It made sense to her now. She pulled her cellphone from her pocket and called Jon.

* * *

Glen and his cofounders had almost completed setting up MindField's new offices. Their South Amphlett Drive office in San Mateo was what Glen thought of as a convoluted warren, although their landlord called it a corporate startup incubator. There were as many as twenty startup offices on each floor of the old four-story building, and there were twelve buildings in the complex. The office they had taken was on the third floor of building number eight, next door to eleven other startups on just that floor. Within the office there were six separate rooms, the largest of which had been used by its last occupant as a conference room, and another that was nearly as large as the kitchen. The other four rooms were smaller and each cofounder has his or her own.

Glen had proposed that at 8 a.m. each morning, the group would gather for a short meeting in the conference room to discuss their progress and their obstacles. Today's meeting was about to start.

Glen sat at the head of the large conference table with Samantha, Harvey, and Ford. They were all pleased, and showing it.

Harvey flashed a gleam of smile. "I'm pleased to report that the prototype works. Well, sort of works."

Everyone leaned closer across the table.

"What does 'sort of' mean, Harvey?" Glen's expression

showed his concern. "Even with the investment that InTelQ made in us, we haven't much money."

"Yeah. Well, remember that the original intent was to produce a physical hackproof nano-firewall that can be programmed to let only telecomm signals set up as 'desired' to pass between its users and their 'friends'?"

Everyone nodded.

"Well, the original plan was to have the physical device protect its wearer from hostile comm signals. But, using a shear thickening fluid to paint the device on human skin failed."

Glen muttered a single word. "Shit!"

"Yup. That's what I thought." Harvey smiled. "But, I found that the nanodevice would work if it was swallowed."

"Did you test this on someone?" Glen seemed surprised. The others pulled away from the table as if they smelled something foul.

Harvey nodded. "Me. I tested it on me."

"You tested this on yourself? Crap, Harvey. What were you thinking?" Glen's eyes were wide.

"Who the fuck else could I test it on?"

Glen shook his head. "Are you crazy?"

Harvey took a deep breath. "I am proof of concept. The device acts as a firewall to keep hackers from my insulin pump."

The others knew Harvey was a Type 1 diabetic.

Glen immediately saw the value in the breakthrough. "So then you think it will work on pacemakers and other medical devices?"

Harvey nodded. "Absolutely. We've achieved our first major milestone."

Glen's smile bubbled through his face so much he could feel it. *I can't wait until I tell Ann.*

CHAPTER 25

Glen Sarkov's apartment,
137 Homer, Palo Alto, CA

September 28, 3:24 a.m.

Ann woke up gasping for breath. The recurring nightmare she had occasionally had since she was a teenager had visited her once again. It was accurate in every detail to her memory of the real-life event that triggered it. She shivered in the bed next to Glen.

Glen rolled to face her. "What happened?"

She huddled against him. "Glen, when I was twelve, my birth mother died from a drug overdose as my younger brother and I watched. I thought Joshua and I might be separated by child services and to keep that from happening, we found what we thought was a safe place."

Glen pushed away and stared at her face. "So?'

Ann shivered. "There are tunnels under Grand Central Station. Old tracks no longer used by the railroad. Homeless people used to live there, and we joined them. It turns out, it wasn't safe at all. A man raped me, and when Joshua tried to stop him, the man snapped his neck. That was the night Cassie found me. Without her, I'd surely be dead now. The nightmare I just had is a carbon copy of my rape and Joshua's murder." She began to whimper.

Glen hugged her. "You're safe here with me."

"Yeah, well duh." But that dream returns whenever I sense that something isn't right. Something bad is brewing."

Glen said, "When I grew up in Russia, we lived at the edge of danger, too. It's why we left. My father was a journalist. He set up our travel and sent us away in the dead of night. He was supposed to follow right after he posted the story he was working on. But he never made it out of Russia. To keep the story from getting into the press, he was murdered. I was twelve. Not nearly as bad as what happened to you." He hugged her closer. "How long were you living in those tunnels?"

"It was nearly a year. Cassie left after a few weeks. I didn't know then, but when she returned to get me, I found out that she had worked for one of America's intelligence services. She was outed by a mole in her own agency. The mole sold her identity to terrorists who thought she was just a financial consultant, and they had started to hunt her down. She needed to find a way to recover her life. The odds for her were long, but she succeeded. Then she returned, found me, and adopted me."

He pulled away and studied her face. "Any other secrets?"

"Actually, there are a few. Well, maybe more than just a few."

"Tell me."

Ann smiled. "Not tonight. But I will, someday. One secret is enough for a single night."

Glen was silent for a few seconds. "Well, I can lighten the mood. I've got great news."

Ann smiled. "And what would this 'great news' be?"

"We've completed the prototype. Our original design was flawed. The STF didn't work to paint the nanodevice onto human skin. But Harvey discovered the device could be swallowed. And that worked well."

Ann paled. She began to shake.

"What's wrong, sweetie?"

Ann tried to calm herself, but to no avail. Through tears, she spoke while shivering. "I have another secret that you need to know now. One which very few people know. You must promise never to tell anyone! Never! Do you agree?"

He moved farther from her, startled by her. "Well, okay."

"Remember how I told you that I was modified using a nanodevice?" She sobbed. "The whole story is that a hacker fed me a thousand of them—Bug-Loks—to see if they would kill me or modify my repertoire of skills."

Glen said nothing. His jaw remained open, working his mouth open and closed.

"If I survived, the devices were supposed to give me the ability to access the internet using my brain. One of them might have been enough. But, they latch into the brainstem and, after about six weeks, they detach and are eliminated. But each one scars my brain. And, a thousand of them? That many had an unintended consequence. I was able to shoot fire from my fingertips. For decades, the CIA and KGB tried psychokinetic experiments to make things like that happen. That's why you can never tell anyone. Understand?"

Glen nodded, but she stared at the confusion in his face.

"I'm no longer human in the usual sense of the word. Six weeks passed, the Bug-Lok devices are gone from me but I can still do that nasty trick."

Glen's eyes remained agog.

He said nothing, but Ann could easily read his expression. He must be thinking, *my girlfriend, the freak.*

* * *

"Do we have enough of these?" Jon pointed to the bag of Bug-Loks, each encased in a liquid-filled, very tiny slide-lock bag.

"Yes," Cassie said. She handed the bag to Jon. "I'll talk with each pretender while you get us coffee. Make sure you empty the bag's contents into the coffee and hand the pretender the one containing the Bug-Lok."

Jon nodded. Cassie and Jon left the hotel room and headed toward the elevator.

The two spies met to discuss the progress of the eight startup CEOs over coffee and doughnuts in the Stanford University Cafeteria. The CEOs each left their meeting with the Mossad's version of the Bug-Lok nanodevice floating though their bloodstreams on its way to their brainstems.

When Jon and Cassie returned to Jon's room, they tested communications between the devices each CEO had swallowed and Jon's notebook computer. All of them worked to spec. Cassie said, "We did it. Let's tell Avram."

Jon nodded and plucked his cellphone from his pocket. Phase two of Jon's plan was now complete.

* * *

Robert Randall looked at his reflection in the mirror and sighed without making a sound. His fifth meeting with Daniel Strumler would begin whenever the candidate let him into the hotel room where he lived prior to the election. Randall had been pacing in the outside hallway for nearly an hour. He had considered the obvious reasons why their other meetings had been nearly disastrous. Perhaps it had simply been a mutual dislike. Perhaps Strumler was as arrogant and stupid as he appeared. Perhaps Randall had simply not been pre-pared. Maybe Strumler had sensed Randall's dislike for him and felt obliged to respond in kind. It could be any of these, or maybe all.

To keep from wearing his dislike for Strumler, Randall focused on the issues he would present in his daily intelligence threats report. The list was short. He spent the time while he waited rehearsing his statement.

The door opened and Strumler's choice for vice president left the room, shaking his head. The man stage-whispered, "You're next. He's not happy today."

Randall forced himself to smile and entered the room.

Strumler's face was red with anger. "Why are you so happy?"

Randall gulped. "Not happy, sir. But, I've been looking forward to meeting with you again."

"Yeah, well, fuck you very much. Take a load off and tell me what's happening today that threatens to kick our collective asses as a country."

At that moment, Randall wished he were anywhere else. Even a shootout with a gang of foreign terrorists would have been sweeter.

CHAPTER 26

CIA headquarters, Langley, VA

October 30, 1:15 p.m.

When his daily meeting with Strumler ended, Robert Randall felt chest pains from his frustration. He was beginning to hate "the candidate who had no chance," as the news had often described him. He parked the car in the CIA head-quarters lot and walked through the lobby to the security gate.

He took the elevator up from the lobby, but before it even settled to a stop, his cellphone was buzzing.

"Randall."

"It's William Smythe." Randall remembered that the man had recently become the assistant director over him. "Where are you?"

"I'm in the building. If you want, I can be in your office in under a minute."

"No, that's not necessary," responded the ass dire. "But, tell me: How'd the meeting with Strumler go?"

"Sir, it went badly. To think that this dolt has even as much as a rat's chance of being president makes my head spin. I've never met anyone this frustrating or ignorant."

"Relax, Robert. The election is less than a month away. No way anyone will vote for him. Once the election is over, you can go back to your other projects, and the agency will always be grateful you did this for us."

"Yes. I'm sure it will."

"Just hang in there." The ass dire terminated the call.

Randall walked to his own office. He plunked himself into a chair and sat, waiting for his mind to clear. His only thought, reverberating continuously through his brain was, *What happens to me if Strumler actually wins? What happens to my country?*

* * *

The sky in New York City was a dark gray, but the forecasted rain had yet to start. Frank Lucessi sat in the back of a taxi and watched the brownstones fly by as his driver turned a corner.

"We're here, boss."

Frank passed the driver two twenties. "Keep the change."

He exited the car and scanned the street, looking for the number of the house this startup used for offices. He found the startup incubator in what used to be a very nasty section of Brooklyn.

Frank climbed the stairs and rang the bell. A short man with a beard smiled and opened the door. "Mr. Lucessi! Welcome to GrayStem. Please, follow me." The man led him through what smelled like a chem lab, down a long hallway, and past a smallish kitchen to what was once a bedroom and now was set up to serve as a startup's conference room.

Frank entered and examined the room. Near the entrance was a presentation screen, and in the center of the room was a conference room table big enough to seat eight people. Frank sat on one of the long sides of the table, across from the entrance. He flipped open his attaché case and pulled a file folder and his notebook computer from within.

He smiled at the thought that this board meeting was

the final one he had scheduled, and that by early evening he'd be headed home. Home to Laura. He missed her. And he was troubled by the fact that his phone calls to her—every one of them—had rolled into voicemail. His housekeeper had called to tell him that Pedro watched over Laura and she was safe but moody. He remained troubled by the feeling that something must be terribly wrong. *Well, just a few hours more and I can see her. I just hope she's at my home, waiting for me.*

* * *

Laura thought she saw her father standing in the compound's formal dining room. But no, it was just her imagination. She blinked her eyes and he disappeared. Then, he was back, screaming that she was a murderess. She shook her head, thinking, *no, I'm not! You are! You murdered my mother.* The image she'd conjured smiled back and then laughed. She screamed, her entire body shaking before she fainted.

When she became conscious, she wondered yet again if it was really her and not her father who had murdered her mother.

I must speak with Daddy. Haven't spoken with him since he was taken to prison. She walked to Frank's office and took the landline phone from its receiver. She knew the number by heart. When the prison officials wouldn't let her talk to him, she felt her world grow smaller, tightly crushing her. She decided to go to shopping in Asunción to take her mind off what was happening inside her,

Pedro drove her from the compound in Areguá to Asunción. She visited the art gallery on a tiny side street where she had bought her vase a few weeks ago. For a while she felt better. Once again, she made no further purchases.

As she strolled back up the alleyway toward her car and the driver, she saw a squirrely looking pawn shop and wandered inside. At first she saw nothing of interest and was about to leave when, under the glass in the counter, she saw a gun.

She'd begun studying Spanish and decided to practice her skills. In Spanish, she asked the pawnshop owner, "What's that?" She pointed to the gun.

"Señorita, it is a Beretta nine millimeter. Very cheap. It works well."

"How much?"

When she left the pawnshop, her purse held the handgun and a box of ammo. She had no idea how to use it, but she somehow felt safer from her hallucinations.

PART III

He knows nothing; and he thinks he knows everything. That points clearly to a political career.
—George Bernard Shaw,
Major Barbara

CHAPTER 27

**Daniel Strumler's campaign headquarters,
201 East 57th Street, New York City, NY**

November 6, 3:48 a.m.

Autumn was starting to turn to winter, and Election Day turned into Election Night for Daniel Strumler. He hadn't visited his apartment in Manhattan in nearly a month. These days, his hotel room in Washington DC had turned into his temporary home when he wasn't stomping for his campaign.

He'd eaten a light meal before arriving at his campaign headquarters. Strumler's eyes bugged as he read the red LED news ticker. It glowed, "Strumler Wins Upset By Four Electoral Votes." Cheers from his supporters and advisors made it impossible for him to be heard. It wouldn't have mattered. His lips moved but he emitted no actual sound. His expression was full of simple surprise. He watched a tsunami of red balloons fall from the ceiling. *What have I done? Now I'll actually have to do this damned job. Oh fuck, fuck me!*

One of his assistants tapped his shoulder. "Mr. President-Elect, you have to make a speech. The teleprompter is loaded with the speech you wrote."

In a daze, feeling like a wounded animal, Daniel Strumler stumbled up to the microphone. He took a deep breath and tried to steady himself by gripping the edges of the lectern. The teleprompter screen rolled past, but it displayed the concession speech he'd spent two weeks writing. He's been so sure he would never be asked to deliver the speech of a winner.

He shook himself and stopped speaking while he thought what he could say. As the teleprompter scrolled on, he edited on the fly. "Thank you, my loyal supporters. Now is the time to fix all that is wrong with America. I will hire the brightest and bring them to Washington. The clock is running and we have until January twentieth to prepare ourselves."

* * *

Robert Randall had been in Washington working at the CIA's headquarters in Langley. He ate leftovers in his apartment in the outskirts of Washington before settling in on Election Day.

His temper exploded as he watched America's future unfold on television. He saw Strumler fumble his way through his victory speech.

He took his cellphone from his pocket and entered the phone number for the ass dire.

"Robert, I was expecting your call. My apologies, but you'll have to continue your role as CIA threat advisor to the president-elect. At least until we can figure out what we want to do next. You understand?"

Randall swallowed several times to make it easier to speak. "Yes sir." But he was sure the ass dire could hear the discomfort in his voice.

"Don't worry, Robert. One thing is for sure: He'll never serve a complete term. Be patient. Keep me up to date, Robert. Be a team player."

After the ass dire terminated the call, Randall sat riveted to his apartment's couch, watching Strumler's election celebration. His feelings of rage caused his right hand to cramp.

He worked on refining his plan to deal with Strumler. The first step would be to contact Alan Skorkin. He punched in Skorkin's number and was routed into voicemail.

"Alan, it's Randall. I have another task for you. You know that batch of stuff I left with you?" The word "stuff" was code, referring to a batch of one hundred Bug-Loks he'd bought on his own dime from a Chinese CSIS intelligence agent. "Please stuff the turkeys, one in each. Then see if their stuffing works and send me a file." This was code to log each Bug-Lok's serial number with the name of the startup CEO who was "infected" with it. From that time on, Randall could record each CEO's every word and location where the CEO spoke.

He'd no longer need Frank Lucessi.

* * *

Glen took an unexpected left turn off University Drive onto Bryant and used the rear-view mirror to watch the car that had been following him for seven blocks. It was the same car he'd seen the last two days during his commute to and from the new offices of MindField. Glen pulled the car to the curb and watched the car in his rear view as it flew by him. Glen snapped a photo of the driver using his cell. He snapped another photo to get the license number.

Then Glen continued home as the rush-hour traffic thinned out the setting sun.

When he had parked his car in the garage, he enlarged the photo to see the driver's face. A male, narrow face, probably between thirty-five and forty years old. He checked the photo of the plate number. It was clearly focused.

He walked up the stairs. He could smell the aroma of cooking from the apartments in the complex. He entered his own apartment. Spaghetti sauce, possibly homemade. Ann stood at the stove. He marveled at the simple dish. *I didn't even know she knew how to cook!*

Ann turned and faced Glen. "Hey, sweetie. I got ambitious. Fresh pasta from the market at the Stanford Mall and a bottle of spaghetti sauce from Safeway. Hungry?"

Glen nodded. "Can I help?"

"Nope. Just sit. It's all done. What was your day like at MindField?"

Glen sighed. "We're all hard at work. But I noticed something over the last two days. Someone's been following me." He showed her the two photos.

She pulled her own cellphone from her pocket and transferred copies of both to her own phone. "Probably nothing, but let me send a copy of these to Cassie."

After their quiet dinner, Ann sent an email to Cassie with both photos attached, and a request to see who the person was.

Ann also formulated a plan to deal with whomever this was. *First step, find out where he's staying and follow him.*

The next morning as they ate breakfast before leaving for work and school, Ann's phone buzzed and she saw a text from Cassie:

> Ann—
> I got your message but was busy last night. I'll get
> you some intel as soon as I have a break this
> morning.
> —Mom

Ann did a trace on the license plate number of the stranger's car. She loaded a TrackMe, a piece of hacker software William Wing had given her. The car was only a block away from Glen's apartment. She took the stairs down to the lobby and walked to the car's last registered location. She found the car and approached head on. She passed by and took a turn around the corner. Ann watched from an alleyway. She saw Glen leave their apartment and watched the stranger in the car start the engine. *Yes, he's definitely following Glen.*

Ann decided there was not much more she could do until Cassie told her something—anything—about who this stranger was and why he was following Glen.

Later, while she sat in class, she felt her phone buzz against her body. She read the message:

Ann—
The man whose photo you sent me turns out to be a "consultant" based in Washington. Why are you interested in him?

William Wing hacked him for me. His name is Alan Skorkin, but he also goes by many other names. Wing searched and found his identity, then read his email and text messages for the last two months. The results indicate he may have been used as a cleaner for several intelligence services. This man is very dangerous. Stay Away!
—Mom

Ann thought about this while her teachers droned on. When her class ended, she went to the next class, but by the end of the day she realized she hadn't taken any notes.

She decided to follow Skorkin very carefully, now that she was aware he was dangerous.

She saw that he spent time around startup CEOs. She recognized several as members of her entrepreneurship class. She trailed Skorkin into the cafeteria and watched him dump something into one of the CEO's coffee mugs. Ann remembered when she had been administered a thousand Bug-Loks in her morning coffee by the CypherGhost a year ago. Although she couldn't be certain, she was guessing that Skorkin was administering Bug-Lok devices to the startup CEOs just as the CypherGhost had done to her. She texted her sitrep to Cassie.

* * *

It didn't take long for Alan Skorkin to locate every one of the startup CEOs. He followed each one until they stopped at a coffee stand or went for lunch, and then, when he could do it without the CEO seeing what was happening, Skorkin dropped the liquid from the container into the CEO's coffee or their beer or wine. When he had "taken care of" the ten Silicon Valley CEOs, he drove to San Francisco, where he dosed five more, and then he took a flight to Cleveland, Ohio, where he repeated the process for three CEOs whose addresses Randall had sent him. Next, he planned to head to south Florida, then to New York's Tri-State Area, and finally fly to Atlanta where the final two were located. While he waited at the terminal in the Cleveland airport, he called Randall with a progress report.

CHAPTER 28

51st Floor, Strumler Tower Capital Hotel, Washington, DC

November 10, 11:38 a.m.

Daniel Strumler sat in his hotel room. From his first visit long ago, he'd realized that this city was recalcitrant. Unable to conceive of a better way to do things, it would always refuse to change. He had promised to change all that. Now he was realizing that he would inevitably fail.

He realized he was totally unprepared to be president. There was too much to do, too many people to direct. *It's not like one of my corporations, where I can fire someone for their bad performance. Bad enough that I can't fire those I appoint, because they'll write a book about me. No, the worst are those who were elected to Congress. If they serve their own tiny group well, those slackers will continue to elect them.*

These thoughts caused him to fall into a rage he couldn't control. Worse, his inability to control his temper further enraged him. He even saw enemies where there were none.

I'm sure that CIA guy Randall bugged my office. What if he can somehow record what I'm thinking and feeling? Didn't the CIA run experiments long ago to try doing just that? What was it called? Psychokinesis?

* * *

Robert Randall reported back to William Smythe, his ass dire. "Sir, the man's not playing with any cards in his deck. He's not stable. He's a... a loon."

He heard nothing for nearly thirty seconds from Ass Dire Smythe. Then finally, in his most soothing tone of voice, Smythe told him, "There's always the twenty-fifth amendment if he is truly bonkers. But, his staff will have to initiate it. Why don't you gather evidence of Strumler's instability? If you find enough material to convince me, I might be able to find a way to route it to the appropriate parties."

And Randall thought, *I'll have to find some way to collect evidence.*

* * *

Cassie had decided to follow the man who'd been feeding CEOs what appeared to her to be Bug-Loks.

It had been nearly a decade since she had last used her countersurveillance techniques. She knew her skills were rusty. She knew that following a suspect was best done using a team of at least three. She would need to try without any other operative, so she would have to be more diligent.

She stayed nearly a full block behind her target, using tricks like the reflections off storefront windows to offer brief snatches of her target's image. When he drove to SFO, she followed, always at least sixty feet behind. When he bought a ticket at the counter, she watched, then told the ticket counter agent, "My husband just bought a ticket right here. I'm sure he's cheating on me. I want to follow him. Can you sell me a ticket to his destination? On his flight?"

She bought a last-minute ticket to Atlanta and stopped by a clothing store in the terminal. She bought a suitcase and several hats and light jackets, and dropped them in the suitcase.

She donned a different jacket and hat, and then boarded the same flight. She sat, six rows in front of him. When the flight landed, she followed him to his hotel.

She saw him park his car at a cheap motel and stayed in her car in the parking lot, across from his. When she heard him start the car engine, she woke instantly and followed him to an office park. She changed hats and jackets.

There, her target met with one startup CEO. She followed him and watched him drop something into the CEO's coffee during their meeting. Cassie knew that Bug-Lok nanodevices were stored in small clear semipermeable containers that would dissolve in any liquid.

Remembering her own experience of being infected with a Bug-Lok, her fears were exacerbated. She waited until the man left his hotel room. Once more, she changed her hat and jacket.

Cassie approached the door to his now-empty room. She pulled her 9mm Beretta from her jacket holster, loaded a round into its chamber, and flicked the safety off. She grabbed her electronic keycard from her pocket and fit it into the door's key panel. The lock gave a satisfying click and the door popped open. She searched the room thoroughly and found a stash of what she identified as Bug-Loks in their dissolvable packaging. The labeling of the packets was in Mandarin, a language Cassie could speak and write.

Cassie searched the room for something that would identify her target. In one of the drawers she found a paperback. The book, DS Kane's *Bloodridge*, had a business card that was being used as a bookmark. The business card had Alan Skorkin's name engraved on it, along with his phone number and a Washington DC address. No email address and no internet address. She photographed the business card with her cellphone's camera.

Casssie took one of the liquid tubes with her to have it analyzed. She left the room as quickly as she could and called Michael Drapoff of the Ness Ziona as soon as she was out of the hotel.

Drapoff told her to ship the package to him.

Cassie took the first flight back to SFO.

CHAPTER 29

51st Floor, Strumler Tower Capital Hotel, Washington, DC

November 11, 7:03 a.m.

This time, Robert Randall wasn't kept waiting to brief President-Elect Strumler. He wondered why he was being permitted to see the man after such a short wait. *Is he taking his election seriously?*

Even more surprising was Strumler's attitude. The man literally beamed at Randall, and asked if he'd like coffee while they spoke.

Randall nodded, but as Strumler placed two cups on the coffee table between the two couches in his hotel room, Randall found the opening he'd prayed for. Before Strumler could sit, Randall asked Strumler, "Do you still have the manila folder I gave you at our first meeting?"

Strumler nodded.

Randall said, "Good. May I see it, please?"

Strumler rose from his seat and walked to the desk in the hotel room. He began opening drawers and searching for the folder. By the time he returned to the coffee table, Randall dropped the contents of a tiny clear plastic bag into Strumler's coffee.

"Please read the note at the top of the first page. I'll wait until you have."

After scanning the first page of the threat assessment guidelines, Strumler asked, "So?"

Randall tried so hard to keep from smiling that his face hurt. "Done correctly, the meetings we have only last ten minutes unless something drastic has changed in the world. I'd like us to meet every day at the same time, at a time of your choosing. We'll meet wherever you are, and if you are out of the country, I will travel with you. Can you agree to that guideline, as it is printed on the first page?"

Strumler appeared to think for a few seconds. "Yeah. Sure."

"Good."

Randall left this meeting knowing that he'd have a digital record of everything the president-elect said or heard for the next six weeks, until the nanodevice passed out of his body.

* * *

Frank Lucessi's flight debarked at Silvio Pettirossi International Airport just west of Asunción. It was a warm, humid day with a clear blue sky. Frank took a deep breath and was welcomed by the astringent odor of jet fuel. *It's good to be home.*

He walked through the terminal to the exit and waved to his driver. The limo stopped. Pedro emerged and stuffed Frank's suitcase into its trunk. Frank saw that the driver was alone. "Where is Laura?"

Pedro shrugged. "I'm not sure. I haven't seen her inside the house or anywhere on the grounds of the compound today."

Frank felt his stomach lurch. *Hope she hasn't just wan-*

dered into the woods outside the compound. It was where he'd gone hunting for wild game, much of it quite dangerous.

The half-hour drive home seemed like an entire day to Frank. He jumped out of the limo before it even came to a full stop. Entering the front door, he trotted up the staircase to the bedroom level and went first to his bedroom. The bed was made and there was nothing out of order, so Laura must have slept in one of the other bedrooms. He found the second-largest bedroom and entered. All the window shades were closed tight, so he turned on the electric lights. The room was in disorder, and he could smell his own fear. And he could also smell Laura's fear. *Laura must have been truly frightened for her aroma to be so easily detected.* It was an odor unlike anything he had experienced before, and Frank wouldn't have described himself as having an exaggerated or even merely accurate sense of smell. *What could have caused her this much fear?*

He paced around the room, looking for anything that might give him a better sense of what she had been thinking. He saw a beautiful blue vase on the nightstand. He picked it up and examined it. It was heavy. The label on the bottom stated it was sold by an art dealer in Asunción. Not a dealer he'd ever visited. He carefully placed it back on the nightstand and left the room. Frank searched the entire compound, room by room. There were fifteen-some-odd wine bottles missing from the wine cellar, so Laura must have downed at least one bottle every other day. There had never been any missing wine before and he knew his staff didn't drink. No weapons were missing from the small armory adjacent to the wine cellar. Laura was nowhere on the grounds.

Frank ran to the guard's room and mustered a search party. There were five guards available on the premises. He took three with him. They provisioned backpacks and weapons, and left the compound as the sun reached its zenith. "We'll search sixty square miles around the compound." He pointed and said to two of them. "You search from the swamp seven miles northwest to the dry desert plain fifteen miles southeast. Then report back to me by radio." Then he motioned to the last of the three. "We'll head toward San Pedro's boundaries due north."

Frank feared that it would be a long and difficult search. He opened the gun safe and handed rifles to each of the three men and took one for himself. Then he picked boxes of ammunition from the safe and distributed those as well, in case they encountered wild animals in the swamp or the desert. He thought, *there are worse dangers than death from dehydration. I hope we're not too late.*

* * *

What a blowout of a party! Glen and his startup team's celebration had been getting less organized as they consumed more and more alcohol. Glen smiled at his three cofounders. He sipped his fifth shot of Islay single malt scotch and staggered to the center of the private party room at Chef Chu's on San Antonio Road and Camino Real. He tried to grab the microphone but missed and fell to the floor. Harvey tried to get him back on his feet, but Harvey was as drunk as Glen, and the result was two grown men rolling on the floor.

When Glen's consciousness returned, he found himself walking back to his apartment. Someone had taken his car keys but he couldn't remember whose idea it was. He was certainly far too drunk to drive himself home. It was a moonless night, and the intersections were both dark and quiet. He reminded himself that he needed to be careful, given his state of mind. *Where the fuck am I?* He stopped at a street corner and examined the street sign. *I'm on Homer. Head north three more blocks and I'll be at my apartment.* He crossed the street and continued, heading north until he saw the row houses that had been converted to apartments. He took the stairs up a flight and searched for his house keys. *Rats! Whoever took my car keys now also has my apartment keys. Ann must be home. She can let me in.* He tried reading the time from his wristwatch. It was just past 3 a.m.

Glen knocked on the door. No answer. He repeated the process, only louder and for a longer time.

Ann opened the door, wearing a bathrobe. She sniffed the air. "God, you stink of booze."

"Am slightly tips. Trispy. Tispy." He could feel himself falling to the floor. Looking up, he smiled at Ann. And at least two shots of single malt spewed from his mouth.

Ann's head seemed to get very close to his. "Glen! Glen, open your eyes."

When he became conscious again, he found himself on a cot in Stanford Hospital's emergency room.

Ann stood at his bedside, a look of concern combined with a quiet sense of rage like nothing Glen had ever seen before. She still wore her bathrobe.

"How long?"

"You've been here for..."—she looked around the room and stared at the clock—"twenty minutes. If you hadn't awakened in ten more, the ER team would have dropped by this room for more work on you. They pumped your stomach. What they found disturbed them. Seems like the fluid in you was a combination of straight scotch and something they had to run through a spectrometer to determine its composition. They weren't familiar with the stuff, but I told them we're married and they sent me a copy. I'm familiar with this. It's the type of liquid used to store nanodevices. Glen, I think you've been infected with a Bug-Lok."

Glen's head felt like a spinning top. He tried to rise off the bed, but nothing happened. "Whazza Bug-Lok?"

Ann shook her head. "Look, I'll be back. But they have a

rather strict policy of cellphones remaining off in the ER. I've got to get out into the open to call Cassie and Jon. I'll be gone for just a few." Without waiting for him to respond, she turned on her heel and disappeared.

Just before sunrise, Ann left long voicemail messages for Jon and Cassie and then headed back toward the ER.

* * *

Cassie, Jon, and Lee conference-called Avram. Cassie told Avram about the small pouches of liquid she found the mystery man administering to the startup CEOs, Avram took this new twist on their assignment as "worth relaying up the food chain."

Avram conferenced Michael Drapoff into the conference call with Cassie, Jon, and Lee. After Cassie had explained what she had seen, Drapoff spent nearly a minute in silence, then another minute talking with his hand muffling the receiver before relaying back his analysis of what was in the pouches: "It's an early version of the Bug-Lok, probably about six or seven years old. Early model, no kill capsule and no internet-based person-to-person communication. Just see, hear, and transmit over the nearest wireless communication to a static endpoint, and the endpoint would be the lone handler. I'm sure it's the Chinese version."

Cassie sat deep in thought for several minutes. She said to Jon, "I wonder if Ann's boyfriend Glen has been infected? If he has, it means Ann's name is on the transcripts Skorkin's handler now has."

She walked out of Jon's hotel room into the hallway and used her cellphone to call Ann.

But Cassie's call immediately rolled into Ann's voicemail. Cassie left Ann a text message asking her daughter if there was any way she could get Glen to a hospital. Her text mentioned that he might have a Bug-Lok lodged in his brainstem. Then she checked her own voicemail and found Ann's message. She ran back to tell Jon, Lee, and Avram.

CHAPTER 30

Swamp, 6 miles northeast of Lucessi compound in Areguá, Paraguay

November 12, 2:38 a.m.

Laura had no idea where she was. It was the middle of the night and there was no moonlight to make the landscape visible. She felt tired, hungry and thirsty.

It had been days since she had slept in Frank's large house.

She had heard her mother moaning in pain and rose. She walked into the hallway outside her bedroom. Her mother stood in the hallway facing her. There was a long gash across her neck. Laura realized that she held a jagged piece of glass covered with blood—her mother's blood—and at that moment she screamed. She fled down the stairs and fumbled with the front door's handle.

Once outside, she ran from the compound as fast as she could, not looking back. When she was exhausted, she stopped running. She looked around her. The night sky was pitch black. She had no idea where she was or how she could find her way back.

Since then, she had continued to walk, hoping she was headed back toward Frank's compound. But when she felt the ground go from hard-packed soil to lush soft bog, she realized she was hopelessly lost. She walked on and the swamp became not just damp but hot and wet. She stumbled and fell. She was now covered in mud.

As she backed out of the swamp's edge, she could hear animals and insects. They owned this place and she had no business here. She tried to quell the panic that built to a frenzy inside her. *Where? How?*

* * *

During the two days that had passed since Frank landed back in Paraguay, his search team had found no trace of Laura. As the third day dawned, a team manning his helicopter returned to their campsite, the pilot shaking his head as it landed. The pilot exited the chopper as the engines slowed and stopped. He told Frank, "Señor, no sighting so far."

Frank scratched another grid off the search map. The security cameras showed she had headed toward the swamp and that's where his team was now. But he was starting to lose faith that they would find her before she either starved or was eaten.

* * *

After the conference call, Avram Shimmel sat in his office on the twenty-ninth floor of the United Nations Secretariat Building in east midtown Manhattan. He stared into the void pondering what he had learned and deciding his next move. After a few minutes, he picked up the landline receiver and dialed Samuel Meyer, the director general of the Mossad. They exchanged pleasantries, designed to authenticate their identities to each other.

Avram said, "The mission is currently in progress. We have determined that it is possible that the CIA owns InTelQ and that they are using Bug-Lok nanodevices to infect startup CEOs from whom they can obtain current status on the readiness of their products for use in defense or as weapons. Then it appears InTelQ sends out a cleaner to terminate the team and bury all evidence of the cofounders' lives. We have identified their cleaner's identity. Michael Drapoff has determined where the Bug-Loks were manufactured. But one thing doesn't ring true. Why would the CIA murder startup crews by job lots? I'm wondering if this is a false flag, or even worse, an off-the-books op."

Meyer said, "Try to get something hard on who is behind this. I worry that time is running out. I've received evidence that points to other intelligence services having noticed the weapons development strategy InTelQ is using. If they copy it, there'll be tons of competition for those startups whose products can be weaponized."

* * *

Michael Drapoff sat in his small office in the subbasement of an unnamed and anonymous building in Herzliya, Israel, and searched for active and unknown global Bug-Lok signals. He'd been at this task for several hours and had let several cellphone calls from Samuel Meyer go to voicemail. He knew the task was urgent, but the range of Bug-Lok transmissions was unknown, and he had to search sector by sector, with the planet divided into six hundred sectors. He was now searching sector 22, in and around Washington DC.

"Crap on a cracker!" He smiled. Several hundred endpoints bloomed on his screen.

He coordinated the identities of the signals and was able to identify that they were all manufactured as part of the same batch, with Lev Robinson's signature in their data. He reread the case. Robinson was a Ness Ziona employee, convicted of treason. He had died in an Israeli prison two years ago. Michael read more of the case and discovered a listing of over two thousand Bug-Lok serial numbers. One hundred sixty of them matched those in his assigned case.

One last question: Who were the devices sent to? Just a bit more reading and he found the answer. The batch was delivered to Gilbert Greenfield's unnamed intelligence service six years ago.

Michael pulled his phone from his pocket. It was 3 a.m. in California, so he sent his findings via an email to Avram, Jon, Cassie, and Lee, with a separate copy for Samuel Meyer.

CHAPTER 31

51st Floor, Strumler Tower Capital Hotel, Washington, DC

November 12, 8:03 a.m.

Robert Randall completed another of what he was now privately referring to as "torture sessions" with President-Elect Strumler. From the questions the idiot asked, Randall estimated the man's intelligence as "grossly inadequate for the job."

He cursed himself for his fate. After all, he *was* cursed, by his own ass dire. And he cursed his charge, the president-elect. *Call a pig a pig.*

Randall already had enough evidence for a charge of treason against the man. The growing accumulation of Bug-Lok transcripts proved beyond doubt that Strumler was controlled by Moscow. The problem was that the transcripts were illegally obtained. There had been no search warrant. Bug-Lok was designed to be a covert tool. It had no standing with law enforcement and his evidence was limited to what the Bug-Loks had yielded him. In their face-to-face meetings, Strumler never said anything that indicated he was treasonous. Strumler said very little.

Since his plan had been to accumulate enough evidence to gain an indictment, the missing piece was for the attorney general to demand a search warrant. But there still was a disconnect: no way to get the AG to ask for evidence, especially from the CIA. In fact, Randall's off-the-books operations violated many of the CIA's operating rules. No domestic missions were permitted under law. Assassination of US citizens without legal process was not legal. The list of his violations was unending. His plan was flawed.

Standing in the lobby of the president-elect's hotel, he called Ass Dire Smythe on his cellphone to report his status. "Hello sir. It's Randall. The president-elect and I had another threat assessment meeting. It was a total disaster. He couldn't remember half the names of the countries in the Middle East. He thought our Israeli embassy was in Jerusalem. He didn't know Jordan was an ally. Iran and Iraq are one and the same for him. My God, the list of his inadequacies goes on forever."

The ass dire was silent for a few seconds, and Randall could hear the sound of keystrokes in the background noise. "This is your assignment. I can't replace you without firing you."

Randall took a deep breath. "Okay. Okay. I'll get back to work and bite the bullet for the agency."

He heard Smythe end the call. He thought, *I could just wipe all the startup teams away. They're loose ends.* But he knew this would draw attention to his enterprise.

Randall stiffened. He knew the trail of evidence would lead back to himself. But an order was an order.

Then he had another idea. One that might work. But he hadn't any excuse for initiating this tactic. He'd have to figure out how to make this work.

He had work to do.

* * *

Husro Mansuri sat with seven others around the conference-room table in a relatively new skyscraper on the out-skirts of Tehran. The view from the window showed rounded mountain tops with very little in the way of residential or business construction.

Mansuri listened to a comment from one of the agents. He thought about it before replying. "You are sure of this?"

"Yes, sir. They have a process that cheaply produces weaponized products."

Mansuri nodded. "And they have actually murdered their developers when the weapons are ready for production?"

"Yes."

Mansuri scratched his nose. "I seem to remember many civilizations have killed the builders of secret products after they finished their work. It is an ancient mode of develop-ment, predating the Egyptian civilization by nearly five thousand years. How difficult would it be for us to copy this?"

"We're ready now. The only question is whether to do this here or abroad. Abroad would be more dangerous for us, but it would offer us the entire range of Silicon Valley tech-nology."

Mansuri needed to be careful. His charter didn't permit murdering his own country's citizens unless they had com-mitted crimes. "Let's start with Silicon Valley. If we can manage to develop a high-tech community in Iran, we can then expand the program here."

The others nodded and rose from the table.

Mansuri walked to the window. It would be decades before Iran had a viable high-tech community. Silicon Valley on the other hand was a ripe fruit, waiting to be plucked. He had already heard that the Germans, the Brits, and the Chinese were working to weaponize Silicon Valley startups. The Israelis had done it for over fifty years with their Ness Ziona. And the United States had organized DARPA to do this. But neither of the last two had ever terminated the lives of their startup executives.

Mansuri wondered why the Russians had no such program. After all, they were truly ruthless. But he was sure they would soon join the fray.

The race was on to develop a fully functional venture capital group for weapons development, and the supply of viable startup targets would not last forever.

* * *

Robert Randall walked through the security gate and took the elevator to the third floor, where his office was located. He had realized that he needed to terminate the evidence trail for everything InTelQ had been involved with. Everything that led back to him. All the startup teams had to be wiped off the earth.

He walked dark carpeted hallways lined with gray-painted walls to the one with his name on the door. He entered and closed the door. He crafted a list of the names and home addresses of every cofounder of every startup in which InTelQ had invested.

Randall sent a text message to Skorkin with the new "kill list" attached. Skorkin would have several months of work to complete, but he had never failed. Randall now considered the implications of InTelQ a "dead deal."

CHAPTER 32

**Stanford University Student Union,
Palo Alto, CA**

November 12, 11:02 a.m.

Ann saw the text message on her cell when she checked the cell between classes. It was from Avram Shimmel:

Call me as soon as you see this.
Your help urgently needed.

Ann thought, *should I respond?* She walked to the hall where her next class was about to start and grabbed a seat. But while the professor lectured, she had difficulty keeping her mind on what he said.

She was behind on writing two papers. She was sure Avram's "help" would be a disaster for her classwork. But, when the class ended, she had failed to take usable notes. *No, this will never do. I have to call him and just tell him to find another resource. Aren't William Wing and Betsy Brown available?*

She keyed Avram's cell number and placed the call. Avram answered before the first ring finished. "Ach, finally. Ann, I need your help."

"I have midterms coming up soon. Why not William or Betsy?"

"William and his wife are out of contact. Under deep cover. Jon and Cassandra are also busy, and Lee is helping them. For this type of work, I need you."

"For what?"

"Cassie has backtraced a text message between two people she was covertly following. She was unable to decrypt the message. We all know you are our best resource in cyphers. I will send you the message in its native format. Please see if it is something you can decode. Yah?"

"Whatever. I'll get to it after dinner."

"Good. Good. Message is on its way now. Good luck."

Ann examined the text. Seemed simple enough. She wondered if this was really beyond Cassie's skills. *After all, Mom was one of my cypher teachers long ago. Maybe Avram thinks if she knows the contents of the message, she'll take action without Avram's authorization?*

She turned off her cellphone's screen and walked to the cafeteria for a sandwich. There would be plenty of time in Glen's apartment tonight. He had been released from the hospital but hadn't been well enough to work today. She would deal with the Bug-Lok in his head before she started working on Avram's assignment.

* * *

When she returned to Glen's apartment, she found him asleep in bed. She roused him.

"Huh?"

"Glen, I want to try and help you. I think you swallowed a Bug-Lok and I can remove it non-invasively. Will you permit me to try?"

"What does it mean? Where would I have swallowed the whatever-the-fuck it is?"

"Bug-Lok. The nanodevice I told you about."

He appeared to be confused.

She had wanted his permission. Suddenly she realized that if he indeed had one of those nanodevices embedded in his brainstem, it was recording and transmitting everything they said to either Skorkin or his handler, whoever that was. She couldn't risk letting this go any further. "I'll take that as a 'yes.'"

She concentrated on Glen and put her mindspace into his. It took time to settle into him. She sought the spot where it would have nestled and, after several attempts, she could read its serial number and date of manufacture. Underneath those she saw Mandarin characters. She turned the device off, then reached her mind below the Bug-Lok's molecular connections to his neurons and gently pried the device loose until it floated away into his bloodstream.

Ann reemerged into normal time and sat still, her energy depleted. When she was able to think clearly again, it was dark. She prepared dinner for them and ate everything that Glen didn't. Then she opened her notebook and opened her Hackertools folder.

It was well after midnight when Ann had finished decrypting the message. In clear, concise language, it was evident to Ann that two parties were behind all of InTelQ's operations. Alan Skorkin, as had been reported to her by Cassie, was a paramilitary contractor who worked occasionally for the CIA doing cleanup work. But Skorkin was working for Robert Randall, a CIA case officer, and—she read the message for the third time—Randall had ordered Skorkin to murder a long list of startup company execs. Butcher entire teams. Over six hundred names. Midway down the first page, she found Glen's name, as well as those of his cofounders. Her first reaction was fear for him. Then, fear for both of them. But both faded into a feeling of absolute rage.

She called Avram on his landline to be sure the call wouldn't roll into voicemail. This would have to be via voice, not text. She had questions and would need answers. Immediate answers. And if Avram didn't want to involve her, she'd damn well get the answers on her own.

* * *

Avram Shimmel answered his incoming call. It was Ann and she seemed to be quite angry. "Calm down. You're talking too fast. I'm missing words."

He heard her sigh. "Avram, Glen is on a hit list. How the fuck did that happen?"

"You mean that guy you're seeing?"

"Well, duh! Yes. It looks like the CIA wants him dead. We need a plan to protect him. Well, not just him. The list I sent to your phone has over six hundred names of people you have to protect. A case officer named Robert Randall and his cleaner, Alan Skorkin, are both involved."

Avram now had confirmation of Cassie's claim that Skorkin was the primary. He thought about what his course of action should be, but realized he'd need a plan and he had none. "I'll get on this. Now."

Ann sounded much calmer. "Thanks. Please keep me in the loop."

* * *

Avram's first act was to call Cassie, first updating her and then trying to reassure her that he and both the United Nations and the Mossad would work on InTelQ's plan of mass assassinations. He asked, "Where is Jon?"

He knew he'd need a plan that could work under any level of contingencies that might emerge from unintended consequences they hadn't imagined. This was Jon Sommers's specialty.

"Jon and Lee are out right now. I'll have him call you just as soon as they return."

"I'll need you all on a conference call. Get back to me ASAP." He knew he'd have to speak jointly with Cassie and Jon as soon as he had amassed the paramilitary force necessary for any operation he might have to assemble. And since the Posse Comitatus Act prohibited US armed force operations on US soil, if he couldn't assemble enough mercenaries, he might need Samuel Meyer's Israel Defense Force to work with his United Nations Paramilitary Force.

To obtain use of the IDF, he'd need Meyer to enroll the Mossad. He called Samuel Meyer. "Director Meyer, this is Avram Shimmel. We intercepted a message that Robert Randall of the CIA sent to Alan Skorkin, a CIA cleaner. Our original mission has escalated."

"Your mission was 'discovery.' Just investigate and report back. How did it escalate? What the fuck have you done?"

Avram had never heard Meyer lose his temper before. He gulped and reassessed his next move. "Sir, I understand our orders. But we found facts that suggested, using our initiative, we needed to follow up and obtain more data. Now we have answers to questions you very likely would have asked us had we just followed your original orders."

Avram heard Meyer take a deep breath. "Okay, okay. Tell me what you found in this little message."

Avram repeated exactly the text that Ann had sent him. "So now we believe Randall wants Skorkin to execute over six hundred of the brightest minds in Silicon Valley. For us to stand by and do nothing would be its own crime. But, we don't have the resources to stop this by ourselves. Is the Mossad interested in helping? You're already on the hook for seventeen of the one hundred thirty-nine names since we promised those venture funding if they played the role of 'pretenders.' That's nearly a quarter of the six hundred eighteen startup cofounders on Randall and Skorkin's list."

Avram could hear Meyer's breathing over the phone line. "Okay. Let me review our status of forces and I'll send you a text detailing what I can offer. Why don't you also use your covert teams at the United Nations to muster a force? What a joke. Israel and the United Nations working on the same mission. The prime minister will never believe this." Meyer terminated the call.

But Avram wasn't finished. Cassie hadn't called him back so Avram decided to call Jon directly. "Jon, is Cassie with you?"

"Ah, no. But she updated me with a voicemail a few minutes ago. Lee and I are returning to their hotel room. You want a plan to deal with the pending massacre. Yes?"

"Yes. Here's a sitrep for you. I just finished a voice call with Samuel Meyer. He is willing to consider offering us Mossad operatives, but he isn't sure how much force is available as yet. Nothing available from IDF. We will know soon enough though. Please plan to discover and screen all six hundred eighteen cofounders."

"It would be lots easier for us to terminate Randall's cleaner. Terminate Skorkin."

"Not enough. Randall would send others. But that might be a part of the problem's solution."

"What about terminating Randall *and* his cleaner?"

"Are you willing to bet that Randall is rogue? What if his orders come from higher up the food chain?"

"Good point. Any new plan will need to factor this as well."

Avram considered how large and complex this new mission might become. Then he remembered one more fact Meyer had told him. "Meyer told me that there are rumors other nations' intelligence services are now looking into using venture funding to develop weapons projects, just as the CIA has. What can you do about that?"

Jon was silent for more than a minute. "As if it wasn't going to become a shitstorm with just the United States wreaking havoc on startups. Lemme think. Ah, yes, I just might have a way to stop the entire cleanup. But it would be a combo of kinetic and cyber ops."

Avram thought about this. "How long until you can refine your plan and call me back to obtain resources?"

"Give me a few hours. Jon out."

Avram wondered if Jon really could craft a double-sided strategy with a tactical plan that could work.

* * *

Jon, Lee, and Cassie gathered around the desk in Jon's hotel room. Jon pointed to the small whiteboard on the desk. "So, our new mission will be to develop a tactical and operational plan to discredit the process of using VCs to develop weapons tech. And, when this emerges as a news item, we'll also have to protect the startup cofounders."

Lee shook his head. "But if the cofounders are alive, won't it prove your story is a lie? And, if they're dead, you'll have no corroborating witnesses. Either way, the cover story is inherently weak."

Cassie nodded. "Yes. Lee is correct. I think I can recruit a reputable reporter to craft and distribute a news story when the time is right. April O'Toole."

Lee smiled. "I remember her. Smart woman."

Cassie nodded. "We'll have to use the timing of the news release and the timing of where and when we provide protection for the cofounders as our best way to convince the entire startup community to stop working with nontraditional equity providers."

Jon pulled the cap off a liquid marker and stood ready at the board. "Give me a specific example."

Cassie placed her fingers under her chin as she thought. "I hate to say this, but we'll need Ann as one of our resources. How about this: What if..."

* * *

Just after dawn the next morning, Robert Randall sat at his desk, culling facts from the various new threat assessment files to be included in the daily threat assessment summary he was due to deliver to Strumler in about an hour. North Korea, Syria, China, Russia, and several other hot spots were the sources of a few items in his upcoming summary.

But then he saw a new one, labled "urgent." As he read it, his eyes bugged. "Oh, fuck me!" The report stated that several of the United States' adversary nations had considered setting up venture capital firms to fund weaponized technology development. But it failed to directly mention InTelQ.

Randall knew that every item marked "urgent" had to be discussed with the president-elect. None of these was optional. But he worried that if this news was now under the purview of the CIA, they might soon uncover the nasty fact that InTelQ was Randall's own off-the-books retirement fund. If the CIA did a little digging, soon the head of the snake would swallow the snake's tail.

Randall was now in an untenable position. He thought about ways to extricate himself from InTelQ more swiftly, but he needed a viable path.

Strumler. He's a business man. Randall's grin was ear-to-ear as he prepared for a different kind of threat assessment meeting.

CHAPTER 33

51st Floor, Strumler Tower Capital Hotel, Washington, DC

November 13, 1:37 p.m.

Due to Strumler's emergency appointment with his hair stylist, Randall's next briefing session with the president-elect was delayed from early morning until midafternoon.

Randall sat fuming in the hotel's lobby as the clock drifted past their rescheduled time. He swallowed an extra cup of coffee, then realized drinking the beverage was a mistake. He now suffered from indigestion combined with a need to visit the restroom. And just when he decided that he had to get up from the sofa in the lobby, his cell buzzed. "Randall here."

"The president-elect can see you now. Please come up to the suite."

The call ended as abruptly as it had started. Randall was torn between the restroom and the elevator. He chose the restroom. He knew it would work out better for him. Late, he arrived at the huge door to the suite on the top floor of the hotel.

The man whose voice he had heard before on his cell now asked him who he was.

"Randall."

"Sorry, sir. You will have to wait. An urgent matter has arisen." The man, who Randall now saw was either a private service bodyguard or Secret Service, pointed to a couch. There were several others sitting in the area. And, to Randall's surprise and consternation, the others were called, in some order that he couldn't discern. It appeared to Randall that he was fifth on the list.

By the time it was his turn, the acid leftover from the coffee was burning through his stomach wall. He marched into the suite, trying to disguise his rage. But the president-elect was not present. After what seemed an eternity, Randall heard the toilet flush. The bathroom door opened and the president-elect emerged, trailed by a noticeably foul odor.

"Mr. Randall. What have you for me today?" Strumler sat on the couch and motioned his hand toward the spot next to him.

As Randall sat, he accidentally inhaled some of the vent cloud that had followed Strumler from the toilet. He tried and failed to keep from gagging. "Ah, sorry. Bad food at breakfast."

Strumler's nose sniffed and wrinkled. "Yeah. Well, what's going on in the world today?"

Randall began his report, starting with the Middle East. Then he covered North Korea. He now had two items left, neither of which would be easy conversations. He decided to let the worst of it sit until the end. "Intelligence services of three of our closest allies have reported to the CIA that the Russians hacked our electoral process. They claim our voting machines and tally databases were—"

"It's fake news. I don't want to hear it. Next?"

Randall took a deep breath. Now was time for the item that could lead directly to him. "There's also a report that several unfriendly intelligence services have been impersonating venture capital firms and investing in high-tech startups that are developing products easy to weaponize. The report claims that when the products are ready for market they dispose of the startup personnel. Sir, I can't claim there is any validity to this one, but I was told to include it in your daily briefing. Ah, we're finished now. Do you have any questions?"

Randall was sure the dolt would not have understood anything he'd been told, let alone have any thoughts about it. But still, he hoped—

"Wait a second. I want to know about the investors that your report claims are foreign intelligence agencies."

It took Randall all his self-restraint not to smile. He almost choked on his own saliva. "Uh, sure. What?"

Strumler sat for a few seconds, thinking. "You know, I'm a businessman. I've invested in lots of companies. Do you know how many startups get funded in the average year?"

Randall tried to recall the briefing notes. "Not sure but my guess is many hundreds."

"No. Thousands. Do you know how many fail?"

"I don't know. I have to believe that most do."

Strumler smiled. "About one-quarter achieve any level of success. Fewer than ten percent become publicly traded. But most are either business-to-business or business-to-consumer. Do you know how many produce military products?"

Unfortunately, this was one fact Randall knew all too well. "About one percent."

"Yeah, I'd already guessed it would be a tiny fraction. But the military pays tons more in total for its products than any commercial product could earn. This is a no-brainer. If I was a venture capitalist, the military sector's products are the market I'd go for." Strumler smiled at Randall. "Okay. Thanks, Mr. Randall. You can go now."

Randall couldn't understand what had just happened.

But he thought he might have succeeded in setting up Strumler.

As he left the suite, he heard Strumler humming.

* * *

After the CIA minder left him, Strumler couldn't stop thinking about this new devious method of weapons systems development. He sat at his notebook computer and researched venture capital and startup funding. He even cancelled two appointments he'd looked forward to.

As the afternoon ended, he made a decision. Strumler picked up his cell from the coffee table and dialed a number in Russia. "Please let me speak to Nikolai Puchenko."

He waited nearly two minutes. Then he heard Puchenko's voice. "Da?"

"Mr. Puchenko, this is Daniel Strumler. I may have something for you."

"Ah, Mr. President-Elect, I was hoping to hear from you soon. What do you have?"

"I've just been told that there are a number of countries that are using their intelligence services to act as venture capitalists, to develop new weapons technology. Are you aware of this?"

"But of course. Our SVR and FSB services both have reported this. Do you have anything else? I'm busy right now."

"Er, no. That was all."

"Then, goodbye. Call me when you have something interesting. And remember, we have a file of information on you that the press in the United States would make a—how you say—field day out of. Goodbye."

* * *

"I've got something." The newest hire in the Shenzien hacker cooperative sent a copy of the audio call to his superior in the Chinese CSIS.

The superior listened to the recording and nodded. "This is good. It's been nearly three weeks monitoring Strumler's phone without anything useful. But this. This is gold. He is handled by Puchenko, a senior SVR spy. Now we have leverage."

* * *

Charles Nottingham, a low-level NSA analyst read through the last page of the telephone intercept and pinched his eyebrows. From the file, he could see that the president-elect had called someone the NSA had been tracking because they believed he was a Russian spy.

Nottingham printed out the transcript and walked it into the office of his boss, Carl Von Truber, associate director of communications intercepts.

Von Truber scanned the transcript. "You never saw this. It's way above your pay grade." After Nottingham exited his office, Von Truber took the elevator to the top floor. He waited outside the DCI's office without an appointment until the receptionist beckoned to him.

The DCI sat and stared at his ass dire.

Von Truber pushed the transcript in front of the DCI. "Sir, this is something you have to see. You won't believe it. It appears that the Russians hacked the presidential election."

CHAPTER 34

**Swamp, 6 miles northeast of Lucessi compound
in Areguá, Paraguay**

November 13, 1:26 p.m.

On the afternoon of the third day, Frank Lucessi and his searchers had finished covering over two-thirds of the area where they thought Laura had most likely been. They had yet to find any clues about her direction and had not even a guess as to how far she had wandered. Their least likely and most dangerous part of the grid was the swamp northeast of the compound. It was here that they intended to search today and tomorrow. If they hadn't found her by the end of tomorrow, Frank knew his searchers would give up. Most of the searchers grumbled that the young woman had probably been eaten by now.

Frank heard someone shout, "Over here."

He wasn't sure where "here" was and stood rooted where he was, looking in every direction, waiting to hear or see something to give him distance and direction. But when all his searchers started running all in the same direction, Frank ran, too, as fast as he could. He reached a group of men standing in a circle by a tree. He pushed his way through the throng. At its very center, at the bottom of the tree's trunk was what appeared to be a hunk of mud in the shape of a human.

One of the searchers had a towel and was wiping mud off the face of Laura! Frank fell to his knees at her side and took a damp towel, wiping her eyes clean of mud.

"Señor, the mud saved her from being eaten. It covered her scent. Also, saved her from the mosquitoes." The searcher smiled. "She's dehydrated, but not enough to kill her. You are very lucky."

Frank had wiped her face clean and could now see that Laura's eyes were empty. Alive, but unresponsive. He could see her lips move and placed her ear close enough to hear her.

"I murdered her. Daddy didn't do it. It was me. I murdered Mama."

Frank was sure she was delusional. At least, he hoped she was.

He called their helicopter on his satellite phone. Soon, the chopper landed and they loaded her in along with Frank. He wondered how long it would take to reach the nearest hospital. But now Frank had hope that she would recover.

* * *

Ann thought Glen was recovering nicely. She was sure he'd be able to return to work the next day. She suggested they have a celebration dinner. Glen nodded. "Okay."

She made a reservation at the Burma Ruby, an upscale exotic Asian restaurant on University Avenue in Palo Alto.

"You're sure that you are up for this?"

Glen nodded. "Yeah. I'm good. I can't just hang around the apartment eating leftovers."

She shrugged. "Okay. Promise you'll go easy."

"I want to walk there. Two days in bed. I need the exercise."

She shrugged again. She had planned this to see if he would be ready to return to work tomorrow. The hospital had told her to have him spend one day in bed and the next taking it easy. She'd seen to that.

It took much longer to walk from the apartment to Burma Ruby than she had thought. Glen struggled and needed to stop frequently. She waited, smiling at him in encouragement, and he smiled back.

She hadn't eaten there before, but she had read reviews. It was expensive, and she wondered it Glen could afford it.

They arrived just after their reservation time and then waited for what seemed like forever. They were led to a table reserved for them near the kitchen. Ann had thought this would work better for them, for she could see how he reacted to the aromas of the food. Glen sniffed the air and smiled. "Curry, I think."

"That's right. Do you want to order or shall I?"

"Surprise me."

Ann nodded. She read through the menu, then selected minted jalapeño pork, walnut shrimp, and eggplant and garlic. The first dish arrived within minutes, but then they waited for the other two after a large party was seated. The large party might have swamped the kitchen, she thought. She had wanted to order a Burmese pad thai, but decided it would take too long.

The food was tasty but the portions were somewhat small. Glen tore into his food as if it were the first solid food he'd eaten in days. *Wait. It is the first solid food he's eaten in days,* thought Ann.

The sun set while they ate. It was mildly chilly and dark when they left the restaurant. They walked toward campus along University Avenue for a few blocks before turning south on Bryant. Glen walked steadily now. He seemed to have recovered. As they waited for the light to change, a large man wearing a hoodie charged into Glen, pushed him into the rush-hour traffic, and then sprinted down the sidewalk. Ann saw Glen roll into the street. She jumped over him, her hands waving the oncoming car to a stop just in front of where Glen lay.

"Glen? Are you okay?"

He got to his knees and slowly stood. "Um. Yeah, I think. What just happened?"

She wondered, *that's what I need to know*. "I think someone just tried to kill you."

"That's preposterous. Why would anyone want me dead?"

She was sure that this was Skorkin. If he'd watched her save Glen from wherever it was he'd run to, she was sure he'd make another attempt.

"We'd better get to your apartment now. And fast." She hailed a taxi.

After they reached his apartment, Glen turned on the television to watch the news.

Ann shook her head. *How much to tell him?* She walked to the kitchen and called Cassie. "Mom, are you free to talk?"

She heard Cassie's footsteps. "Yes. I'm on our room's terrace. How are you?"

"Not sure. Glen and I went out to dinner, but on our way back, a large hooded man pushed Glen into the traffic and I barely saved him. I'm thinking this might have been Skorkin. Do you know anything about what's happening to the other InTelQ-funded startup teams?"

"Yes. I've read the message you decrypted for Avram. He's assembling teams to protect the cofounders. But, there are over six hundred of them. It will take several days for Avram to mount an op big enough to cover all of them. Is Glen alright?"

"Yes, he's okay. But I need a protective detail here tomorrow morning at the latest. Can you make that happen?"

"Not sure. Don't let Glen leave the apartment until you hear from me."

"Okay, Mom. Please. Make it happen."

* * *

Just before the sun could rise, Jon's cellphone buzzed on his night stand. "Sommers here."

"It's Avram. Cassie called me. I need you to head a small protective detail for today. Only today. By tomorrow, we'll have enough military to keep all the pretenders safe. Do you know where Glen Sarkov lives?"

"Not a clue."

Avram gave Jon the address. "How long for you to get there?"

"Figure fifteen minutes. What about his cofounders?"

"Cassie is now rounding them up. The entire team should be at Glen's apartment in a few hours at most. I fear whoever tried to kill Glen last night won't give up easily. Get going now." Avram terminated the call. Jon raced to the bathroom and then dressed. He was soon out of his hotel and in a taxi.

* * *

Alan Skorkin watched the woman herding four of his targets into what he already knew was Glen Sarkov's apartment. He prepared to break in and dispatch them all. First, he checked his weapons. He had a military-issue bladed weapon, a 9mm handgun, and several chemical agents he could use to paralyze a victim at close range.

But before he could forge an operational plan, another person, a man who moved like a soldier, emerged from the elevator on Glen's floor and knocked on the door. The man said, "Sommers. Here to help."

The door opened and the man entered, after which the door closed again. Skorkin, standing behind the fire stairs, cursed. No way he could do this now without making a big mess. He decided to wait for a better opportunity. And, after all, there were over six hundred names on his list. Over two hundred were in Palo Alto, Menlo Park, and Mountain View, all within a fifteen-minute ride. He could always do the low-hanging fruit first and do these later.

* * *

Jon relaxed as the sun set. *Much ado about nothing.* He felt his phone buzz against his hip. "Sommers."

"Shimmel. We chose poorly. While you were cooling your heels, Skorkin murdered eleven pretenders. Four in a startup incubator in Palo Alto, three in another incubator in Mountain View, and three in a house in Menlo Park."

"Bad joss. What do you want me to do next?"

"Stay with your charges overnight. Tomorrow morning at first light I have a Mossad group to replace you and Cassie. Their countersign is 'dark prince.' Let them in and call me for your next assignment. Meanwhile, think about this: We need you to complete your plan to save the rest of the surviving pretenders."

"Okay. Will do."

"Shimmel out."

Jon opened a planning app on his cell. He set about trying to construct something he was sure no one else could. A perfect plan. But, none of Jon's plans had ever been perfect, so he also constructed fail-safes down three levels. As he worked, he hoped for good joss.

CHAPTER 35

Asunción National Public Hospital, Asunción, Paraguay

November 15, 8:36 a.m.

Time was a blur for Frank. He'd arrived by chopper at the hospital's helipad with Laura, got her admitted, and watched as the doctors stabilized her, and then waited forever for a psychiatrist to visit.

A nearly ancient psychiatrist wearing a lab coat spent a brief time with Laura. Laura remained expressionless and silent. The psychiatrist told Frank through a heavy German accent, "She's catatonic. Given what she's been through, I'm not surprised. She will probably recover, but it's too soon to tell. Right now, she needs constant attention. You can have her committed if you are too busy to devote yourself entirely to her well-being."

For Frank, there was no decision to be made. He simply replied, "I will be with her and attend to all her needs and wants."

The psychiatrist shrugged. "As you wish. In that case, I'll sign her release. We can free the bed. There are many others needing attention."

It took Frank the rest of the day to get Laura back to the

compound and set up her bedroom so that he could be her constant attendant.

* * *

Laura's eyes were open, but she couldn't understand anything she saw. It was as if there was another person's body with her eyes splayed open, unable to move. She was trapped within its body. Every few hours, she would surface to this level of attention to the world, and then sink back into oblivion. She wanted to scream, *help me!* but she could make no sound.

Whenever she descended back into her coma, she would see things she knew weren't real. She saw herself slicing her mother's neck open with a shard of glass. She saw her father screaming at her mother. She saw policemen dragging her father off, and then she saw an old ragged woman from Child Protective Services take her from her own bedroom. These visions repeated continuously like a broken record though her mind.

She resurfaced again and saw Frank deliver a spoonful of food to her mouth. He forced her mouth open and pushed the spoon into her. She swallowed, her eyes no longer focusing as she swirled back into oblivion.

Sometime later, she had a different vision. This time, she saw a large, powerful man visit the compound. He wore camouflaged clothing and his face was covered with green, brown, and black makeup. He carried a knife. The vision lasted for just a few seconds before she was back in the oblivion, murdering her mother yet again.

* * *

Alan Skorkin debarked the aircraft at Silvio Pettirossi International Airport just west of Asunción. He exited down the outdoor ramp and walked toward the terminal. The evening was humid and hot. He carried a small suitcase but he'd checked his prize luggage, a long case with a disassembled sniper rifle. Skorkin retrieved it from the pile of luggage unloaded from the aircraft, and searched outside the terminal for the taxi line. There was no such line, but there was a single taxi. He took it into the city and checked himself into a small hotel. He wouldn't be here long.

He had failed to eliminate all the startup cofounders. He'd killed nearly fifty, but now the rest of them were under the protection of some dubious group pretending to be a part of the United Nations. When he'd reported this to Randall, the man had told him to "just kill Frank Lucessi. With him gone, the trail of evidence won't point to us."

Skorkin wasn't sure this was true. And he was absolutely sure somehow the living startup teams would be the evidence that got him and Randall convicted of hundreds of murders. No, after killing Lucessi, Skorkin was going to complete his mission. He'd never failed before. He wouldn't fail this time. But, as Randall ordered, first he'd kill Lucessi before he resumed murdering the remaining startup teams. He was determined to leave no survivors, no witnesses. He'd need a plan to separate them from their "UN" protectors.

The next morning, he rented a car and drove the roads to and around Lucessi's compound, reconnoitering the area's approaches and getaways. He returned to the hotel late in the day and ate a light meal at a busy, local restaurant, a place big enough that he wouldn't be remembered.

Then he returned to the hotel and prepared for a busy night.

* * *

Ann called Cassie on her cell. "We have to meet. I'm sure that whoever tried to kill Glen is still out there. We need a plan that can end this. A protection detail won't work forever."

Cassie said, "I'll bring Jon and Lee and be at Glen's apartment soon. We still don't understand the larger outlines of events. We're close, but no conclusions. It's starting to look like Frank Lucessi is just a pawn."

Ann waited for them to arrive. She tried to call Laura but there was no answer on Laura's cell. Ann left a voicemail describing her fears.

* * *

Robert Randall reviewed his Bug-Lok transcripts from Daniel Strumler. Although he had overwhelming evidence that the Russians controlled Strumler, there was still no way to legally make that evidence actionable without a warrant. And there was no legal cause to obtain that warrant.

While he read through the daily Bug-Lok transcripts, something new and promising caught his eye in a conversation between the president-elect and the chairman of Ruhr-Rohrbach in Berlin, Germany:

Strumler: Willy, this is the best. I mean, it's a business we can't lose at. Normally, venture capitalists aim at producing small-ticket items and until they have established a big enough market, they give the product away. But with military products, there only needs to be a single customer. It's like an on–off switch. Just get the military interested enough to sign a contract and then deliver whatever the startup produces.

And, we're not limited to a single country's military. We can sell to every country.

We keep telling the cofounders that our startup production costs still exceed the revenues and they have to work harder. When we have a production model, we just eliminate the startup team.

William Wrand: You mean kill them?

Randall beamed. *I know how to turn this into evidence!*

CHAPTER 36

Lucessi compound in Areguá, Paraguay

November 15, 6:13 p.m.

Frank fed Laura again after he ate his own dinner. He opened the windows and heard cicadas and the sound of an occasional bird's flapping wings. Sitting with her in her bedroom, he cursed Robert Randall for taking him away from her. In his mind, Randall was responsible for Laura's catatonia.

His landline rang and he ran to the phone in his own bedroom. "Hello?"

"It's Doctor Fernandez. How is Laura?"

"She still hasn't spoken or moved."

"Have you considered my recommendation for her care?"

"Committing her? No way!"

"She will need constant attention. Perhaps for the remainder of her life."

"No! No, I won't commit her. I'm determined to care for her myself."

"All right, Señor. I was just following up."

"Yeah. Well, thanks and goodnight." Frank ended the conversation. He turned to Laura. "Don't worry. I'll always be here for you."

* * *

In the back of her consciousness, Laura had recorded the scene. She felt like a prisoner. Her captors were her own body and Frank Lucessi, the man who had taken her here from Stanford, the man who had left her alone while he gallivanted around in the United States. She had suffered alone. She was beginning to hate Frank Lucessi.

Later, while she stared into the empty night, she could hear him read a book to her. She wanted to scream.

* * *

As sunset flashed its last, Alan Skorkin lay prone in the grassy field outside Frank Lucessi's compound, assembling his sniper rifle. He'd brought two boxes of long-range ammo, but he was sure he'd not need more than half a box.

He wore a ghillie suit as sniper camo, making him nearly invisible in the moonless night. Underneath it, he wore a black tee shirt. He knew he'd have to remove the camo before he charged the compound.

He studied the compound. Three guards walked their rounds. When his wristwatch chirped once at midnight, he took aim at one of the guards during the guard's route.

He squeezed the trigger and watched for the bullet to cross the quarter mile to the compound. He heard no sound as the guard's head disappeared in a blush of red.

Skorkin watched as the second guard approached the point where he had another clean shot. The second guard died thirty feet away from the first.

He needed to kill the three guards who were outside doing their rounds and then—before the guards in the guardhouse tried to communicate with the guards making the rounds and found that they weren't answering—he planned to charge silently to the compound's walls, scale them, and kill the other three guards in the guardhouse before any of them had a clue he was there.

Then, when he'd terminated all the guards, Skorkin planned to enter the building where Frank would be asleep.

A simple plan. Skorkin took aim at the third guard.

CHAPTER 37

Starbucks, Stanford Mall, Palo Alto, CA

November 15, 6:45 p.m.

When the dust settled after Glen's "accident," Jon counted the dead and thought, *we were lucky*.

He walked to his final meeting with a startup CEO, Arthur Creeg of Underwire Software. Jon bought them coffees and found a quiet place in the otherwise busy and noisy coffee bar.

He'd expected the meeting to take less than an hour. "So, I'm glad you're alive. As we agreed, the Mossad will offer you two million for a seed round of thirty-five percent series A convertible. If you can produce a piece of computer code that is capable of hacking the Ness Ziona's web servers, we'll buy the code and talk about other projects. Okay so far?"

Creeg nodded.

"Although I'm pretty sure you won't need a protection detail after this month, we'll need to provide one until we're sure. Is that okay for you and your cofounders?"

Again, he nodded.

"Good. I've instructed your detail to escort you to New York where we have a system of safe houses. Please tell your cofounders to pack for a stay of about two weeks."

Jon thought, *soon, all this will be over. Soon.*

* * *

On the flight to JFK, Ann sat in the row with Glen and his cofounders. She was pleased he'd accepted Jon's offer. Glen's group would be in a safe house in Brooklyn Heights with three other groups and a team of seasoned United Nations Paramilitary Force mercenaries.

She remained troubled at Glen continued denials that there was any real danger. He told Ann, "There never has been any danger."

When he told Ann, "I think you're unhinged," she stifled the rage she felt. She turned away and watched the clouds skip past the aircraft.

* * *

Skorkin took aim at the last guard doing rounds and then pulled away from the scope to make a small adjustment after he detected an unexpected breeze. Once again, he took aim, and then slowly squeezed the trigger.

He felt the satisfying tug on his shoulder and watched through the scope as the final guard's head exploded. He dropped the sniper rifle. He'd have plenty of time to pick up the Dragunov and disassemble it when he left. He racked one round into the chamber, then pulled the clip from his 9mm Ruger and pushed a bullet into the clip where the racked round had been. The he reloaded the clip, giving him one extra round for a total of eighteen. He began trotting toward the guardhouse. The guards relaxing there would be surprised when he opened the door and slaughtered them all. He knew he could kill all of them before they could react.

As he neared the guardhouse, he screwed a silencer onto the handgun's barrel. The door wasn't locked. He opened it and saw three men intently watching a series of monitor screens. The first two were dead before the third noticed he was there. But that last guard in the entryway hadn't even time to open his mouth before he, too, was dead.

Skorkin just nodded and moved on to the small barracks with nine bunkbeds. He saw two sleeping and one not present. Skorkin shot the sleepers on their beds, then walked to the door to the bathroom, where he knocked on the door and waited.

"Gimme a minute, I'm washin' up." The last guard opened the door and died.

Skorkin placed his 9 mil in his jacket pocket and drew his Benchmark knife from its sheath on his belt. *Now, on to the main house to complete this part of the assignment.*

* * *

Robert Randall reviewed his files of unauthorized evidence and tried for the umpteenth time to figure out some way to take down Daniel Strumler. *I could sell it to someone. I know that no journalist with a shred of ethics would buy it, but perhaps the Russians would want to save Strumler enough to pay me what I'd need to retire.*

But, in the end, he decided his best idea was the one he had thought of days ago. He sent an email to Strumler bouncing it through a set of servers located around the world:

> Sir—
> It has come to my company's attention that you are interested in the acquisition of a venture capital firm that invests in weapons technology. Ours has been successful in developing products for over two years and a listing of our portfolio of products is attached to this message. We are about to auction the company and retire with the funds. If you are interested in a preemptive bid to purchase our company, the price will be twenty-five million USD ($25,000,000.00).

We have attached the documents you must sign, scan, and return as attachments in an email, and also the details of our receiving bank, for your convenience. This price remains effective until the end of today.

Sincerely,
Board of Directors
InTelQ Investments

The sun had set into a scattering of clouds before he felt his level of frustration ebb.

Next, he cleaned and dumped a copy of the transcript files of Strumler's conversations onto a virgin thumb-drive and pocketed the drive in his suit-jacket pocket.

He heard his desktop beep an incoming message. Strumler had signed the agreement and sent the cash.

He waited until his boss was out of the office. He entered and dropped the drive on the center top of his boss's desk.

Then he exited and waited for holy hell to break loose.

CHAPTER 38

Lucessi compound in Areguá, Paraguay

November 15, 7:01 p.m.

Laura heard strange noises and woke from her trance. She rose from her bed and moved toward the door into the hallway.

As she walked, her visions returned. She voyaged without volition, without footsteps. She saw their old furniture and she could smell the aromas of the meal her father had cooked for them earlier that night. Onions, some kind of inexpensive beef, and potatoes. She drifted through the hallway and heard more noise.

As she moved toward the noise, her dream momentarily faded. She saw herself standing in a different hallway, this one in Paraguay. When the dream returned, she had entered her parents' bedroom. In front of her, she saw her mother being stabbed by her father. He raged at his wife, screaming his own name. But then her father transformed into herself and now it was Laura stabbing her mother. Laura tried to scream but she couldn't. She saw her mother scream as blood sprayed from her neck.

Laura watched her mother fall to the floor. Laura remained rooted to the floor where she'd been standing. Her dream-self finally mustered the power to scream and flee, as her father entered the bedroom, telling her to stop. Now she could feel the sharp edge of the shattered glass vase she had just used to murder her mother.

A muffled sound broke through the dream once again, and now, her eyes sprang open wide. She heard a shot, followed by another. She found herself at the doorway from her Paraguay bedroom looking into the hallway. Now she was able to move, able to walk. She was no longer imprisoned in her dreams.

* * *

Frank heard shots in the distance. He ran from Laura's bedroom to his own, picked up his cellphone from the night-stand, and called the guardhouse.

There was no answer. He trotted to the gun safe near the bathroom, and opened the safe, removing a 9mm Beretta and a clip.

He ran back to Laura's bedroom, worried about her safety.

On the way down the hallway, he saw a camo-dressed man carrying a knife in one hand and a gun in the other. The man was huge, his face painted in camo. The interloper now stood in front of him.

In a soothing voice, the man said, "Mr. Lucessi, I'm Alan Skorkin. I was sent here by our Mr. Randall to make your acquaintance. He told me to tell you that your project has been cancelled, and, unfortunately, you are a loose end. Randall gave me strict orders to execute you. So sorry."

Frank realized he held his Beretta in his hand. He took aim but, as he began to pull the trigger, the man laughed and kicked the gun from his hand.

* * *

Laura heard muffled voices in the hallway. She still had fragments of the dream screaming "danger" at her. The vase she had bought at the art gallery in Asunción stood on her nightstand in easy reach. She picked it up and walked silently through the doorway, into the hallway.

She saw a stranger confronting Frank. Though she was behind him, she could see that the stranger held a gun and a knife. He kicked a pistol from Frank's hand and moved closer to him.

The scene in front of her swirled and she was now back in her dream, with her mother holding a knife, about to stab her father. She stepped forward and brought the vase down on her mother's head as hard as she could. The vase shattered, stunning her mother. Laura now held just a large pale-blue edge of glass. She plunged the shard into her mother's neck. Laura said, "Goodbye, Mother. Now you can never hurt Daddy again."

Once more she stirred from her dream and saw a strange man sprawled at her feet, his eyes bulging and blood spraying out of his neck.

CHAPTER 39

Lucessi compound in Areguá, Paraguay

November 15, 7:22 p.m.

Laura rubbed her eyes, unwilling to believe what she saw in front of her. A man she had never met appeared to be dead. She could see that she held the shard of glass that killed him, but she could not remember anything that happened.

She opened her mouth and tried to speak. "Who? Who he?"

Frank ran to her side and held her gently. "He said his name was Alan Skorkin."

"Who is?"

"He said he was sent here by someone I'd been working with. Thank you, Laura. You saved my life." Frank gently pried the shard of glass from her tight grip. Then he guided her to a chair.

"I did what?"

"You saved my life. You killed him before he could kill me."

"No. No! I didn't kill anyone."

Frank stood speechless.

Finally, he found words. Words might clear this up for both of them. "What's the last thing you remember?"

"I was starting to hate you for leaving alone me in this

godforsaken place. I left the compound and needed to walk, to refresh myself and have a chance to think. But I got lost and started wandering."

"That was five days ago. I returned and found you missing. I organized a search party and we found you two days ago. You were catatonic until now."

Laura could see the body and the pool of blood on the tile floor in front of her. She just couldn't figure out what had happened. "I did that?" She pointed to the body.

Frank nodded. "I need to get a crew here to do some cleanup."

* * *

Avram Shimmel shook hands with the last startup's CEO and cofounders. "When the aircraft lands in Tel Aviv, there will be a Mossad team to meet you at Ben Gurion. They will guide you through the process of relocation."

The CEO smiled. "Thanks for saving our lives. How long until we have office space in Herzliya?"

Avram shrugged. "I'm not sure, but not too long. You'll have enough funding to complete your product, and the IDF has already promised that if it works to their satisfaction, you can live in Israel permanently as the senior executives of your own company."

He watched them board the El Al aircraft at JFK. This was the last startup group of the nearly hundred that Jon and Cassie had been able to save. He took a deep breath as he watched the aircraft disengage from its boarding gate.

Samuel Meyer, the Mossad's director, had made the decision to move them to Israel so that the products produced by the startups could be more closely monitored. He had personally negotiated the terms of the deal with each startup CEO while Avram was kept out of the loop. That way, there would be less chance for the United Nations members to discover just how powerful a background role Israel had within international corridors.

Nearly two hundred cofounders had been viciously slaughtered. Avram shook his head. *What a waste.*

* * *

Ann felt uneasy about her next plan. She sat in Glen's apartment, waiting for him to return after his second day at work. The dinner she'd cooked for them was cold and ruined. It was nearly midnight. She'd eaten without him. She heard the door to the apartment unlock and she waited, a 9mm Beretta Nano concealed carry in her hand tucked under her leg. She still feared the danger they had just avoided. *I hope it's Glen. But if it isn't...*

When Glen appeared, she uncocked the trigger and placed the handgun in her purse on the table next to her. She rose and hugged him. "You're late."

"Um, sorry. It was my second day back and I had a massive backlog of things to get through." He sniffed the air. "Smells like dinner. Sorry. I picked up a sandwich from the fridge in the office kitchen."

"Glen, you're not taking your safety seriously. There could still be a cleaner out there."

"Ann, that's a crock. Just because I fell in the street doesn't mean—"

"Yeah, but it doesn't mean we were wrong. According to Avram, nearly two hundred of InTelQ's startup teams were butchered. Every one of the rest of them has been relocated to somewhere outside the United States."

"None of my cofounders wanted a relocation program. And neither do I."

She considered everything that had happened since she had become involved with him. *It isn't working. It never really worked.* She sighed. "Okay, then. I guess we gave it our best shot. Look, I've packed my stuff. I plan to be gone in a few minutes. I'll see you in class."

She walked into the bedroom and lifted her rolling spinner suitcase off the bed. Glen wouldn't look at her as she left.

* * *

Samuel Meyer read the report Avram Shimmel had filed on his computer. He shook with rage. Shimmel had cost Israel tens of millions of dollars with a return payback that was problematic at best. Worse, there was still the risk from intelligence agencies in Iran, Germany, UK, and China developing their own versions of InTelQ. Although Russia hadn't been part of the rumored move to seed weapons development through venture capital, he was sure they would soon join the fray. And the final failure was that, according to Shimmel, at least one of InTelQ's cleaners was still out there.

He plucked the secure landline receiver from its cradle and called Shimmel. "Avram, is there any news on the cleaner InTelQ has been using?"

"Nothing. He was recorded at the airport in Paraguay, but since then, no traces."

"Can you have one of your hackers trace all the messages to or from Robert Randall?"

"I have my best person on it."

"Get back to me as soon as anything develops."

* * *

Avram had left a voicemail for Ann. She saw the message while she was getting seated for her computer forensics class. The move back into her old apartment had taken most of the morning and this was the only class she could attend today, so she left the message unopened for the duration of the class.

She took notes while the professor droned on.

Then, as the class broke up, she put the phone to her ear and listened. "It's Avram. I had Michael Drapoff track the Bug-Lok devices that were in the group that had Glen Sarkov's device. Please call Drapoff and have him send you the details of every other device placed from that Bug-Lok group. I need to know who each device was placed into and if possible, get transcripts of every word said and where it was said. Then I need you to destroy their Bug-Loks so whoever was tracking them can no longer do it. Avram out."

She sighed. This would take all night, at least. She walked to her apartment. *I'll do it after I eat something.*

She sat in thought but then frowned. She called Michael Drapoff. As she sat at her desk eating a ham-and-cheese sandwich on toasted sourdough, his phone rolled into voicemail. The voicemail announcement was in Hebrew, so the only word she understood was "Drapoff."

"Hello, it's Ann Sashakovich. Avram asked me to call you about the devices you tracked for him. Please call me back ASAP so I can finish this assignment and get back to my studies."

She waited. Then her cell buzzed. "Hello, Ann. It's the middle of the night here. I was asleep. What details are you wanting?"

"I think Avram wants to know literally everything. Like who was the host for each device, and a list of every transcript for every device."

"That'll be a ton of data. It was over sixty terabytes at last count."

"Can I download them?"

After a long silence, Michael said, "It will take forever and you'll need several storage devices. I'm setting you up with a temporary account. Username "leveya," password "bat9327." I'll keep the account active until I return to work in five hours. That should be long enough for you to download everything. Oh, and one more thing. It turns out that your president-elect currently walks with one in his brain. Happy hunting."

Ann wasn't even given the opportunity to say "thanks."

She started the download and went to sleep. When her cellphone alarm buzzed just after six the next morning, she took a look at her notebook computer's progress bar before she took her morning trip to the restroom. "80%." She realized she would be hard at work soon and started a pot of coffee. By the time she returned from the bathroom, the progress bar registered "download completed."

She used the Windows search tool to scan the database by "target's name" first, to complete the primary task Avram wanted. She assembled the details of the report. She now had each Bug-Lok target's name, their device number, and the date they were infected. Then she attached a link to every transcript on her storage devices for that infected person until she had all the links in a huge single anthology file. She closed the file and sent it to Avram.

Ann knew that using her mind to enter another person's Bug-Lok took an enormous amount of her energy. But the last task Avram had assigned her would do just that. She sat in a meditation stance and pushed her mind into the Bug-Lok of the first CEO on the list she had scanned. She located the CEO's Bug-Lok and removed it. Then she drank a half-bottle of orange juice. She looked within the refrigerator and then inside the pantry. There might be enough calories in every-thing to give her the energy she'd need to complete the task.

She repeated the procedure again and again. When the last Bug-Lok embedded in the last CEO on the list had been destroyed, she felt tipsy.

Her task was complete. But she found herself scanning the list of names. "Glen Sarkov" was there. She couldn't stop her fingers from pressing the key that opened his file. It was mostly conversations about the startup. Most of the conversations were about current status and plans.

Then she found several conversations with Samantha Trout, Mindfield's chief financial officer. None was innocent. She could tell that Samantha and Glen had been having an affair. The relationship was longstanding. As she read through the long set of conversations, she realized that Glen had been serious about Samantha, but his ardor hadn't been returned recently. In fact, the only reason he had pursued Ann was to make Samantha jealous.

Ann felt tears in the corners of her eyes.

She was about to close down her notebook and head out for classes when she saw another name that piqued her interest: "Daniel Strumler."

"Damn!" There were over a thousand files. She opened the first conversation. The date of the file was over six months old, long before the election:

Nikolai Puchenko: I asked if your campaign might be able to use some help.

Daniel Strumler: If I accept, you'll own me.

Nikolai Puchenko: If you don't accept, let me remind you that we already have enough just in photos and videos to end your campaign. We also have signed contracts between your businesses and our oil companies. Not to mention—

Daniel Strumler: Yeah, not to mention what we were just talking about. But, all of that is just gossip. If I agree to your "help," then you really own me.

Nikolai Puchenko: But if you do, your odds of winning rise
from "slight" to nearly a "sure thing." Remember,
we only back winners.

Daniel Strumler: (silence).

Nikolai Puchenko: Well? Mr. Strumler, do you wish to
become president?

Daniel Strumler: You fuckin' piece of shit. Of course I do.
But what you're asking me to do is treason!

Nikolai Puchenko: It's survival of the fittest in regards to all
political dealings. Do you have what it takes to be
your country's leader?

Daniel Strumler: What the fuck do you want from me now?

Ann emitted a low whistle. Was Strumler a traitor? She
decided to skip her classes. She would need all day to do the
research. And none of this research would require her notebook computer. She drank an entire pot of coffee and had an
enormous meal. This procedure would leach most of her
remaining energy.

CHAPTER 40

Ann Sashakovich's apartment,
#211, 3950 Louis Road, Palo Alto, CA

November 16, 4:36 p.m.

Ann was sure that Daniel Strumler's Bug-Lok was still operational and could have collected more recent conversations. She concentrated on Strumler's Bug-Lok device. At first, nothing happened. Focusing on the Bug-Lok's serial number, she tried using a zazen approach, which she had learned in number of meditation classes. Nothing at all happened. She guessed she was out of practice.

But that's just an excuse! A lame one at that. I must try harder.

Once more she set herself to work. She tried to focus on the serial again, but this time she mouthed Strumler's name as if it were something dear to her.

Slowly, she could see the device as if it was in front of her. She read its serial number. *A match!*

She read the most recent transcript, in which Strumler had just ordered a plate of steak, potatoes, and string beans. Then, the less recent ones. And yesterday she found her most recent mention of Russia, Russians, or Nikolai Puchenko:

Daniel Strumler: Please let me speak to Nikolai Puchenko.

Nikolai Puchenko: Da?

Daniel Strumler: Mr. Puchenko, this is Daniel Strumler. I
            think someone in my own government is trying to
            get me impeached. I need your government's help.

Nikolai Puchenko: Ah, Mr. President-Elect, I was hoping to
            hear from you soon. But, what do you expect my
            government to do?

Daniel Strumler: Help me. Can your government send out
            bots to spread fake news like you did just before
            the election?

Nikolai Puchenko: Nyet. Our SVR and FSB services have
            recently considered doing just that. But since the
            DEFCON report about how easy our hacks of your
            voting machines came out, we have decided to stop
            completely until the next election. Do you have
            anything else? I'm busy right now.

Daniel Strumler: Er, no. But, I'm your best investment in
            controlling the United States. Surely, there is
            something you can do?

Nikolai Puchenko: Nyet. Goodbye. Call me when you have
            something interesting. And remember, we have a
            file of information on you that the press in the
            United States would make a—how you say—field
            day out of. Goodbye.

    She read through seventy-three other transcripts, all
related to Strumler and Puchenko's conversations. Now she
knew for sure that Strumler was Russia's candidate. She

thought of sending Avram a message, but decided that sending a message to Jon would be more effective.

She was sure Jon would forward her report to Sam Meyer. To be sure the message reached Meyer, she copied Michael Drapoff.

* * *

Daniel Strumler's mind continued to swing between scenes of being arrested for treason and ones where he sat in the Oval Office with people bowing before him.

He tried relaxing while he sat in his bathrobe, wondering how it would feel once he was president. *Yes, I've never been more than a huckster until now. But now I can make them grovel before me!* He thought about the real work he'd have to do. *I'll need professionals. Lackeys who know something about ruling a nation. But, who?*

He considered Robert Randall for just a moment. *No, the man's a professional spy. A nut job.* And then he remembered that Randall was due any moment to deliver one of those useless, boring daily threat assessments. *Aghhhh!*

He dressed in a suit. Then he sat in his big overstuffed chair and watched television news for reports about himself as he waited.

One of the stupid assholes from the Secret Service knocked on his door. Strumler said, "What?"

The door opened and the neatly dressed Secret Service officer popped his head through the door. "Sir, your CIA briefing is available. Shall I send him in?"

Strumler watched the television screen. It was a story about how comedians would make a fortune with him in office. He felt his gut roiling. "No, can't you see I'm busy? Let him wait."

When the short TV report ended, Strumler decided to call stories about him that ignored his vast series of accomplishments "not real news." No, that wasn't a good idea. He decided to think more about how to cope with stories that failed to mention him as their hero.

Then he remembered Randall was waiting. He picked up his cell and dialed his Secret Service butler. "Okay. Send him in."

Randall appeared and stood, obviously waiting for Strumler to invite him to sit. Strumler ignored the man long enough to see him struggling to restrain his own anger.

* * *

Robert Randall was glad he wasn't allowed to see the president-elect while carrying his sidearm. He would have found it difficult to keep himself from drawing his weapon and pulling the trigger until the clip was empty.

He had been given a new set of orders from William Smythe, his ass dire. Smythe told him, "Provoke Strumler by failing to mention anything he's done that smacks of a hint of success. Prod him. Belittle him if the chance presents itself. But for God's sake, don't mention that the NSA is tracking him."

Randall smiled at Strumler. "Sir, may I ask, have you any political experience? Any at all? I know you have been a businessman, but did you ever have any contact with anyone in an elected position while in conduct of your job?"

"Why, of course I have. My corporations needed permits and such to conduct business."

"Ah, well maybe that will work. You see, we in government have to work with others in government to get the job done. Our meetings, the daily threat assessments, are designed as a short course."

"Yeah. Well, I intend to alter the way our government works, from top to bottom. The government is a failure. It's too big and totally ineffective."

Randall forced a smile. "Well. Well, I guess you'll find out, as so many before you, that your task will be harder trying to change the system than working from within the system."

Strumler's face reddened. He took a deep breath and remained.

Randall thought himself now ready to deliver his first aggressive comment.

He leaned forward and said in a low whisper, "You know, we follow everyone and record nearly everything. Even you have secrets. We can help or hinder, depending on how our relationship goes. We—"

Strumler's jaw dropped. "Whatcha mean, 'everyone'?"

Randall remained silent.

Strumler stiffened. "Follow me all you want. You won't find anything."

"Oh, Mr. President-Elect, I didn't mean that the CIA would follow you. No. Not you. But there are others in our government who conduct domestic oversight." Randall felt like doing a happy dance. He nodded his head. He'd followed Smythe's orders to the letter, and yet he'd still delivered the message he was ordered to keep secret.

* * *

As soon as Randall left Strumler's room, the president-elect told his guards not to annoy him while he napped. Immediately, he plucked his cellphone from his pocket and tapped in a number.

"Get me Puchenko."

Seconds later, he heard his handler. "Da?"

"It's Strumler. I may have been compromised."

PART IV

I have been authorized by the Department of Justice to confirm that the FBI, as part of our counterintelligence mission, is investigating the Russian government's efforts to interfere in the 2016 presidential election and that includes investigating the nature of any links between individuals associated with the Trump campaign and the Russian government and whether there was any coordination between the campaign and Russia's efforts.

—James Comey, former FBI director,
testimony before Congress,
April 2017

CHAPTER 41

**Lubyanka conference room,
Kremlin, Moscow, Russia**

November 16, 4:59 p.m.

Nikolai Puchenko, director of the Russian SVR, sat at the long table with only one other person in the room. In the night outside, the Kremlin, coated in drifting snow, was bathed in electric floodlights. Murmurs filled the hallway outside the Lubyanka conference room. The president of Russia wore a frown as he listened to Puchenko's report.

"So then, you have concerns running forward?"

Puchenko nodded. "Mr. President, I don't know if Strumler has been compromised. But if he even believes this to be true, it would be prudent to cut ties with him."

"What a waste. After all the time and money we spent getting him into the White House."

There was silence in the room.

"If he is impeached or indicted for treason, he might tell his interrogators about us. It might be better to simply assassinate him. The Republicans would blame the Democrats, the Democrats would blame the Republicans, and we could watch the fight from afar."

Puchenko sighed his regret. "We should have done what China did. Develop a nanodevice."

The discussion about assassinating Strumler went on without any conclusion. Then the president said, "Let me think about this. I'll let you know what I want when I decide. I might just simply cast Strumler adrift, but right now I think he might become a serious irritant. Of course, if he does, there are more aggressive methods of dealing with him."

* * *

After her morning class, Ann walked to the Stanford University library with about four thousand calories of sugary snacks placed conveniently in her backpack. She found an empty carrel. She concentrated on Strumler's Bug-Lok and soon found her consciousness within the device. Once there, she examined the route to his handler and retrieved the records of what the handler heard and saw. She followed the route back to the handler through the internet. She saw a communication stream from Washington DC back to the Kremlin in Russia. The computer at the receiving end belonged to the SVR. The user ID of the person operating the computer was Nikolai Puchenko.

While her consciousness resided inside Puchenko's computer, she examined everything she found there. All the files, all the contact lists, even the MP3 files Puchenko listened to. She decided she hated his taste in music. She transferred copies of these new files to her own computer before leaving her Bug-Lok trance.

But she couldn't speak or read Russian, and Cassie had told her the old KGB leftovers still working Russia's upper echelons used their own terminology. She sent copies of these new files to Cassie and Jon. Both spoke Russian:

> Guys, I'm sending you both a set of files. MP3s of
> Russian conversations, and text files in Cyrillic. I hope
> you aren't busy.

She waited and wondered what their reaction would be. It took two days. Cassie sent her a copy of translated documents with a brief message:

Good work. Now get back to your studies. We'll take care of the rest.

Ann's eyes skimmed the translation. At times her eyes bulged with the audacity of Strumler's deeds.

She thought, *this will be a major shitstorm in the political world of Washington DC.*

She could see how it would play out: one way if she took no role in the events that she knew with certainty were about to happen, and another way if she got off her ass and changed the future she had clearly envisioned.

Ann packed a suitcase, grabbed it and her notebook computer, and took a taxi to SFO.

CHAPTER 42

**Lubyanka conference room,
Kremlin, Moscow, Russia**

November 18, 9:59 a.m.

Outside the Kremlin a hard autumn snowstorm fell from a sky that was an ominous deep shade of gray.

Nikolai Puchenko had thought of all the trouble he'd have driving home later. But he listened to his direct superior, the minister general of SVR activities, and his eyebrows rose as he listened. He thought, *did they get the Russian president's permission? Does he even know?* When the minister general finished speaking, Puchenko scanned the faces around the conference room table. "So, you planned Daniel Strumler's termination? If they can trace it back to Russia, they'll declare war on us."

The minister general simply nodded. "Puchenko, do as we just told you. Say nothing to Strumler. If the Americans find out, they would declare us national heroes." The man chuckled.

Puchenko nodded and rose. When he left the conference room, the snow was falling even harder.

* * *

Samuel Meyer sat at his desk in Herzliya and read through

the texts a second time. He'd never met Ann Sashakovich but he had met her mother Cassandra at Yigdal Ben-Levy's funeral. He thought, *she is even more talented than her mother.*

Meyer had been appointed to head the Mossad seven years ago, when Ben-Levy retired as the Mossad's director and was made Israel's UN ambassador. Meyer saw himself as a plodder, conservative and careful, compared to Ben-Levy's passionate but reckless leadership.

He thought, *can I believe what I'm reading? How did she backtrace the data trail into the SVR mainframe servers? I'm not sure it's possible. But Jon Sommers is very reliable, and he's the one who forwarded these reports to me.*

He reread the hack from Nikolai Puchenko's computer. Killing Daniel Strumler was an audacious move. Ben-Levy had assassinated a sitting US president and never been detected. The assassination Ben-Levy commanded was attributed by the Americans to an anaphylactic allergy to insect bites.

Meyer wasn't sure whether to help save the president-elect or let the Russians terminate him.

He sat in silence as a red fiery sunset came and went. *I can tell the Secret Service. Will they believe me?* He doubted it. Would they see the death of Strumler as an act of divine assistance? He wasn't sure what the Americans believed, and after all, they had elected him.

As the sky darkened, he decided that *exposing the traitor will work better for Israel. If the Americans don't believe the evidence I will send them, so be it.*

He decided to use the United Nations to send his message. First, he called Israel's prime minister to see if he could secure the backing he needed. "It's Meyer. Put Abba on the phone for me. I only need two minutes."

In just a few seconds he heard a gruff voice come on the line. "Cain?" *Yes*, in Hebrew.

Meyer answered in Hebrew. The prime minister had once been an IDF sniper. Before winning his first political victory, he'd recorded over thirty kills of Israel's enemies. The PM was known to be short tempered and rigorously right wing. "Samuel, what is the nature of your call. Is Israel in any new danger?"

"Ah, no, sir. But our foremost occasional ally is. We have uncovered a plot to assassinate the American president-elect. I'd like to expose this plot. We also have documentation that the president-elect is a traitor to his country. I'd also like to make this new information public."

"How are you proposing to do this?"

"The same way Ben-Levy did. It worked then and it could work now."

After a longer than normal silence, the PM said, "You want to send someone to the United Nations? Ben-Levy would have been prosecuted here in Israel if he had not been assassinated on the steps of the United Nations after his speech."

"I'm looking for your permission. Ben-Levy ignored your threat."

"You cannot use Israel's UN ambassador. We're on thin ice with the UN right now."

Meyer let the silence sit. He'd anticipated every word of the conversation so far. But this was where he needed to be careful. He spoke more slowly. "I'd like to send Avram Shimmel. He's been staff to the United Nations for almost two years and he has earned the respect of most member nations. Please appoint him 'temporary assistant ambassa-dor.' If you tell me now that you will, then I'll take responsibility for the outcome."

"Let me see if I understand. You want Shimmel to tell

the world that the Russians want to assassinate the president-elect of the United States, who you have evidence to prove is a traitor to the nation that elected him?"

"Almost. Try this: I want Shimmel to tell the world that the Russians have sent an assassination team to the United States to murder the president-elect of the United States, and that we have evidence to prove that the man the Americans elected is a Russian agent, and therefore a traitor to the nation that elected him."

Meyer waited through the silence that followed. Then the PM said, "Samuel, when Ben-Levy spoke at the United Nations, it was against my orders. But I was wrong and it ended up working. So, I'll let you try. But if this fails, you will resign your position as director of the Mossad. Are you willing to gamble your future?"

Meyer sighed. "Yes."

"Okay then. Go with God."

Samuel Meyer had a long record of hypertension. He'd been treated for this at the Ness Ziona Medical Center in Herzliya for several years. He thought his heart disease was a feature of his job. He took a few minutes to let his blood pressure fall back into the normal range. Then he tapped Avram Shimmel's phone number into his landline and waited for the phone to be answered.

"Shimmel."

"Avram, it's Sam Meyer. I have received permission from the prime minister to appoint you temporary assistant Israeli ambassador to the United Nations."

"You what? Why?"

"I want you to schedule an appearance at the General Assembly session now in progress. Schedule it for the earliest date available. Tomorrow would be best. I will send you the speech I want you to deliver. You will read it verbatim."

Shimmel had served within the Mossad eight years ago

as a covert operative. Meyer knew that Shimmel understood the Mossad had the right to restore any former operative to active duty whenever they wished. There was no right of appeal.

Meyer heard Shimmel cough. Meyer said, "You have no options."

"Are you sure you want me to deliver the speech and not our current ambassador?"

"This order, just as I read it to you, came from the PM, not me. I'll send you a package through the dip pouch tomorrow. It should be in your hands before dawn. You will do exactly as I just told you."

Meyer heard Shimmel sigh. "Yes, sir. Exactly as you have ordered."

Meyer terminated the call. Then he called his country desk manager for Israel's relations with the United States to his office. "Shmuel, I have a set of files I want you to encrypt. Use the dip pouch to deliver the file to our embassy in New York. I'll also send you another, much shorter document. Encrypt that also and address them both to Avram Shimmel, an overt of the Mossad."

Shmuel nodded. "I'll start as soon as the files hit my inbox."

* * *

When he arrived at the United Nations Secretariat building the next morning, Avram had an encoded message from Samuel Meyer waiting for him in his inbox. He followed the decryption process, running the message through a mask in his cellphone. Mossad communications were always overly encoded. The resulting text was a very short message:

Israeli Consulate, New York City. Retina encoded.

Avram took a taxi to the Israeli consulate at 800 Second Avenue and identified himself. The consulate was in an older skyscraper at 43rd Street, one block west of the United Nations. After passing through the security gate, he was met by a guard and admitted to a small room with gray metallic wall paint that prevented any tracking of electronic signals.

He sat in front of a monitor and placed his eyes near a tiny lens embedded in the screen. He stood motionless until he heard a "beep" and the screen displayed "Recipient Identified." The printer emitted three pages and a USB drive dropped from a reader/writer below the screen.

Avram placed the paper and the drive in his lead-foil-lined attaché case and walked back to the United Nations. He took the elevator to the twenty-ninth floor, which he shared with the United Nations General Assembly administration.

"Hello, Yi Shun. I've just been appointed to Israel's ambassadorial department to the United Nations."

Yi Shun, a tall and very thin woman from Taiwan, simply nodded. "You may regret this. But, congratulations."

Avram smiled and nodded. "My prime minister has asked me to schedule speaking time at the earliest possible available time to introduce myself. When, and how much time can you make available?"

She looked at the computer screen on her desk. "Tomorrow. A half hour, starting at two in the afternoon."

Avram said, "Thanks, Yi Shun."

Avram Shimmel walked to his own office and started practicing his speech.

* * *

Ann's flight to JFK landed and she called Avram before she even debarked. She was dumped into voicemail. *Damn!* "It's Ann Sashakovich. I think there's going to be an attempt on Daniel Strumler's life, probably tomorrow. I'm not exactly sure where it will take place, but I'd bet the farm it will be at the hotel where he's staying. I'm in New York now. We need to talk. Call me back."

New York City was where she was born. Brooklyn was where her mother, her brother, and she resided, at a very old, brick, six-story apartment at 6701 Colonial Road in Bay Ridge, Brooklyn. She was familiar with the city, but it destroyed her youth when her birth mother overdosed, her brother was strangled, and she was raped.

Ann hated New York City.

* * *

It was a bright, sunny afternoon when the Cessna aircraft with Russian tail markings taxied the runway to the private air terminal at Washington Dulles International Airport. When the aircraft came to a stop and the rolling staircase was placed against the aircraft, Victor Kreslin signaled to his team and they moved to the exit in formation.

There was an unmarked helicopter waiting to pick up the team at the private air terminal.

Victor Kreslin and his team debarked the aircraft and trotted to the helicopter. They boarded, ready for transport into Washington DC. Soon, the chopper hovered over the rooftop heliport at the Russian embassy.

Of the eight men under Kreslin's command, Kreslin believed he himself was the most highly skilled in the killing arts.

He sat in the helicopter's shotgun seat and waited for it to complete its touchdown on the roof. Kreslin signaled his second in command, Igor Nelovich, to gather the men and prepare to debark. Then he said, "Nelovich, see to the weapons and ammunition."

Igor nodded. The platoon entered the embassy through

the rooftop door and took the staircase in formation to the lobby.

They all found seats in the Dodge Caravan owned by the embassy. Nelovich loaded the two large crates of weapons and one carton of ammunition into the Caravan. Kreslin drove it from the embassy.

Nelovich said to Kreslin, "Our primary objective is to kill the man as quietly as we can. Our best intelligence, received just before we landed, is that he remains in his hotel suite on the top floor of the Strumler Tower on Constitution Avenue. We'll wait until night and use the darkness as camo."

Kreslin smiled and continued driving toward downtown.

CHAPTER 43

51st Floor, Strumler Tower Capital Hotel, Washington, DC

November 21, 2:09 p.m.

Daniel Strumler ate a toasted cheese sandwich overstuffed with heirloom tomatoes while he watched the afternoon news. A Fox News commentator said that the new Israeli ambassador to the United Nations was speaking about Strumler. During the presidential campaign, Strumler had told his supporters that he would rather develop jobs in America than ship arms to defend Israel.

He feared this speech might be a vehicle for Israel's payback.

He immediately changed the channel to watch the speech.

The man speaking dwarfed the two Israeli bodyguards at the edges of the stage. He was huge and his uniform couldn't hide his muscles. But, since when did a diplomat wear a military uniform? Strumler examined the man's face and decided that the man seemed too young to be a seasoned diplomat. *I wonder if their new ambassador is former Mossad?*

He turned up the volume.

"...for you today. First, I have urgent information concerning a set of messages Israel intercepted about a pending attempt to assassinate the president-elect of the United States. We discovered this intelligence threat while we were tracking Russian communications. As a result, I also have evidence to present. Convincing evidence. We have discovered that the reason why this assassination attempt is about to occur, is that the American president-elect is owned by the Russians and the Russians want to keep him from being arrested and tried as a traitor. Moving to the first of these items, here is the evidence..."

As Strumler watched the ambassador speak at the United Nations General Assembly, his fear and rage turned to acid in his throat. He grabbed his ever-present bottle of antacid tablets and ate them like candy.

The Israeli Ambassador continued his speech and Strumler rose and began throwing things around the room. Vases, lamps and even the remains of the toasted cheese sandwich and the plate it was delivered on—all went flying through the air.

Secret Service and Strumler's private bodyguards crashed through the door in response to the noise. "Sorry, sir," said one of the Secret Service agents. "We heard the speech. We thought it might be some threat."

"Leave me be!" Strumler's eyes were nearly popping out of his head.

* * *

Laura couldn't stop crying. She sat frozen in her seat in the international terminal at SFO after her flight from Paraguay landed.

She was still angry with herself for moving to Paraguay. She hated Frank Lucessi and Paraguay. But most of all, she now knew how dangerous she could be to others. Skorkin's body was proof of that. Frank's response of calling in a cleanup crew left her wanting to murder him. She had left him instead.

Only one person she knew had been able to deal with her without triggering a potentially violent response.

She had purchased a new cellphone at the airport. Now, she used it to called Ann. "It's Laura. I'm back at Stanford. Do you still need a roommate? Paraguay didn't work out. Anyway, call me back. Please. Call me back."

When she decided to return to Stanford, she had no firm direction on what her future would be. She knew it wouldn't include studying art.

* * *

After Ann reached the United Nations Secretariat Building, she waited for Avram to return her call.

She sat in the lobby of the tall building, her notebook computer on and plugged in, charging from a nearby wall outlet. Her notebook buzzed. She examined the screen and saw a backtrace she'd initiated while waiting for a taxi at JFK. The backtrace was covering all telephone calls made from Nikolai Puchenko's cellphone and his landline. Since her first download of messages from the Kremlin, Ann had downloaded and installed a Russian-to-English translator app onto her notebook. The backtrace had intercepted a new message from Puchenko's voicemail. She read the text:

> Puchenko, it's your boss. Your ultimate boss. I have decided to send a small assassination team to terminate the existence of your American puppy. Do not have any further contact with the man. The team should be arriving in Washington any time now. I decided not to tell you until after they arrived and were on the ground. Don't worry. I'll not punish you for your own failure.

Ann realized her vision of the events now in progress was incorrect. *Damn! I'm in the wrong city!* She exited the building and ran toward the street to flag a taxi.

On the sidewalk in front of her, she saw a throng of people surrounding a very tall man. It was Avram! She scooted through the people flinging questions at Avram. When she was face-to-face with him, Ann yelled "Avram!"

He stopped, and faced her. "Ann, what are you doing here?"

"I left you a voicemail. Didn't—"

"I was speaking before the General Assembly."

The throng of reporters remained silent, focusing on the exchange between the two.

"I'm on my way to Washington DC. Listen to the message. Decide how you want to handle the problem. I'm sure you'll do the right thing. And, don't worry, I'll tell Cassie and Lee." She backed away and headed to the curbside. She flagged down a taxi and bounced into the back seat. "JFK, any domestic terminal."

The cab rocketed up First Avenue toward the 59th Street Bridge.

While the taxi driver drove Ann down the Brooklyn–Queens Expressway, she called her parents. Cassie picked up the line. "It's Ann. I'm headed toward JFK to take a flight to Washington DC. You guys all need to be in DC. There's a Russian assassination team on their way to Strumler's hotel to kill him. We need to save him so he can be tried for treason. Get yourselves from the United Nations to Strumler's hotel in DC. Call me back when you're en route."

She could see the terminals of JFK flashing by outside the cab's windows. She packed away her phone and notebook. When the cab stopped, she tossed a Franklin to the driver and bolted from the cab.

Inside the terminal. Ann approached a check-in desk

and waited her turn in line. "Hi. I just received word that my mama had a heart attack. I have to get to Washington DC as soon as I can. Please sell me a ticket on the next available flight."

She offered her credit card, grabbed the boarding pass, and headed to the TSA precheck security gate.

As she passed through security and trotted toward the departure gate, her cell buzzed. Ann stopped and pulled her cell from her pocket. She examined the screen while she ran. "Mom! Where are you and dad?"

"We're in New York. We got your message. We also got a message from Avram. We'll be meeting up at the private air terminal at JFK. He was able to muster fifty of the two hundred paramilitary he commands in New York at the United Nations. We also have Jon with us. Avram has a Cessna about to take off. Look, Ann, I'm not comfortable with you engaging in a military operation. Go home to Stanford and your studies."

"No way, Mñom. I'm the best hacker you have available and I can help by telling you where the assassins are located in real time. Remember, I can hack them without a computer. Remember the Bug-Loks the CypherGhost fed me? So use me! I promise I'll stay out of the line of fire."

"Ann, no. Avram called the Secret Service and they're coordinating the op together. You aren't needed. Let the professionals handle this."

Ann thought about her vision of pending events. It had reformed, revised to accommodate the new set of facts that had emerged. She was sure this new ability would stay with her. "If I'm close enough, I think I may be able to envision their conversations. Don't know how it happened, but I'll know where the assassins are. You need me."

She heard Cassie and Lee talking softly in the background. "Okay. But you'll take orders from Lee and me. You agree?"

Ann smiled. "Yes!"

"We'll meet you inside the Strumler Tower's lobby."

She had become a member of the paramilitary team.

* * *

After Ann's flight landed, she took a taxi to the Strumler Tower. Avram deployed Cassie, Lee, Avram, and two hundred mercenaries from the UN Paramilitary Force into strategic locations within the building.

Cassie ordered Ann to sit in the stairwell on the 49th floor, out of harm's way.

Ann found no further trace of the assassination team. It made sense that the team would go dark before their op, so she was sure they had already assumed their positions within the hotel.

She constantly monitored the security feeds throughout the hotel from her position two floors below Strumler's suite on the fifty-first floor. Half of Avram's paramilitary force was scattered through the hotel's fire stairways. The other half were hidden within the four stairwells leading up to Strumler's suite. Jon was with them. Cassie and Lee were at Avram's command station in the hotel's delivery platform behind the lobby.

Now, all they could do now was wait.

* * *

Five hours ago, Victor Kreslin and his team arrived at Strumler Tower. The team had purchased a pizza from a stand nearby. One of his team mugged a pizza delivery worker and stole his hat and a pizza in a box. The team walked twenty floors up the staircase and the "pizza delivery man" knocked on a door in one of the hotel suites. When its occupant said he hadn't ordered any pizza, the "delivery man" told the occupant, "Might be a mistake but the pizza is getting cold. You might as well accept the delivery."

The occupant opened the door.

Kreslin's team murdered the occupant and the occupant's companion, who both appeared to be tourists.

Kreslin and Igor Nelovich reviewed the plan as they waited for the cover of nightfall.

* * *

Kreslin stood by the window, watching the sun descend. "Use the restroom and eat a snack. Once we leave this room, we can expect things may have changed since we constructed our battle plan. So, be prepared to adjust."

The other seven Russians nodded, then lined up to use the room's single bathroom.

* * *

Ann's notebook computer buzzed. She examined the screen and sent a text out. All her texts were addressed to Cassie, Lee, Avram, and Jon Sommers:

> Russians moving up the southwest stairwell. Now on forty-one.

Now she had a fix on where they were. She watched them climb the stairs and texted a revision:

> They're still heading up the staircase. Now at forty-fourth floor. Eight in total. One with a Dragunov sniper rifle. Others armed with semiautomatic handguns.

Although she'd agreed to stay out of combat, Ann's feet moved her, unbidden, to the hallway outside the southwest stairwell on the fiftieth floor. She sought cover at a spot where the hallway turned a corner.

She continued monitoring the security cams. She could hear shots now. At first, single shots with seconds between each report. Then the shots were more continuous and louder. The Russians were getting closer to her position.

She heard the stairwell door closest to her spring open. She backed away, down the hall, fear chilling her.

Ann heard running footsteps coming in her direction. Turning the corner of the hallway and trotting toward her, she saw an armed man wearing a mask and holding a hand-gun. He stood in front of her, aiming the pistol.

She was frozen where she stood.

Ann was unarmed. But she could use her ability to shoot fire from her fingers to save her. She could see he was still too far away for a dead-on headshot at her. Unfortunately for Ann, she was too far away for her own magic to work.

She placed her notebook computer on the floor and concentrated on her fingers. But her fingertips were blue. She frowned and placed her hands in front of her while she waited for the armed man to close the distance.

When he was less than forty feet away and still running toward her, she thought, *FIRE!* But, she could only smell her fear. Nothing happened.

The Russian took aim. A headshot. She was less than ten feet away. There was no way he could miss. She thought, *I should have listened to Cassie*. Ann closed her eyes. She couldn't face her own death.

But then she heard the stairwell door open again. She opened her eyes and saw Jon running toward her. The Russian reacted to the footsteps approaching him from behind. He whirled around and took aim at Jon.

Her fear converted fast into rage at the Russian. Her fingertips turned from blue to a glowing orange. She aimed her hands at the back of the Russian's head and once again thought, *FIRE!*

A bolt of fire streamed from her fingertips and the Russian's head exploded. Pieces of his skull and brains clung to the hallway walls and floor.

Jon Sommers stood above the Russian, holding his own 9mm Beretta. No smoke wafted from its barrel. He looked at the headless dead body, and then at Ann.

Jon shook his head with disbelief. "Hello, Ann. Neat trick. Are you unharmed?"

She was still in shock and couldn't speak. She took inventory. No wounds anywhere on her body. She nodded and smiled.

When she could once again speak, she said, "What now?"

"Your trick. It's our little secret. For me, it's back into the stairwell. There may still be hostiles at work. For you, stay hidden. I promise I'll return soon." Jon headed back the way he'd come.

Ann continued to monitor the action from her notebook. She heard the shots diminish in frequency until there were none. Cassie's voice said, "We're done. Let's make sure Strumler is alive."

Ann took the elevator to the lobby. As she emerged, she saw a group of men wearing FBI jackets enter the same elevator she'd exited.

Ann sat in one of the plush armchairs in the lobby and waited for the inevitable. Her body began to shake more and more violently. She reached into her backpack and pulled a bag of sour gummies from it. After eating the entire bag's contents, the shaking began to subside.

She was beginning to feel normal again when the elevator doors opened again. The FBI agents emerged from the elevator leading Strumler in handcuffs. The president-elect was screaming, "I'll sue you for this! I'll sue you all!"

It was all over. She shook herself to loosen her cramping legs and arms.

CHAPTER 44

**Stanford University Student Union,
Palo Alto, CA**

November 24, 2:09 p.m.

Ann was back at the Stanford campus, looking at the grades posted in the Student Union lobby. She grinned when she discovered she had aced her midterm on computer forensics. After attending her afternoon classes, she walked back to her apartment and passed a newsstand.

The headline on one of the newspapers stated, "Strumler Arrested for Treason." She decided to read the news online when she had reached her apartment.

When she unlocked the door, she heard someone humming in her kitchen. The familiar voice belonged to Laura Hunter. "Hi, Ann. Did you get my message?"

"Ah, no, Laura. I just returned from a trip back east. What's in your message?"

"Me. Paraguay didn't work out. I'm back, attending Stanford. Do you need a roommate?"

Ann smiled. "Sure."

She turned on the television and watched the story of the FBI arresting Daniel Strumler. She thought, *it's even better on-screen in color than it was when I was there.*

Laura cooked them dinner. While Laura was busy, Ann

called Cassie. Her mother was still angry with Ann for viola-
ting the promise she'd made to stay out of harm's way.
"Mom. I'm sorry. I know it was irresponsible of me. I promise
I'll never disappoint you like that again."

"Crap, Ann. How can I trust you?"

"Yeah. Well, I thought I was in a safe place. I was wrong."

"Okay. Did you get your midterm grades?"

"Yeah. I did fine. And Laura's back. So it's pretty much
back to normal."

"I like normal." She heard Cassie laugh.

Ann smiled. Her mom had already let her anger go.

* * *

Robert Randall knocked on Smythe's door. The ass dire shout-
ed, "Come," and Randall entered but remained standing. He
removed an envelope from his jacket pocket and handed it to
Smythe. "What's this?"

Randall said, "It's my resignation."

"Why?"

"Please, sir. Just accept it and let me be on my way to
something not involved with international intelligence."

Smythe remained silent, thinking. "Are you sure?"

Randall nodded.

"Right, then. I accept your resignation." Smythe sighed.
"We'll miss you." He rose and extended his hand.

Randall shook hands with Smythe, then returned to his
desk. In two weeks, he would be a rich man, retired and free.
The millions in cash from his sale of the off-the-books InTelQ
project waited in his offshore account.

* * *

Avram Shimmel and Jon Sommers sat in the conference
room on the twenty-ninth floor of the UN Secretariat Building. Bright sunshine drenched the room.

Avram handed Jon a small stack of papers. "I have received approval from Israel's prime minister. The termination is approved. Our collections department located your target. Bring a bathing suit with you. Oh, and we've sent you the package of accessories to your hotel via FedEx."

Jon opened and read the first page in the stack. "It's rare that a termination is approved. In fact, I've only done one before."

"Yah. This is retribution for the deaths of our covert operatives in Sunnyvale. Make sure he knows why he's being terminated before you complete the assignment. No one should die this way without knowing why."

Jon nodded, rose, and exited the conference room. He grabbed his Burberry and fedora and took the elevator to the immense lobby. He stepped outside, with over one hundred national flags flapping overhead. He flagged a cab and bounced inside. "To JFK, international terminal, Air Jamaica."

The cabby nodded and sped up First Avenue toward the 59th Street Bridge.

* * *

Robert Randall sat in a cabaña by the shoreline. He held a piña colada in his right hand and the day's newspaper in his left. The paper's headline stated, "President-Elect Was Russian Mole." The line under the headline elaborated: "Strumler Operated Assassination Program Murdering America's Brightest Entrepreneurs."

He chuckled and sipped his drink. The tent shielded him from the sun while its open side left him with a view of the ocean, but it obscured his view of the elegant hotel behind him.

He watched the ocean waves beating against the shore. *I'm free and I'm rich. Nothing could be better.*

He felt a pinch in his neck. Probably a mosquito. He

swatted at his neck and a small dart popped from his neck onto his lap.

He suddenly felt groggy. A well-built man in a bathing suit appeared in front of the cabaña. The stranger held a neatly folded towel in his hand and Randall noticed the handgun hidden under it.

The stranger smiled at him. "So sorry. Mr. Randall, I'm Jon Sommers. I work for the United Nations but I once worked for the Mossad. I was a *kidon*. An assassin. The small dart I shot you with has a nearly undetectable poison developed by the Ness Ziona in Tel Aviv. You will die slowly, in terrible pain, and you will be paralyzed until you are dead. The reason why I've been ordered to end you is because your cleaner murdered two of our operatives in Sunnyvale. Your orders. I'm just returning the courtesy. Oh, and I recently was informed that your cleaner, Alan Skorkin, was himself cleaned. I have to leave now. Enjoy your day." Randall watched the man turn and walk away.

Randall felt a numbing in his fingers and his toes. The numbness was spreading toward his torso. Within seconds the numbness turned into a flaming sensation of pain in his joints. He tried to scream but he couldn't make a sound. His vision began to stipple and he felt as if his eyeballs would explode. Breathing became difficult and his lungs felt like they were burning.

Randall watched the afternoon fade to sundown before he breathed his last.

* * *

The table separating Strumler from his attorney was small. It was bolted to the floor, and Strumler's cuffs were bolted and locked into the table's gray metal top. There were armed guards standing at the doorway, watching everything said and every movement.

The lawyer said, "Sir, I recommend you accept the deal. It expires in an hour."

"Fuck the deal. What's the worst they can do? I'm still president!"

"No, sir, you aren't. As I've already told you twice before, Congress has impeached you even though you haven't taken office. While I'm not sure if this is legal, today's headlines are that Congress is about to void your election and declare a special election in six months. And, I'm not sure if that's legal either. But in any case, you are no longer the president-elect, and you have been charged with treason.

Strumler appeared to be confused. "What?"

The attorney shrugged. "Okay. Do you want to accept the deal? Please. If you're convicted of treason, the penalty could be a firing squad."

"That's funny." Strumler chuckled. "I'd truly be fired." His laughter was explosive.

The attorney rose from the meeting table and beckoned to the guards. "Okay, then. I'm done. Get me out of here."

* * *

Avram Shimmel was once again back at work at the United Nations. He made himself comfortable in his overstuffed office chair as he admired the view from his office window. The East River sat twenty-nine floors beneath him, the streets due east of him filled with skyscrapers. It was an unseasonably warm day and he saw pedestrians wearing light jackets as they walked the sidewalks below.

His phone buzzed. "Shimmel here."

"It's Meyer. Our UN ambassador has resigned. She was unhappy that you delivered a speech she had wanted to make, and she decided to run for a seat in the Knesset. We are currently without a United Nations ambassador. The PM suggested you."

"Me? I'm not a diplomat!"

"Yes. Are you deaf?"

"But who will run the UN Paramilitary Force?"

"That's a problem for you to solve. What's your answer?"

Avram knew that there was no way he could deny a command assigned to him by the Israeli PM. He sighed. "I accept."

"Good. You will be stationed at the Israeli embassy in New York. Report there as soon as you can." Meyer terminated the call.

Jon's office was adjacent to Avram's, albeit somewhat smaller. He was also admiring the view when his landline rang. "Sommers."

"Jon, drop by my office as soon as you have a moment."

Jon recognized Avram's thick Israeli accent. "On my way now."

He walked in, smiling, and took a seat. "What's up?"

"I've been asked by Israel's PM to accept the position of Israeli ambassador to the United Nations."

"Wow. Congrats, big guy. That's quite a coup."

"Maybe, maybe, but it leaves me with a problem. I have to replace myself. Do you have any preference as to who becomes your next boss?"

Jon's face showed surprise and confusion. "I've not had any time to digest this."

"Well, if there is no one you'd prefer for your next boss, then I guess I'll just have to appoint you. Congratulations, you are now director of the UN Paramilitary Force."

Avram saw Jon's eyes bulge. It was all Avram could do to keep a grin off his face. But within a second, he could no longer help himself. His own smile beamed back at his friend.

Jon shrugged. "You sure about this? I've never commanded anything larger than an operations team. Five at most."

Avram nodded. "Congrats. You're it. I have to leave now and start preparations to move my office to the embassy. Good luck, my friend."

Avram rose, shook Jon's hand and started walking from his—now former—office.

Jon turned and faced Avram's receding form. "Wait. What's my job description?"

Avram stopped, turned, and faced Jon. "You'll figure it out, just as I did."

An hour passed, with Jon unable to move from his seat across from Avram's desk. No. Now it was Jon's desk.

He rose and reseated himself in his new chair. He was too short for its current setting. Jon adjusted the seat until he was finally comfortable. He opened the desk drawers and pulled all the folders from it. It took him through the day and long into the evening to read through them, open the computer's file directory and take inventory of the contents.

He sent a text message to Ann.

As the sun set and the night stars shone over Manhattan, Jon Sommers smiled and thought to himself, *I wonder if this will turn out to be a blessing or a curse.*

* * *

Ann's cell buzzed as she entered her computer audit procedures class. She read the text and smiled:

Ann—Thanks for saving my life. Don't worry about
your secret. I expect we'll work together again, soon
and often. —Jon.

Ann thought, *yes, Jon. Now you owe me one and I owe you one.*

Glossary A.
Terms Used in the *Spies Lie* Series

AFI. Intelligence branch of the Israeli Air Force.

air-gapped. A computer with no external connections to WiFi or CAT5e connections is referred to as "air-gapped."

aleph. Lead *kidon*, the assassin leading an execution mission for the Mossad.

Aman. Intelligence branch of the IDF (Israeli Military Intelligence).

asset. A civilian in a foreign country who claims to have valuable contacts or information useful to a case officer. The primary objective of most case officers is to develop in-country assets.

ayin. Tracker (surveillance) for the Mossad.

backstopping. Fake identification papers.

bat leveyha. Female agent for the Mossad.

better world, send to a. Euphemism for murdering an enemy agent.

blind dating. Meeting place chosen by an agent to meet his or her handler.

bodel. Courier for the Mossad.

BP. Israeli paramilitary Border Patrol.

Bug-Lok. Also called DeathByte, the device is a nanobug that can be ingested or injected into a subject. Bug-Lok was developed by the Ness Ziona in Herzliya on contract with Gilbert Greenfield's intelligence service. When ingested or injected, the nanobug then finds its way to the medulla oblongata of the subject and attaches itself to the neural bundles that carry visual and auditory signals into the subject's brain. The nanobug transmits these signals to the nearest local area network (LAN) and from there to the handler, who gathers video and audio of the subject's activities, in addition to the subject's GPS location. Bug-Lok can be fitted with a tiny concentrated ricin dose to kill the subject, activated by a remote when the handler no longer needs the subject. NOTE: When I first crafted the features and functions of this device, it was pure fiction, but was based on several devices then in development. I have recently been told that a device similar to this has since been specified and may have completed its development.

burn notice. A termination notice for an official operative or an NOC; the burned spy has his or her bank accounts confiscated and identity documents redacted, and, in extreme cases, is subject to a terminate-on-sight order.

C-6. A more powerful and concentrated form of the C-4 explosive.

Chinese Secret Intelligence Services (CSIS). Chinese Secret Intelligence Service. The Chinese version of the FBI and one of the Chinese government's many espionage and technical research organizations.

CHIPS. The Clearing House Interbank Payments System, used by money-center banks to settle all outstanding transactions between them at the end of their day.

Collections Department. Intelligence Department abroad.

cutout. An intermediary, usually an innocent person, either a volunteer or paid by a covert operative to deliver or retrieve something valuable such as a message or a gadget, from a covert operative or an asset.

DARPA (Defense Advanced Research Projects Agency). Defense Department's agency for advanced research projects, charged with development of weapons systems.

daylight alert. Highest-priority alert.

DDOS (Distributed Denial of Service). A brute-force method of bringing down a website, by overloading it with traffic. Rarely used successfully by any except the most desperate and skillful of hackers.

dry cleaning. Countersurveillance techniques.

ECHELON. An identity-tracking system developed by contract programmers and used by the United States as its primary terrorism-prevention system prior to 9/11. There are currently in excess of forty systems developed since 9/11, used by the NSA to track the identities of US citizens and foreigners.

EFT (Electronic Funds Transfer). The basic term denoting a non-check payment.

EMP (Electromagnetic pulse). A high-energy discharge that fries all electronic devices within its range.

exfiltrate. To retrieve an agent from hostile territory.

false flagging. An operation falsely made to appear mounted by another country.

Farm, The. A camp in Virginia used to train CIA case officers and the case officers of intelligence services friendly to the United States.

Fifth Estate. A sociocultural reference to groupings of outlier viewpoints in contemporary society, and is most often associated with bloggers, journalists publishing in non-mainstream media outlets, and the social media. (WikiPedia)

FISA (Foreign Intelligence Surveillance Act). The Foreign Intelligence Surveillance Court (FISC, also called the FISA Court) was established and authorized under the Foreign Intelligence Surveillance Act (FISA) of 1978 to oversee requests for surveillance warrants against suspected foreign intelligence agents inside the United States by federal law enforcement agencies.

Five Eyes. The intelligence alliance of the United States, United Kingdom, Canada, Australia, and New Zealand.

FSB. The Russian internal security and counterintelligence service, created in 1994 as one of the successor agencies of the Soviet-era KGB.

fumigate. Sweeping an area for electronic bugs.

GNU Radio. Developed by Eric Blossom, it is a free and open-source software development toolkit that provides signal-processing blocks to implement software radios. It can be used with readily available low-cost external radio-frequency hardware to create software-defined radios, or without hardware in a simulation-like environment. Prior to his involvement with software radio, Blossom was the cofounder and CTO of Starium, Ltd., where he oversaw the design and development of a line of cryptographic equipment for the commercial marketplace. He is also the founder of an international consulting company called Blossom Research.

go bag. A lightweight luggage carrier used by covert operatives to carry travel essentials, including emergency clothing, sundries, and weapons and ammunition. When not being used, it is typically stored, fully loaded, near a door or under a window for fast access.

heth. Logistician for the Mossad.

honey trap. Sexual entrapment for intelligence purposes.

IDF. Israel Defense Forces; the Israeli army.

InTelQ. CIA's wholly owned venture capital firm.

katsa. Case officer for the Mossad.

KGB. The Soviet Union's secret police, the Komitet Gosudarstvennoy Bezopasnosti was established in March 1954 in Moscow and was attached to the Council of Ministers, but operated independently. With over 500,000 employees, it was the largest spy agency in the world.

kidon. Operative specializing in assassination for the Mossad. (plural: *kidonim*.)

Krav Maga. Martial art developed by Aman, the Israeli military intelligence directorate, and used by IDF and Mossad. Now taught to many of the global spy agencies.

Liquid armor, or shear thickening fluid (STF). Developed by the US Army in 2003, STF can stop a .38-

caliber bullet, but improved versions can stop anything up to a .50-caliber shell.

MI-6. Also known as Great Britain's Secret Intelligence Service.

Mossad. The Institute for Intelligence and Special Operations; originally called the Institute for Coordination; called "the Office" by those who work there.

Ness Ziona. Israeli weapons laboratory, located in Herzliya, Israel.

neviot. Surveillance specialist for the Mossad.

NI. Intelligence branch of the Israeli navy.

NOC (non-official cover). The status of a contractor working with the CIA in-country and without sanction or cover from the Agency.

NSA (National Security Agency). Formed under the Truman administration and used as the technology management arm of the United States government.

Office, The. The name of the Mossad used by most of its case officers (*katsas*).

qoph. Communications officer for the Mossad.

RAID (redundant array of independent disks). Used as a physical non-cloud device for backup of high-value data.

RSA. An encryption algorithm, or key, used to safely send messages between parties on the Internet.

S-13 Russian World War II Submarine. S-13 was a Stalinets-class submarine of the Soviet Navy. Her keel was laid down by Krasnoye Sormovo in Gorky on 19

October 1938. She was launched on 25 April 1939 and commissioned on 31 July 1941 in the Baltic Fleet, under the command of Captain Pavel Malantyenko. At about 840 tons, this sub carries 12 torpedoes and 6 torpedo tubes, and has a mounted 100mm machine gun and a 45mm cannon on its deck. S-13 was decommissioned on 7 September 1954. (Wikipedia.)

S-56 Russian World War II Submarine. S-56 was a Stalinets-class submarine of the Soviet Navy. Her keel was laid down by Dalzavod in Vladivostok on 24 November 1936. She was launched on 25 December 1939 and commissioned on 20 October 1941 in the Pacific Fleet. During World War II, the submarine was under the command of Captain Grigori Shchedrin and was moved from the Pacific Fleet to the Northern fleet across the Pacific and Atlantic Oceans via the Panama Canal. At about 840 tons, this sub carries 12 torpedoes and 6 torpedo tubes, and has a mounted 100mm machine gun and a 45mm cannon on its deck. Now decommissioned. (Wikipedia.)

safe house. Apartment or house used covertly for a base of operations.

sayan. A helper for the Mossad. (plural: *sayanim*.)

Shabak. Also known as GSS or Shin Bet; the Israeli agency responsible for internal security and defense of Israeli installations abroad, including embassies, consulates, and other organizations.

siloviki. Russian word (the term *silovik*, literally translates as "person of force") for politicians from the security or military services, often the officers of the former KGB, GRU, FSB, SVR, the Federal Drug Control, or other security services who came into power. It can also refer to security-service personnel. *Siloviki* are used to run errands between the Russian mafiya and the Russian government. Some work for the Russian mafiya.

sitrep. Situation report.

slick. Hiding place for documents.

souk. A Middle Eastern marketplace, usually an open-air farmer's market that also sells craft items.

surveillance detection route. A method used by covert agents, walking back and forth several city blocks, looking at reflective surfaces to discern if they are being followed.

SWIFT (Society for Worldwide Interbank Financial Telecommunication). A European agency that sets standards for global financial messages used by banks for near-real-time settlement of electronic funds transfers. The transaction types (debit memo, credit memo, etc.) have numbers to identify them; for example, MT100 is a credit memo sent by one bank to another to indicate payment via real-time book entry.

systema. Martial art used primarily in Russian military and covert operations.

Tze'elim. Israel's Urban Warfare Training Center in the Negev Desert.

Va'adet Rashei Hasherutim. The committee of the heads of service in Israel's intelligence community. Mossad is a prime member.

virus (computer). A piece of code that is capable of copying itself and typically has a detrimental effect, such as corrupting the system or destroying data.

Vory. Russian criminal brotherhood, compatriots.

Wahhabi. Puritan doctrine of Islam, founded by Muhammad ibn Abd al-Wahhab (1703–1792) in Saudi Arabia.

wash. Recycling of a valid passport obtained by theft or purchase.

worm (computer). A standalone malware computer program that replicates itself in order to spread to other computers. Often, it uses a computer network to spread itself, relying on security failures on the target computer to access it. Unlike a computer virus, it does not need to attach itself to an existing program.

yahalom. A covert computer hacker, or cybercriminal working for the Mossad's Yahalomim unit.

zombie patriot. A person with a terminal disease who decides to sacrifice his or her life to earn money that might benefit surviving loved ones.

Glossary B.
Terms Related Specifically to Hacking

(From Motherboard)

Attribution. The process of establishing who is behind a hack. Often, attribution is the most difficult part of responding to a major breach since experienced hackers may hide behind layers of online services that mask their true location and identity. Many incidents, such as the Sony hack, may never produce any satisfactory attribution.

Backdoor. Entering a protected system using a password can be described as going through the front door. Companies may build "backdoors" into their systems, however, so that developers can bypass authentication and dive right into the program. Backdoors are usually secret, but may be exploited by hackers if they are revealed or discovered.

Black hat. A black-hat hacker is someone who hacks for personal gain and/or who engages in illicit and unsanctioned activities. As opposed to white-hack hackers (see below), who traditionally hack in order to alert companies and improve services, black-hat hackers may instead sell the weaknesses they discover to other hackers or use them.

Botnet. Is your computer part of a botnet? It could be, and you might not know it. Botnets, or zombie armies, are networks of computers controlled by an attacker. Having control over hundreds or thousands of computers lets bad actors perform certain types of cyberattacks, such as a DDoS (see below). Buying thousands of computers wouldn't be economical, however, so hackers deploy malware to infect random computers that are connected to the internet. If your computer gets infected, your machine might be stealthily performing a hacker's bidding in the background without your ever noticing.

Brute force. A brute force attack is arguably the least sophisticated way of breaking into a password-protected system, short of simply obtaining the password itself. A brute force attack will usually consist of an automated process of trial-and-error to guess the correct passphrase. Most modern encryption systems use different methods for slowing down brute force attacks, making it hard or impossible to try all combinations in a reasonable amount of time.

Bug. A bug is a flaw or error in a software program. Some are harmless or merely annoying, but some can be exploited by hackers. That's why many companies have started using bug bounty programs to pay anyone who spots a bug before the bad guys do.

Chip-off. A chip-off attack requires the hacker to physically remove memory storage chips in a device so that information can be scraped from them using specialized software. This attack has been used by law enforcement to break into PGP-protected Blackberry phones.

Cracking. A general term to describe breaking into a security system, usually for nefarious purposes.

According to the *New Hacker's Dictionary* published by MIT Press, the words "hacking" and "hacker" (see below) in mainstream parlance have come to subsume the words "cracking" and "cracker," and that's misleading. Hackers are tinkerers; they're not necessarily bad guys. Crackers are malicious. At the same time, you'll see cracking used to refer to breaking, say, digital copyright protections—which many people feel is a just and worthy cause—and in other contexts, such as penetration testing (see below), without the negative connotation.

Crypto. Short for cryptography, the science of secret communication or the procedures and processes for hiding data and messages with encryption (see below).

Dark Web. The Dark Web is made up of sites that are not indexed by Google and are only accessible through specialty networks such as Tor (see below). Often, the Dark Web is used by website operators who want to remain anonymous. Everything on the Dark Web is on the Deep Web, but not everything on the Deep Web is on the Dark Web.

DDoS (Distributed Denial of Service). This type of cyberattack has become popular in recent years because it's relatively easy to execute and its effects are obvious immediately. A DDoS attack means an attacker is using a number of computers to flood the target with data or requests for data. This causes the target—usually a website—to slow down or become unavailable. Attackers may also use the simpler Denial of Service (DoS) attack, which is launched from one computer.

Deep Web. This term and "Dark Web" or "Dark Net" are sometimes used interchangeably, though they shouldn't be. The Deep Web is the part of the internet that is not indexed by search engines. That includes password-protected pages, paywalled sites, encrypted networks, and databases—lots of boring stuff.

DEF CON. One of the most famous hacking conferences in the US and the world, which started in 1992 and takes place every summer in Las Vegas.

Digital Certificate. A digital passport or stamp of approval that proves the identity of a person, website, or service on the internet. In more technical terms, a digital certificate proves that someone is in possession of a certain cryptographic key that, traditionally, can't be forged. Some of the most common digital certificates are those of websites, which ensure your connection to them is properly encrypted. These get displayed on your browser as a green padlock.

Encryption. The process of scrambling data or messages to make them unreadable and secret. The opposite is decryption, the decoding of the message. Both encryption and decryption are functions of cryptography. Encryption is used by individuals as well as corporations and in digital security for consumer products.

End-to-end encryption. A particular type of encryption in which a message or data gets scrambled or encrypted on one end—for example, at your computer or phone—and gets decrypted on the other end—such as at someone else's computer. The data are scrambled in a way that, at least in theory, only the sender and receiver —and no one else—can read it.

Evil maid attack. As the name probably suggests, an evil maid attack is a hack that requires physical access to a computer—the kind of access an evil maid might have while tidying his or her employer's office, for example. By having physical access, a hacker can install software to track your use and gain a doorway even to encrypted information.

Exploit. An exploit is a way or process to take advantage of a bug or vulnerability in a computer or application. Not all bugs lead to exploits. Think of it this way: If your door was faulty, it could be simply that it makes a weird sound when you open it, or that its lock can be picked. Both are flaws but only one can help a burglar get in. The way the criminal picks the lock would be the exploit.

Forensics. On CSI, forensic investigations involve a series of methodical steps in order to establish what happened during a crime. When it comes to a hack, however, investigators are looking for digital fingerprints instead of physical ones. This process usually involves trying to retrieve messages or other information from a device—perhaps a phone, a desktop computer, or a server—used, or abused, by a suspected criminal.

GCHQ. The UK's equivalent of the US National Security Agency. GCHQ, or Government Communications Headquarters, focuses on foreign intelligence, especially around terrorism threats and cybersecurity. It also investigates the digital child pornography trade. "As these adversaries work in secret, so too must GCHQ," the organization says on its website. "We cannot reveal publicly everything that we do, but we remain fully accountable."

Hacker. This term has become—wrongly—synonymous

with someone who breaks into systems or hacks things illegally. Originally, hackers were simply tinkerers, or people who enjoyed "exploring the details of programmable systems and how to stretch their capabilities," as the MIT *New Hacker's Dictionary* puts it. Hackers can now be used to refer to both the good guys, also known as white-hat hackers, who play and tinker with systems with no malicious intent (and actually often with the intent of finding flaws so they can be fixed), and cybercriminals, or black-hat hackers, or "crackers."

Hacktivist. A hacktivist uses his or her hacking skills for political ends. A hacktivist's actions may be small, such as defacing the public website of a security agency or other government department, or large, such as stealing sensitive government information and distributing it to citizens. One often-cited example of a hacktivist group is Anonymous.

Hashing. Say you have a piece of text that should remain secret, like a password. You could store the text in a secret folder on your machine, but if anyone gained access to it you'd be in trouble. To keep the password a secret, you could also "hash" it with a program that executes a function resulting in garbled text representing the original information. This abstract representation is called a hash. Companies may store passwords or facial recognition data with hashes to improve their security.

HTTPS/SSL/TLS. Stands for "Hypertext Transfer Protocol," with the "S" for "Secure." The Hypertext Transfer Protocol (HTTP) is the basic framework that controls how data is transferred across the web, while

HTTPS adds a layer of encryption that protects your connection to the most important sites in your daily browsing—your bank, your email provider, and social networks. HTTPS uses the protocols SSL and TLS not only to protect your connection but also to prove the identity of the site, so that when you type "https://gmail.com" you can be confident you're really connecting to Google and not an imposter site.

Infosec. An abbreviation of "Information Security." It's the inside baseball term for what's more commonly known as cybersecurity, a term that irks most people who prefer infosec.

Jailbreak. Circumventing the security of a device, like an iPhone or a PlayStation, to remove a manufacturer's restrictions, generally with the goal to make it run software from non-official sources.

Keys. Modern cryptography uses digital "keys." In the case of PGP encryption, a public key is used to encrypt, or "lock," messages and a secret key is used to decrypt, or "unlock," them. In other systems, there may be only one secret key that is shared by all parties. In either case, if an attacker gains control of the key that does the unlocking, they may have a good chance at gaining access to the contents of the message.

Local area network (LAN). A network of computing devices arranged to facilitate communications among the devices and with external-to-the-network devices.

Lulz. An internet-speak variation on "lol" (short for "laughing out loud") employed regularly among the black-hat hacker set, typically to justify a hack or leak done at the expense of another person or entity. Sample use: *y did i leak all contracts and employee info linked to Sketchy Company X? for the lulz*

MAC (Medium Access Control). An algorithm for identification of a wireless network. When used in reference to hardware (computers), it is the identifier of a specific computer used in telecommunications. MAC provides encryption possibilities and deals with channel contention by using control packets with RTS (Request To Send) and CTS (Clear To Send) designators.

Malware. Stands for "malicious software." It simply refers to any kind of a malicious program or software, designed to damage or hack its target. Viruses, worms, Trojan horses, ransomware, spyware, adware, and more are malware.

Man-in-the-middle. A man-in-the-middle, or MitM, is a common attack in which someone surreptitiously puts themselves between two parties, impersonating them. This allows the malicious attacker to intercept and potentially alter their communication. With this type of attack, one can just passively listen in, relaying messages and data between the two parties, or even alter and manipulate the data flow.

Metadata. Metadata is simply data about data. If you were to send an email, for example, the text you type to your friend will be the content of the message, but the address you used to send it, the address you sent it to, and the time you sent it would all be metadata. This may sound innocuous, but with enough sources of metadata—for example, geolocation information from a photo posted to social media—it can be easy to piece together someone's identity or location.

NIST. The National Institute of Standards and Technology is an arm of the US Department of Commerce dedicated to science and metrics that support industrial innovation. NIST is responsible for developing information security standards for use by the federal government, and therefore it's often cited as an authority on which encryption methods are rigorous enough to use, given modern threats.

OpSec. OpSec is short for "operational security," and it's all about keeping information secret, online and off. Originally a military term, OpSec is a practice and in some ways a philosophy that begins with identifying what information needs to be kept secret, and whom you're trying to keep it a secret from. "Good" OpSec will flow from there, and may include everything from passing messages on Post-Its instead of emails to using digital encryption. In other words: Loose tweets destroy fleets.

OTR. What do you do if you want to have an encrypted conversation, but it needs to happen fast? OTR, or Off-the-Record, is a protocol for encrypting instant messages end-to-end. Unlike PGP, which is generally used for email and so each conversant has one public and one private key in their possession, OTR uses a single temporary key for every conversation, which makes it more secure if an attacker hacks into your computer and gets ahold of the keys. OTR is also generally easier to use than PGP.

Password managers. Using the same, crummy password for all of your logins—from your bank account, to Seamless, to your Tinder profile—is a bad idea. All a hacker needs to do is get access to one account to break into them all. But memorizing a unique string of characters for every platform is daunting. Enter the password manager: software that keeps track of your various passwords for you, and can even autogenerate super complicated and long passwords for you. All you need to remember is your master password to log into the manager and access all your many different logins.

Penetration testing or pentesting. If you set up a security system for your home, or your office, or your factory, you'd want to be sure it was safe from attackers, right? One way to test a system's security is to employ people—pentesters—to hack it purposely in order to identify weak points. Pentesting is related to red teaming, although it may be done in a more structured, less aggressive way.

PGP (Pretty Good Privacy). A method of encrypting data, generally emails, so that anyone intercepting them will only see garbled text. PGP uses asymmetric cryptography, which means that the person sending a message uses a "public" encryption key to scramble it, and the recipient uses a secret "private" key to decode it. Despite being more than two decades old, PGP is still a formidable method of encryption, although it can be notoriously difficult to use in practice, even for experienced users.

Phishing. Phishing is really more of a form of social engineering than hacking or cracking. In a phishing scheme, an attacker typically reaches out to a victim in order to extract specific information that can be used in a later attack. That may mean posing as customer support from Google, Facebook, or the victim's cellphone carrier, for example, and asking the victim to click on a malicious link—or simply asking the victim to send back information, such as a password, in an email. Attackers usually blast out phishing attempts by the thousands, but sometimes employ more targeted attacks, known as spearphishing (see below).

Plaintext. Exactly what it sounds like—text that has not been garbled with encryption. This definition would be considered plaintext. You may also hear plaintext being referred to as "cleartext," since it refers to text that is being kept out in the open, or "in the clear." Companies with very poor security may store user passwords in plaintext, even if the folder they're in is encrypted, just waiting for a hacker to steal.

Pwned. "Pwned" (pronounced "pawned") is computer nerd jargon (or "leetspeak") for the verb "own." In the video game world, a player that beat another player can say that he pwned him. Among hackers, the term has a similar meaning, only instead of beating someone in a game, a hacker that has gained access to another user's computer can say that he pwned him. For example, the website "Have I Been Pwned?" will tell you if your online accounts have been compromised in the past.

Rainbow table. A rainbow table is a complex technique that allows hackers to simplify the process of guessing what passwords hide behind a "hash" (see above).

Ransomware. Ransomware is a type of malware that locks your computer and won't let you access your files. You'll see a message that tells you how much the ransom is and where to send payment, usually requested in bitcoin, in order to get your files back. This is a good racket for hackers, which is why many consider it now an "epidemic," as people typically are willing to pay a few hundred bucks in order to recover their machine. It's not just individuals, either. In early 2016, the Hollywood Presbyterian Medical Center in Los Angeles paid around $17,000 after being hit by a ransomware attack.

RAT. "RAT" stands for "Remote Access Tool" or "Remote Access Trojan." RATs are really scary when used as malware. An attacker who successfully installs a RAT on your computer can gain full control of your machine. There is also a legitimate business in RATs for people who want to access their office computer from home, and so on. The worst part about RATs? Many malicious ones are available in the internet's underground for sale or even for free, so attackers can be pretty unskilled and still use this sophisticated tool.

Red team. To ensure the security of their computer systems and to suss out any unknown vulnerabilities, companies may hire hackers who organize into a "red team" in order to run oppositional attacks against the system and attempt to completely take it over. In these cases, being hacked is a good thing because organizations may fix vulnerabilities before someone who's not on their payroll does. Red teaming is a general concept that is employed across many sectors, including military strategy.

Root. In most computers, "root" is the common name given to the most fundamental (and thus most powerful) level of access in the system, or is the name for the account that has those privileges. That means the "root" can install applications, and delete and create files. If a hacker "gains root," they can do whatever they want on the computer or system they compromised. This is the holy grail of hacking.

Rootkit. A rootkit is a particular type of malware that lives deep in your system and is activated each time you boot it up, even before your operating system starts. This makes rootkits hard to detect, persistent, and able to capture practically all data on the infected computer.

Salting. When protecting passwords or text, "hashing" (see above) is a fundamental process that turns the plaintext into garbled text. To make hashing even more effective, companies or individuals can add an extra series of random bytes, known as a "salt," to the password before the hashing process. This adds an extra layer of protection.

Script kiddies. This is a derisive term for someone who has a little bit of computer savvy and who's only able to use off-the-shelf software to do things like knock websites offline or sniff passwords over an unprotected WiFi access point. This is basically a term to discredit someone who claims to be a skilled hacker.

Shodan. It's been called "hacker's Google," and a "terrifying" search engine. Think of it as a Google, but for connected devices rather than websites. Using Shodan you can find unprotected webcams, baby monitors, printers, medical devices, gas pumps, and even wind turbines. While that's sounds terrifying, Shodan's value is precisely that it helps researchers find these devices and alert their owners so they can secure them.

Side channel attack. Your computer's hardware is always emitting a steady stream of barely perceptible electrical signals. A side-channel attack seeks to identify patterns in these signals in order to find out what kind of computations the machine is doing. For example, a hacker "listening in" to your hard drive whirring away while generating a secret encryption key may be able to reconstruct that key, effectively stealing it, without your knowledge.

Signature. Another function of PGP, besides encrypting messages, is the ability to "sign" messages with your secret encryption key. Since this key is only known to one person and is stored on their own computer and nowhere else, cryptographic signatures are supposed to verify that the person who you think you're talking to actually is that person. This is a good way to prove that you really are who you claim to be on the internet.

Sniffing. Sniffing is a way of intercepting data sent over a network without being detected, using special sniffer software. Once the data is collected, a hacker can sift through it to get useful information, like passwords. It's considered a particularly dangerous hack because it's hard to detect and can be performed from inside or outside a network.

Social engineering. Not all hacks are carried out by staring at a Matrix-like screen of green text. Sometimes, gaining entry to a secure system is as easy as placing a phone call or sending an email and pretending to be somebody else—namely, somebody who regularly has access to said system but forgot their password that day. Phishing (see above) attacks include aspects of social engineering, because they involve convincing somebody of an email sender's legitimacy before anything else.

Spearphishing. Phishing and spearphishing are often

used interchangeably, but the latter is a more tailored, targeted form of phishing (see above), where hackers try to trick victims into clicking on malicious links or attachments pretending to be a close acquaintance, rather than a more generic sender, such as a social network or corporation. When done well, spearphishing can be extremely effective and powerful. As a noted security expert says, "give a man a 0day [zero-day] and he'll have access for a day, teach a man to phish and he'll have access for life."

Spoofing. Hackers can trick people into falling for a phishing attack (see above) by forging their email address, for example, making it look like the address of someone the target knows. That's spoofing. It can also be used in telephone scams, or to create a fake website address.

Spyware. A specific type of malware of malicious software designed to spy, monitor, and potentially steal data from the target.

State actor. State actors are hackers or groups of hackers who are backed by a government, which may be the United States, Russia, or China. These hackers are often the most formidable, since they have the virtually unlimited legal and financial resources of a nation-state to back them up. Think, for example, of the NSA. Sometimes, however, state actors can also be a group of hackers who receive tacit (or at least hidden from the public) support from their governments, such as the Syrian Electronic Army.

Tails. "Tails" stands for "The Amnesic Incognito Live System." If you're really, really serious about digital security, this is the operating system endorsed by

Edward Snowden. Tails is an amnesic system, which means your computer remembers nothing; it's like a fresh machine every time you boot up. The software is free and open source. While it's well-regarded, security flaws have been found.

Threat model. Imagine a game of chess. It's your turn and you're thinking about all the possible moves your opponent could make, as many turns ahead as you can. Have you left your queen unprotected? Is your king being worked into a corner checkmate? That kind of thinking is what security researchers do when designing a threat model. It's a catch-all term used to describe the capabilities of the enemy you want to guard against, and your own vulnerabilities. Are you an activist attempting to guard against a state-sponsored hacking team? Your threat model better be pretty robust. Just shoring up the network at your log cabin in the middle of nowhere? Maybe not as much cause to worry.

Token. A small physical device that allows its owner to log in or authenticate into a service. Tokens serve as an extra layer of security on top of a password, for example. The idea is that even if the password or key gets stolen, the hacker would need the actual physical token to abuse it.

Tor. "Tor" is short for "The Onion Router." Originally developed by the United States Naval Research Laboratory, it's now used by bad guys (hackers, pedophiles) and good guys (activists, journalists) to anonymize their activities online. The basic idea is that there is a network of computers around the world—some operated by universities, some by individuals, some by the government—that will route your traffic in byzantine ways in order to disguise your true location. The Tor network is this collection of volunteer-run computers. The Tor Project is the nonprofit that maintains the Tor software. The Tor browser is the free piece of software that lets you use Tor. Tor hidden services are websites that can be accessed only through Tor.

Verification (dump). The process by which reporters and security researchers go through hacked data and make sure it's legitimate. This process is important to make sure the data is authentic, and the claims of anonymous hackers are true, and not just an attempt to get some notoriety or make some money scamming people on the Dark Web.

Virus. A computer virus is a type of malware that typically is embedded and hidden in a program or file. Unlike a worm (see below), it needs human action to spread (such as a human forwarding a virus-infected attachment, or downloading a malicious program.) Viruses can infect computers and steal data, delete data, encrypt it, or mess with it in just about any other way.

VPN. "VPN" stands for "Virtual Private Network." VPNs use encryption to create a private and secure channel to connect to the internet when you're on a network you don't trust (say a Starbucks, or an Airbnb WiFi). Think of a VPN as a tunnel from you to your destination, dug under the regular internet. VPNs allow employees to connect to their employer's network remotely, and also help regular people protect their connection. VPNs also allow users to bounce off servers in other parts of the world, allowing them to look like they're connecting from there. This gives them the chance to circumvent censorship, such as China's Great Firewall, or view Netflix's US offerings while in Canada. There are endless VPNs, making it almost impossible to decide which ones are the best.

VPN, undetectable or anonymous. A VPN in and of itself is not necessarily anonymous. To be anonymous, it requires a set of architectural parameters and constant shifting of network nodes within the constraints of those parameters. The entire VPN must continuously deconstruct and reconstruct itself with new nodes. Also, the access node has to be part of that activity to make it appear that the access node is a different machine each time—as it generates a new IP address and corresponding false physical-location GPS data every so many seconds or minutes.

Vuln. Abbreviation for "vulnerability." Another way to refer to bugs or software flaws that can be exploited by hackers.

Warez. Pronounced like the contraction for "where is" ("where's"), warez refers to pirated software that's typically distributed via technologies like BitTorrent and Usenet. Warez is sometimes laden with malware, taking advantage of people's desire for free software.

White hat. A white-hat hacker is someone who hacks with the goal of fixing and protecting systems. As opposed to black-hat hackers (see above), instead of taking advantage of their hacks or the bugs they find to make money illegally, they alert the companies and even help them fix the problem.

WiFi. A wireless network

Worm. A specific type of malware that propagates and

replicates itself automatically, spreading from computer to computer. The internet's history is littered with worms, from the Morris worm, the first of its kind, and the famous Samy worm, which infected more than a million people on MySpace.

Zero-day. A zero-day or "0day" is a bug that's unknown to the software vendor, or at least it is not patched yet. The name comes from the notion that there have been zero days between the discovery of the bug or flaw and the first attack taking advantage of it. Zero-days are the most prized bugs and exploits for hackers because a fix has yet to be deployed for them, so they're almost guaranteed to work.

Appendix A.
Character List for *MindField*

Lee Ainsley. Former operative in Gilbert Greenfield's unnamed intelligence service in Washington DC. Now the husband of Cassandra (Cassie) Sashakovich and father of their adopted daughter Ann Sashakovich. Lee and Cassie work for Avram Shimmel and the UN Paramilitary Force.

Ford Bane. MindField's senior vice president of sales and marketing.

Yigdal Ben-Levy. Former associate director of the Mossad. Now deceased.

Elizabeth ("Betsy") Rochelle Brown. Call-sign Butterfly; hacker married to fellow hacker William Wing.

Arthur Creeg. CEO of the startup Underwire Software.

CypherGhost. Call-sign of Charlette Keegan-Ashbury, hacker extraordinaire and former lover of Ann Sashakovich.

Cyrus DeSpain. Father of the CypherGhost.

Michael Drapoff. Former Mossad *kidon* (assassin); now of Ness Ziona, an Israeli defense research institute.

Gilbert Greenfield. Director of an unnamed intelligence agency in Washington DC. Now deceased.

Willy Hangshaw. CEO of the startup XXY.

Carl Hernandes. President of the United States.

Judy Hernandez. One-time lover of Cassandra Sashakovich; currently on special assignment for Avram Shimmel.

Frederick Hunter. Laura Hunter's father, serving time in prison for the murder of his wife.

Ingrid Hunter. Laura Hunter's mother, deceased. Her husband Frederick was convicted of her murder.

Laura D. Hunter. Ann's roommate at Stanford University; girlfriend of Frank Lucessi.

Harvey Kalinsky. Chief technical officer of MindField.

Victor Kreslin. Leader of the Russian team sent to assassinate President-Elect Daniel Strumler.

Lily Lee. Former Hong Kong call girl and former girlfriend of William Wing; now the girlfriend of Jon Sommers.

Frank Lucessi. Small-time arms dealer and drug dealer hired by Robert Randall of the CIA to represent InTelQ, an off-the-books venture-capital firm.

Paul Marotta. Corporate attorney who vets MindField's contract with InTelQ.

Samuel Meyer. Director of the Mossad.

Roxy Mills. Assistant to President-Elect Daniel Strumler.

Husro Mansuri. High-ranking spymaster in Iran's Ministry of Intelligence and Security, known as MOIS.

Igor Nelovich. Second in command to Victor Kreslin on a Russian assassination team.

Charles Nottingham. NSA analyst reporting to Carl Von Truber.

Pedro. Frank Lucessi's driver in Areguá, Paraguay.

Nikolai Puchenko. Director of the SVR, Russia's foreign intelligence service.

Robert Randall. CIA agent and provider of intelligence briefings to President-Elect Daniel Strumler. Randall runs an off-the-books venture-capital enterprise, InTelQ, for which he hires Frank Lucessi as a representative and Alan Skorkin as a "cleaner."

Lev Robinson. Ness Ziona scientist who helped develop Bug-Lok.

Frederico Santos. Small-time drug dealer for Frank Lucessi.

Glen Sarkov. CEO of MindField and Ann Sashakovich's boyfriend.

Ann Silbey Sashakovich. Hacker with growing abilities to access the internet with her brain and shoot fire from her fingers; adopted daughter of Cassandra Sashakovich and Lee Ainsley.

Cassandra ("Cassie") Sashakovich. Hacker, and adoptive mother of Ann Silbey Sashakovich; she and husband Lee Ainsley work for Avram Shimmel and the UN Paramilitary Force.

Avram Shimmel. Israeli general and the director general of the UN Paramilitary Force.

Alan Skorkin. Cleaner (hired assassin) for Robert Randall's InTelQ.

William Smythe. Assistant director ("ass dire"), CIA; Robert Randall's boss.

Jon Sommers. Former *kidon* (assassin) for the Mossad, now associated with Avram Shimmel and the UN Paramilitary Force.

Richard Stein. CTO and EVP of the startup Sturgess Technology.

Daniel Strumler. President-elect of the United States.

Josh Taggert. CFO of the startup XXY Dimensions.

Daniel Tremain. CEO of the startup StarClaims.

Samantha Trout. MindField's chief financial officer.

Carl Von Truber. Associate director of communications intercepts, NSA.

William Wing. Hacker; married to fellow hacker Betsy Brown.

William Wrand. Chairman of Ruhr-Rohrbach in Berlin, Germany.

Yi Shun. Employee of the UN General Assembly administration.

Appendix B.
Internet Links Composing a Primer on Hacker Operations, Government, and Venture Capital Relationships

- **Operation Start Up: BizSprint, Doolittle Institute, July 7, 2017 (courtesy of J.J. Snow: @jensnow47)**

  http://www.sofwerx.org/opsu/

- **Russia steps up spying efforts after election, CNNPolitics.com, July 7, 2017**

  http://www.cnn.com/2017/07/06/politics/russia-steps-up-spying-efforts-after-election/index.html

- **The 18 hottest enterprise startups of 2017, according to how investors value them, Business Insider, July 4, 2017**

  http://www.businessinsider.com/18-hottest-enterprise-startups-2017-2017-6

- **Startup Street: Israeli Spy Agency To Fund Startups Building Cool Spy Gadgets, – Bloomberg, July 2, 2017**

  https://www.bloombergquint.com/business/2017/

07/02/startup-street-israels-mossad-startup-fund-
spy-technologies-zomato-cybersecurity

- **Voodoo Manufacturing raises $5 million for robot factory, CNBC, June 24, 2017**

  http://www.cnbc.com/2017/06/22/voodoo-
  manufacturing-raises-5-million-for-robot-
  factory.html

- **Wikileaks: The CIA can remotely hack into computers that aren't even connected to the internet, qz.com, June 24, 2017**

  https://qz.com/1013361/wikileaks-the-cia-can-
  remotely-hack-into-computers-that-arent-even-
  connected-to-the-internet/

- **Here's a List of Every Single Trump Lie Since He Took Office, HuffPost, June 23, 2017**

  http://www.huffingtonpost.com/entry/every-
  single-trump-lie_us_594d85cce4b02734df2a7bc1

- **Vladimir Putin gave direct instructions to help elect Trump, report says, CBS News, June 23, 2017**

  http://www.cbsnews.com/news/vladimir-putin-
  gave-direct-instructions-help-elect-donald-trump-
  report/

- **Meet The Biohacking Pioneers Who Are Redesigning Their Own Bodies, fastcodesign.com, June 22, 2017**

  https://www.fastcodesign.com/90130651/meet-the-people-who-voluntarily-put-computer-chips-in-their-bodies

- **Why So Many Top Hackers Hail from Russia, Krebs on Security, June 22, 2017**

  https://krebsonsecurity.com/2017/06/why-so-many-top-hackers-hail-from-russia/

- **A Cyberattack 'the World Isn't Ready For,' *New York Times*, June 22, 2017**

  https://www.nytimes.com/2017/06/22/technology/ransomware-attack-nsa-cyberweapons.html

- **8 futuristic technologies from sci-fi movies that actually exist today, mic.com, June 22, 2017**

  https://mic.com/articles/178972/8-futuristic-technologies-from-sci-fi-movies-that-actually-exist-today

- **Security experts warn lawmakers of election hacking risks, ZDNet, June 21, 2017**

  http://www.zdnet.com/article/security-experts-sign-warning-letter-amid-election-security-failings/?loc=newsletter_large_thumb_related&ftag=TREc6

4629f&bhid=26199999350103284654847101531876

- **Humanity's next Stage of Evolution Could Be the Cyborg, futurism.com, June 18, 2017**

  https://futurism.com/humanitys-next-stage-evolution-cyborg/

- **How to Browse the Web and Leave No Trace, gizmodo.com, June 18, 2017**

  http://fieldguide.gizmodo.com/how-to-browse-the-web-and-leave-no-trace-1795721220

- **How to Spot and Remove Stalkerware,** *gizmodo.com, June 18, 2017*

  http://fieldguide.gizmodo.com/how-to-spot-and-remove-stalkerware-1796167351?rev=1497792368757

- **If your home wifi router is on this list, it might be vulnerable to CIA hacking tools, qz.com, June 18, 2017**

  https://qz.com/1008273/complete-list-of-wifi-routers-included-in-wikileaks-cherryblossom-release-possibly-vulnerable-to-cia-hacking-tools/

- **Michael Dorf: When Talking With Trump, Be Sure to Wear a Wire,** *Newsweek,* **June 11, 2017** http://www.newsweek.com/michael-dorf-when-talking-trump-be-sure-wear-wire-623810

- **Top Dem Donor Calls on Lawmakers to Take Up Trump Impeachment, HuffPost, June 9, 2017**

  http://www.huffingtonpost.com/entry/trump-impeachment-dem-donor_us_593b1863e4b0240268797312

- **How Russia Hacks Elections in the US and Around the World, WIRED, June 9, 2017**

  https://www.wired.com/story/russia-election-hacking-playbook/

Acknowledgments

First and foremost, this entire series was spawned by a series of conversations with my "drink of the month" friends, mostly from the Naval Postgraduate School in Monterey, California, as well as conversations with cypherpunk hacker Steven Schear. The story for this book was inspired by a story told by my wife, Andrea Brown, who is also the final arbiter of the quality of my writing.

But, so many other people were also crucial in preparing this manuscript for you, the reader.

My critique partners, Ned Huston, Al Steagall, Marianne Van Gelder, and Evelyn Helminem were instrumental in the final polishing of this manuscript into readable fiction. Also, fellow members of BookPod contributed betareader critiques. My friends also helped with this task, including Will Calhoun, Barry Groves, Grant Rosen, Lee Engdahl, and most of all, my writing teacher Eric Witchey.

I want to thank my publication team, consisting of my editor, Sandra Beris; copyeditor Karl Yambert; graphic designer Jeroen Ten Berge; my formatters Kimberly Hitchens and Barb Elliott of BookNook.biz, my website designer and host Maddee James of xuni.com; my marketing expert Rebecca Berus; and Paul Marotta and Megan Jeanne of the Corporate Law Group, who incorporated The Swiftshadow Group.

I am grateful for all the suggestions and advice I have received but I alone am responsible for the resulting work.

About MindField

MindField is a technothriller taking place mostly in Silicon Valley. When Stanford University sophomore and budding computer hacker Ann Sashakovich meets Glen Sarkov, a senior who is also the CEO of a startup seeking venture capital, she is smitten. Glen and his team find a venture capitalist who is not what he seems, and the strings attached to the funding offer might be lethal.

The world's intelligence services have all been looking for a less-obvious way to fund weapons development. The Mossad's relationship with Ness Ziona and the CIA's relationship with the wholly owned InTelQ venture capital firm are an updated form of the Fed's captive DARPA in providing new weapons tech. What would happen if this new model spread like a virus?

About DS Kane

For a decade, DS Kane served the federal government of the United States as a covert operative without cover. After earning his MBA and earning a faculty position in the Stern Graduate School of Business of NYU, Kane roamed as a management consultant in countries you'd want to miss on your next vacation, "helping" banks that needed a way to cover their financial tracks for money laundering and weapons delivery. His real job was to discover and report these activities to his government handler.

When his cover was blown, he disappeared from Washington and Manhattan and reinvented himself in Northern California, working with venture capitalists and startup companies.

Now he writes fictionalized accounts of his career episodes, as the Amazon bestselling author of the **Spies Lie** series. With seven books previously released in the series, Kane now presents Book 8, **MindField.**